Praise for Ella King

'Beautiful, disturbing, impossible to put down . . . heralds a seriously impressive new talent'
CHRIS WHITAKER

'A blistering psychological thriller'
NEW YORK TIMES

'Searing'
ELLE

'Paring-knife sharp'
ABIGAIL DEAN

'A chilling literary thriller'
GRAZIA

'A tense and tender novel with beautiful writing'
LAURA SHEPHERD-ROBINSON

'She writes with mastery'
***BOOKLIST*, starred review**

'A beautiful, bewitching, unsettling and unputdownable dream of a book'
LISA JEWELL

'Ella King is a genuinely exciting new voice'
KATE HAMER

'A taut, compelling story that's beautifully written'
HARRIET TYCE

Dear Darling

ELLA KING is the acclaimed author of *Bad Fruit*. Her essays on race and motherhood have been featured in *Shado*, *ELLE* and *Harper's Bazaar* and she has taught at Faber Academy, University of Arts London and Spread the Word. She has also worked as a corporate lawyer and for anti-human trafficking and domestic violence charities.

Follow Ella on Instagram @therealellaking.

Also by Ella King

Bad Fruit

Dear Darling

Ella King

HarperCollins*Publishers*

HarperCollins*Publishers* Ltd
1 London Bridge Street
London SE1 9GF

www.harpercollins.co.uk

HarperCollins*Publishers*
Macken House, 39/40 Mayor Street Upper
Dublin 1, D01 C9W8, Ireland

First published by HarperCollins*Publishers* Ltd 2026

1

Copyright © Ella King 2026

Ella King asserts the moral right to be identified as the author of this work.

A catalogue record for this book is available from the British Library.

ISBN: 978-0-00-847660-1 (HB)
ISBN: 978-0-00-847661-8 (TPB)

This novel is entirely a work of fiction. The names, characters and incidents portrayed in it are the work of the author's imagination. Any resemblance to actual persons, living or dead, events or localities is entirely coincidental.

Set in Adobe Caslon Pro by HarperCollins*Publishers* India

Printed and bound in the UK using 100% Renewable Electricity at CPI Group (UK) Ltd

All rights reserved. No part of this publication may be reproduced, stored in a retrieval system, or transmitted, in any form or by any means, electronic, mechanical, photocopying, recording or otherwise, without the prior written permission of the publishers.

Without limiting the exclusive rights of any author, contributor or the publisher of this publication, any unauthorised use of this publication to train generative artificial intelligence (AI) technologies is expressly prohibited. HarperCollins also exercise their rights under Article 4(3) of the Digital Single Market Directive 2019/790 and expressly reserve this publication from the text and data mining exception.

For every girl trapped in someone else's dream.

PART I

Friday and Saturday

1

Beyond the Brambles

Now

When I leave my life behind, I make sure everything is perfect.

I fold a load of laundry, put away the dishes, then start on the rest of the house. The living room is always the messiest, the nursery is too small for my daughter, Millie's, larger toys so her kitchen, craft box and games are in here. I dislike tidying it at the end of the day – rescuing the wheel of a toy buggy stuck between the balcony railings, fishing under the sofa for a wooden carrot that rolls beyond reach. Today though, I take time over her things. Sorting her play food into miniature crates. Finding the long-lost piece of her Peter Rabbit puzzle. Tenderly gathering up the teddies she invited for a tea party.

She's still asleep after her tantrum so I cook dinner, a huge pot of her favourite – cheesy pasta with sweetcorn. I make it the 'no lumps' way, forming a roux with butter and flour, then adding milk and cheddar. Before I had Millie, I didn't know what a roux was, Kit and I didn't cook, we were rarely home early enough from our firms, dinner would be take-away at our desks. But that doesn't work for a little girl who eats at six, who refuses anything unless it's an acceptable shade of beige and cries at the lumps in her bechamel. I beat the mixture to separate the cheddar, lift the whisk to make sure the sauce is smooth.

Through the patio doors, everything is in bloom: geraniums, campanulas, daisies I pick for small vases. The basil Millie and I have been growing has burst into leaf and the strawberries are starting to crop. I squeeze the trigger on the hose, don't stop watering until the soil darkens, Kit will forget while I'm gone. Then, I make my way to the scrubland separated from the rest of the garden by the blackberry hedge. 'Sharp, Millie, do you see how sharp?' I pricked my finger the first time I caught her staring at it, let her come close to the globe of blood. 'You mustn't come here, mustn't touch.' But I know the way through. I pull on my gloves, push back three branches and step beyond the brambles.

A sense of calm courses through me as it always does when I come here. The foxgloves are alive with bees, the clusters so heavy, the stems bow, and the belladonna is flowering, that beautiful rich purple. I run my gloved hands over them for a second, before wrenching them out and stuffing them into a bin bag. I can't guard Millie from them when I'm gone.

The greenhouse doesn't need much; I'll leave most of the plants to die down. But here is where most of the things I need are. Some look innocent – a packet of disposable gloves, specimen jars, a make-up bag of gardening tools. Then, there's the not-so-innocent. Miniature Ziploc bags filled with leaves, seeds, roots. Pots of vibrant-coloured blooms. The thick wad of cash behind the old watering can. There's a reason the greenhouse has a lock, why only I have the key. I slide out the money, choose the most dangerous items and pack everything neatly into my rucksack.

It's my bedroom that fractures my calm. I move quickly, gathering up my painkillers, two changes of clothes, my hot water bottle, trying not to glimpse Kit's side of the bed. There's too much of him here – the duvet he folded back this morning, his neat stack of behavioural economics books, his empty coffee cup. He kissed me after breakfast by the side of the bed, not the brisk kind he does when he's running late but full on the lips after he kissed Millie. 'One for my little girl, one for my big girl.' I stifle a sob against his pillow. My tears mix with the cotton scent of his hair.

The note, I can't spend much time on. It's 17:45 – Kit has messaged to say he's walking up from the station. How to explain I'm leaving? There are no right words, only wrong ones.

I'm sorry.
I love you and Millie.

I slide on my trainers but a sound arrests me, Millie murmuring, and then the need to see her is gravitational. I drop my bag, make my pained way up the stairs and push open the nursery door.

She's still asleep, her thumb is in her mouth, she breathes heavily against it. I crouch beside her bed, smooth back her hair. The colour never ceases to astound me, it is the darkest blonde, from Kit, from me, from my father who I know almost nothing about. But the Chinese of my mother is in her also, in the perfect oval of her face, her wide cheekbones.

Millie stirs; she's searching for something – Acorn. The squirrel was the first thing I ever bought for her. In the shop, I held its maple colour against my barely swelled stomach, ran its tail between my thumb and forefinger. I find it, lay it next to Millie. She clutches it instinctively to her chest. My eyes are wet as I kiss her cheek. 'I love you, baby, I love you,' I whisper.

I shut the front door, crouch under the front window, pull the bins against my feet. I'm inconsistent, illogical, insane to wait for Kit, I'm abandoning my daughter for God's sake, what's two minutes? But I won't leave her alone.

The heath is studded with traffic running from Greenwich to Blackheath, it's one of the things Kit worried about. That and how tiny the house is. It's called The Wedge because it's wedged between two grand terraced townhouses – a hundred years ago, the neighbour to the left walled it off from their house and sold it separately. But I always felt comfortable in it, I love its narrowness, the fact that there's only one room on each floor – kitchen in the basement, living room on the ground floor, nursery and bathroom on first, our bedroom on the second. I didn't care that at Christmas time, when the neighbours invited us over for parties and drinks, we always felt the poorer cousins among the law firm partners, the hedge fund owners, the auction house presidents. 'What else do we need, our own cottage on the heath?' I always say to Kit. Even now, it looks idyllic, the blooms of blue hydrangea, the blaze of dusk reflected in the windows.

Kit is coming. He's handsome, my husband, in his suit trousers and polished shoes. He's finishing off emails to clients, he doesn't look up to open the gate, just pushes it against his hip. If he wasn't typing, he'd see me, do I want him to, is that why I'm here? He's so close I could touch the white shirt trailing over his waistband, jump out at him like Millie sometimes does, 'Did I scare you?'

Dear Darling

He'd loosen his tie, say, 'Right, you've asked for it,' tickle my ribs and then we'd go into our cottage together, back to our daughter, who will wake to the sound of her parents laughing.

But none of that happens. His eyes are glued to the screen. He turns the key in the lock and calls out, 'Hi.'

The door shuts.

Then, I'm gone.

2

Train

Now

Lewisham Station at six p.m. Commuters stream out of the exits, running to catch buses or queuing for the line of black cabs that will disperse them to various South East London neighbourhoods. I've been at this platform many times, there coming out of the lifts, there at the taxi stand, sometimes with Millie in her buggy. Her face in my mind makes me swoon. I stumble onto the tube.

The carriage is almost empty. Lewisham is at the end of the line; everyone is heading home while I head to the opposite of home. I sit at the front of the carriage, my breath catching at the shock of the tracks laid out before me, the open sky because I have instinctively chosen *our* favourite seat, Millie's and mine, we like to sit at the front and wave at the other tubes or watch for the silted banks of the Thames. Once, we saw a boy pretending to drive the train with a toy driving wheel and I vowed that next time, I'd bring hers. Her delight, when I drew it from my bag a few weeks later, was a spark catching fire, lighting up the carriage, lighting up me, and then I know that for as long as I am apart from her, this will be my fate, the agony of being pulled apart. My body knows who it belongs to – her, always her. Not even my abandonment will change that.

Kit is calling, I watch the missed calls mount on my screen, the voicemails, and then the messages come:

Where are you?
Is this a joke?
Pick up your phone.

My hands are shaking. In law school, we learnt that there are two elements to a crime, the act, *actus reus*, and the mental state, *mens rea*, the concept so simple, Kit and I applied it confidently, won easy distinctions. But now, when I turn the theory on myself, I can't find the knife edge where my thoughts sharpened to intent.

I've known this day would come, I've prepared for it in the soil of the garden, the pots of my greenhouse, further back even, before Millie, before Kit. When I read the letter this morning, it was as easy as pressing a button, the thinking complete. But while I might have planned what I'd take on the trip, I am wildly unprepared for the panic quivering through Kit's messages or the ruin of leaving my daughter.

Disused dockyards and warehouses whip past the tube window before morphing into the glass monoliths of Canary Wharf's investment banks, the business hotels with their white-gauzed windows. At Heron Quays, a woman in a cream trouser suit takes the seat next to me, thanking me when I shift to make room. Can't she see that my side is blown in? My lungs aren't working, my heart has stopped because the air I breathe, the blood in my veins, is Millie and I have left her nine stops back.

My hand is trembling as I click on the Nanny app. Kit and I bickered about getting this baby monitor, he thought it was too expensive but I insisted – Millie had always slept next to me, my hand on her heart – if she was going to move into her own room, I needed the best monitor on the market. So, when the picture flickers on and I see my daughter screaming for me, it is in the highest possible quality.

Kit is on the other side of the bars, I can see the top of his head as he leans over her cot bed, 'Honey, honey, calm down, let Daddy pick you up.' But she isn't having any of it. She kicks out at him, thrashing her head from side to side, her dark blonde hair plastered against her forehead in sweaty strands. 'Mama!' she screams. 'I – want – Mama!' It isn't just her words that tear me apart but the sounds between them – the wet in her throat, her hiccupping breath.

I can't bear it. I stand up – too fast, my stomach spasms. I wince. The woman in the cream suit asks me if I'm okay, but I edge my way past her, push my way to the front. The tube pulls into Limehouse Station. Commuters swarm past me as they spill onto the platform or climb onboard, huffing angrily, because I am blocking exits and entries, one arm protective round my wounded stomach, the back of my fist pressed against my mouth, I am on the brink of getting off. But I don't. What did I think I'd do when I was gone, send her home-cooked meals, read her bedtime stories? There are no half measures. Not with what needs to be done.

The doors slide shut. Ahead, the tracks split, the tube swerves to the right. There's an inevitability to a journey, the lost opportunities, the clutch of chances to take a different path. Kit calls me again. I turn off my phone.

*

From: Kit McDermott   18:17
Where are you? You left Millie on her own? I know it's bad right now, really bad, but we can sort it out. Just come home.

3

Mews

Now

His place is where it's always been, on Holland Park Mews. I hate the word 'mews', sickly sweet, a basket of kittens, when it really refers to the row of converted horse stables behind the grand Victorian villas that exploded into popularity after a spate of noughties British romcoms. The street itself was named one of the prettiest in London, I saw it in one of those coffee table books at King's Cross Station, my heart stammering at the sight of his house on the edge of a photo. Trust him to have chosen well, to have lucked out after being locked up – eighteen years later, after one financial crisis and well into another, the value of his stable conversion has skyrocketed. He always managed to come out on top.

Each house is the same as the next – two floors, ironwork stairs and balconies, front doors painted in charming pastels. The frontages of the ground floor are taken up by stable doors, a distinctive period feature.

I've dreamt about this door. Sometimes, the paint is bubbled up like tumours, splintered in a network of veins. I pick at it lightly.

The paint slides off, like it's aching to give. Other times, I dream that I push the door open. The house is helpless against me; I am not its first intruder – the lock is already jimmied, the door is ajar. Inside, it smells of urine and beer. A mattress with unspeakable stains lies in the debris of empty bottles, cigarette butts, clods of earth. The walls are graffitied with words I don't understand.

But none of that is true. I walk back and forth, nursing the sting of early defeat, because the sight of his house makes me want to give up, go home. The windows are whole and unfractured, the balcony is clean and swept. I turn on my phone, shine it on the stable door. A rich olive. I stumble back. It is the exact colour I chose for my kitchen a few months ago; it framed the greenery of my garden perfectly. But standing here, I am frightened that all of my choices are his.

A light flicks on upstairs. He's in, unbearably close, separated from me by no more than wood, brick, concrete. 'Come on, come on,' I whisper, because I know if I glimpse him now, raw from the guilt of abandoning one daughter, the grief of losing the other, I'll be reckless, I'll be dangerous, I'll throw off all my best-laid plans, press a knife to his throat, a gun to his temple. This will be finished.

But I don't see him. And I don't have a knife or a gun. Only roots and seeds and a plant I am clutching so hard to my chest. Slow-acting weapons.

Tomorrow then. I'll meet him at his favourite place, where he said he'd wait for me. But when we meet, I'll know I was here first, where he was least expecting it. Where he thought he was safe.

*

From: Kit McDermott   19:31

I found your note. I don't understand. You have nothing to be sorry about, you've done nothing wrong, you couldn't help what happened. None of this is your fault, Laurie, do you hear me? Come home.

4

Hotel

Now

It was always going to be East London. Staying in the South-East is too risky, someone will recognise me – Annie, Rees, a mum from Millie's nursery – they'd tell Kit, who in a few hours will go to the police. North is out – unfamiliar – so is West – where *he* lives. If I want a place I know well, that leaves only East London where my law firm, Dulwich & Sullivan, is.

The escalator delivers me up to Bishopsgate. The streets are buzzing, it's Friday night, bankers, lawyers, analysts emptying their skyscrapers for beers and cocktails. I head to Spitalfields, searching for anything familiar – food trucks, stalls, shops – because the guilt is very bad now, I'm retching with it. I move through the market in blurts of speed, then have to stop, steady myself against walls.

Check-in at The Spitalfields Hotel is automated, no receptionists or concierge, just a row of silver iPads, a line of empty baggage trollies. My fingers tremble as I type in my name, swipe the credit card that isn't linked to my joint account. I squeeze my wrist waiting for the key card to appear. At the door, I can't hold the card steady, I have to swipe three times at the lock before it flashes green.

The colour scheme of the room is an attempt at Shoreditch cool – white and neon green. A king-size bed claims the centre backed by a lime headboard, behind is an illuminated map of Shoreditch – the parallel stretch of Commercial Street and Brick Lane, the Truman Brewery, Boxpark. Other than that, the walls are blank. Nothing to remind me of Kit or Millie.

My heart is thundering. I set the angel's trumpets on the desk. I want to unpack but, as the adrenaline fades, the contractions in my abdomen grow sharper. I fumble for my painkillers. The midwife said I'd experience 'discomfort' after the C-section. An understatement; I felt like I'd been sawn in two. Kit had to call the hospital for something stronger. They refused initially, the midwife said it would affect breastfeeding, until Kit said in a low, dangerous voice I'd never heard before, 'Read her notes. She's had a stillbirth. There's no baby to breastfeed.'

I walk to the bathroom, undress. Once, I might have watched myself in the mirror, proud of the curve of my hips, the small roundness of my breasts. Now, I can't bear to see the raw slash of scar, my stomach that, only a month ago, was firm and full. I train my eyes to a single bubble of grout between the tiles while I take off my T-shirt, unzip my jeans, carefully pull apart the abdominal band. Cass, Kit's sister and an A&E doctor, gave it to me at the hospital. 'My obs friends swear by it,' she said, trying to sound normal. 'It supports your core.' Released, my belly still looks like I'm four months pregnant, though it's nothing more than an empty pouch.

Dear Darling

Lochia trickles down my thigh, a beautiful word, when I first heard it, I thought of deep freshwater lochs holding ancient secrets, mythological monsters, magic. But later, when I understood it was the discharge after giving birth – a mix of blood, mucus, uterine tissue – I hated it. Because my body is doing the opposite of keeping or holding. It's draining. It's shedding. It's acclimatising to losing my baby when I have not acclimatised to losing her.

I turn on the shower. The water is a relief, transforming everything into itself, the lochia dissolving into silver before circling the drain. Three weeks ago, in the hospital shower, I watched a different transmutation of blood to water, Kit was in the cubicle with me, his shirt translucent against his forearm, his voice unbearably gentle, *Lift up your arms, babe*, but I couldn't, my mind had unlatched from my body, the circuitry blown, he had to lift them for me, wash for me. But he isn't here now. I turn the temperature up to the max. Water deafens my thoughts. Heat sears away my tears.

It is so quiet when I come out from the shower. I hear a key card sliding into a lock, a door banging against the wall, but that's all. I don't believe it, the silence. It feels like they're about to walk in, Millie will fly at me, bury her head into my thigh, Kit will fling his coat over the back of the chair. My body is on high alert for them. How do I tell it they're not coming?

I wrap a towel round myself and open a bottle of water, trying to enjoy each swallow. *This is just like work*, I tell myself, *you're in a hotel on a business trip, nothing's wrong*, but it doesn't work, the panic is white-hot and blank: *How could you have left? What kind of mother are you? What kind of wife?*

I head to the window, push it open. It's summer, the air outside is barely colder than the humidity of the room but I gulp it down anyway.

The outdoors calms me, like it always does. Every night since I found out I was pregnant with Faye, I'd make my way to the garden. Seasons didn't matter. In November, when the morning sickness was the worst, I'd stand in the greenhouse, let the freezing, soil-scented air take the nausea away. In April, when I was so big, it hurt to walk, I'd sit in the canvas deckchair, looking towards Canary Wharf – the banks with their names blazing across the river, the ruby lights of cranes, the white dome of the O2, its yellow-taloned struts.

A few weeks ago, a storm ripped through an entire section of the O2's sheeted roof, peeling back its metal ribcage, sending sheaves of white floating down into the Thames like the wings of swans, and, standing at the top of The Wedge, I wondered what would happen if I opened the window and gave myself over to the gale. Would it tear through my skin? Would it drive me out of my room? Who would I think of as I hurtled down? Faye, Millie, Kit, of course. But if I'm being truthful, brave, honest in a way I can only be away from home, there is one other person I'd think of before my skull smashed against the pavement.

Him.

*

From: Kit McDermott   **20:04**
I've called everyone I know. No one has heard from you. I'm really starting to freak out. If you don't come home soon, I'm calling the police.

DEAR DARLING

From: Kit McDermott   **20:05**
Have you left me? You can't say you love me and then leave me.

5

Display Case

Then

The start. The beginning. For lawyers like Kit and me, the beginning is always obvious – on X date, the claimant purchased this company, the defendant transferred Y pounds. But in memory with its twists and turns, shafted light and shadowed undergrowth, the beginning is impossible to discern. I've tried countless times, I am constantly revisiting the matted knot of those months when I was thirteen, trying to unravel it into smooth, clean strands. How did it begin? Why?

Perhaps it was the display case. Mama packed it away years ago, along with everything else she'd inherited from her parents back in Singapore, zipped them up into an old suitcase because she couldn't bear to see them. There were lots of things Mama couldn't bear to see. A pair of jade earrings carved in the shape of peaches. A gold peacock brooch, the fanned tail studded with diamonds. A painting of a woman brushing her hair made entirely out of feathers. Mama wrapped that in six copies of *Metro* and slid it under her bed.

But now, she needs the old suitcase; Mama is a violinist, she has a concert in Berlin. By the time I drift into her room, she's already hauled the suitcase down and emptied its contents out onto her bed. Now, she's packing – slipping her velvet concert dress off its hanger, folding it in half. I sit quietly on the corner of her quilt because I like watching her.

She's mesmerising. I love how she moves through the world, forceful, regal, so unlike me with my long arms, my gangly legs. She has delicate features, clear, fair skin, she wears her black hair in a long, lustrous ponytail. I look nothing like her. At St Matthews, it is a running joke that I am adopted; my father, whose face I don't know, nevertheless appears on mine, in my nose that is slightly too large, the dull brown of my hair, my murky-brown eyes. If I say this out loud, Mama flinches, before taking me by the shoulders and looking me full in the face. 'You're beautiful,' she says. 'Everything about you is beautiful.'

So, I am watching her, sometimes smoothing her concert dress, sometimes running my hands over the objects she's emptied out onto the bed. In bubble wrap, they cast strange shadows, their contents impossible to discern. I lift the closest package onto my lap.

'That belonged to my father,' she says quietly, before fitting her shoes into the suitcase, and I glimpse that deep hurt in her, which she tries so hard to hide. Though she's filled my childhood with flowers and music, though she swears that I am her family, the only person she'll ever need, I know the truth. We are unwanted by my father, who left us before I was born, by her family, who never spoke to her after she told them she was pregnant. We are exiles.

'Unwrap it if you want.'

I peel the tape carefully off. Underneath is a display case, mahogany with a glass lid, and, behind the glass, is a pair of butterflies. Their wings are rimmed in a black that seems to seep in from the edges, run along invisible channels to expose grey markings on the top wings, yellow on the bottom. Around the black bud of a body is an almost unbroken circlet of crimson.

'You should keep it. As part of your collection.'

Mama indulges my collection, a wild, unruly thing. It is in my drawers, between the blotting paper of my flower press, in the drawings that cover the walls of my room. She says I started it when I was two, I wouldn't stop filling the pockets of my jacket with flowers and leaves and sticks until she gave me an empty jar to put them in. Now, I can spend an entire weekend collecting in a London park, or organising and reorganising seeds, cones, dried leaves, or trying to commit to paper the details of a single flower. When she asks me what I'd like for my birthday or Christmas, the answer is always the same: colour pencils; botanical books; a new flower press.

'Really?' I say, because I know that she is making an exception for me, she is adding to my collection from her hidden hurting one. Her parents never even told her that they were sick. She just found a letter from a lawyer inside one of the boxes that arrived, informing her that her father had died and then, eight months later, her mother.

'Who else would appreciate them?' she says. She comes to sit beside me on the bed. Together, we stare into the glass, and I think, she's right. This shard of nature – beautifully preserved, eternally captured – feels like it's mine already.

'Take it,' she says, her arms round my shoulders. And although this memory is so precious – the butterflies passed down from my great-grandfather to me, the sweet warmth of my mother's body around mine – if I could turn back time, I know what I'd do. I'd stand up, carry the case through our flat and drop it in the bin.

That is one beginning. But there is never just one beginning, there are hundreds. If I'd thrown away the butterfly case, it wouldn't have happened. But it also wouldn't have happened if my mother hadn't left Singapore to attend the Royal Academy of Music, if she hadn't got pregnant with me, if she hadn't stayed in London to raise me alone, if the autumn I was thirteen, the concerts Mama was due to perform at hadn't fallen through.

But my mother did get pregnant, she raised me in London, her concerts were cancelled. 'Ask if anyone needs any music lessons,' she says as I leave for school. It is the first time I see her certainty that the violin is enough, that I am enough, waver. That afternoon, Mama doesn't greet me, she hasn't made dinner. She is playing Paganini Caprices that light up the flat with technical pyrotechnics – clashing harmonies, vicious scrapes of bow against string. Every day, it's the same, she plays uninterrupted from when I get home until late at night. I eat cereal for dinner, buy box after box whenever we run low; I go to bed with the walls still shuddering from her playing. I want to clap my hands in her face, shout, *Call my father, call someone, ask for help, please*. But I never do. It feels dangerous, like rousing someone from a nightmare. I press my hands over my ears and will Mama to stop.

Eventually, she does. Whatever god Mama is offering her virtuoso performances to finally answers. A few weeks later, the dining table is littered with objects – twelve jade horses, an intricately carved ivory box, the peach earrings, the peacock brooch. The feather painting has been unwrapped and is leaning against the sofa.

'Lauren!' cries Mama, because I am crouching in front of it, smoothing down a spotted feather. I jolt back. Mama blinks at me, then softens. 'Sorry, baby, sorry.' She comes over, strokes my hair. 'I just need to get everything valued. Where are the butterflies?'

I don't say she can't have them, they're mine, even though I've squandered whole afternoons on the library's stuttering internet trying to identify what they are, where they're from, how they've been preserved, even though they have pride of place on the shelf above my desk, between the study of a maple leaf I won a prize for at school and the most perfect pressing of a daisy I have ever accomplished. I just fetch them. She sets them down with everything else.

Mama sells the jade horses and the jewellery at Portobello Market. She shows the feather painting and the butterflies to a dealer, who tells her they should be professionally appraised. Mama takes photos, sends emails. The feather painting sells for £5,000 through a London auction house – Mama buys exotic fruit for me every day for a week. But the butterflies require a specialist. Someone is coming from the Natural History Museum.

The night before the visit, I wait for Mama to go to bed, listening for the end of her violin practice, the turn of the taps, the rustle of sheets. When I'm certain she's asleep, I pull back the covers and tiptoe to the display case. Mama has left it on the coffee table, ready for tomorrow.

The moonlight changes the butterflies, muting the crimson, deepening the black, the segments of the body indistinct in shadow. I flick the catch. My fingers hover over the wings, they shiver under me, I want to snatch them up, crumble them to dust, then Mama can't sell them, they'd be mine, always. But then I remember the fear in Mama's eyes after her concert was cancelled, the empty fridge, the boxes of cereal. I shut the case.

*

From: Kit McDermott   **21:25**
I'm outside the police station. I can't do this. I don't feel normal, I'm shaking, my heart is so loud. Help me, babe, please. Don't make me go in.

6

Binomial

Then

We tidy the apartment before he comes. I tackle the kitchen – wash dishes, wipe down the counters, thin the refrigerator of school timetables and drawings of leaves. Mama is everywhere, bringing bowls in from the dining table, scrubbing the toilet. The air smarts with bleach.

But when I see him, the cleaning seems absurd, the apartment irredeemably shabby against the richness of his brown hair, the clearness of his eyes. His blazer is navy, his shirt a crisp, dove grey. A beige trench coat is draped over his arm. 'Ms Tan? I'm Daniel Prior from the museum.'

Mama, accustomed to her effect on men, is speechless at his effect on her. She beckons him through, directing him to the sofa she spotted outside one of the Westbourne Park mansions. She dragged it through the streets and then up two flights of stairs, her smile infectious as she called me over. After we hauled it through the door, I did a running jump onto it, landed laughing in its soft, velvet blue, she did too and then we sat there, imagining the people it belonged to, doing impressions of their *sotto* voices, smug at possessing something worth so much for free. But now, watching him hesitate before he sits down, I see the sofa through his eyes – the scuffs on its wooden legs, the coffee splatter that never quite washed out, crumbs lining the seams. Later, I would realise it was one of his talents. Taking away your vision. Giving you his.

Mama is speaking faster than normal, offering him coffee, tea, lunch, even though it's only eleven a.m. He accepts a glass of water, declines lunch, engages in small talk, but whenever Mama disappears off to the kitchen, his eyes are on the butterflies.

When Mama finally slides the case across to him, he gives a sharp intake of breath and then hesitates, as if he is aware of this moment and wants to savour it.

'Are they special?' she asks.

'Very. Where did you get them from?'

'They were my grandfather's.'

'Was he Malaysian or Singaporean?'

Mama frowns. She bristles at questions about her origins; too many people assume she can't speak English when she went to one of the best international schools in Singapore; her English accent is cut-glass. But she decides it's about the butterflies, so she answers. 'Singaporean.'

'Was he a butterfly collector?'

'A businessman. He had many beautiful things.'

'That much is clear.' He eases the mount out of the case so he can see the underside of the wings. 'These are from the Pieridae family.'

That's as far as I got to when I researched them because of their yellow markings, their black spots. But I couldn't identify their species or sub-species. I crane my head out of the door so I can hear what he's about to say.

He is tilting the display case this way and that. With each flick of his wrist, he is making hundreds of observations.

'What are they?' asks Mama.

'*Delias johor.*'

'Sorry?'

'That's their binomial, isn't it?' I say from the doorway. Mama told me to stay in the bedroom but I push the door open, step out.

He turns.

'What's a binomial?' asks Mama.

'It's a classification of species using two names, one for genus, one for species,' I reply quickly, stumbling over my words, because the look he is giving me is penetrating, without barriers or boundaries, a scrutiny I've never experienced before.

'Lauren is passionate about plants, she reads about them, presses them,' Mama says proudly. 'I gave the butterflies to her.'

'A botanist with butterflies.' His stare is unbroken.

'Come here, honey.' I go over to where Mama is sitting, stand in front of the armchair opposite the sofa. Mama's knees press into the backs of mine.

'So, these are yours?' He holds the butterflies out to me.

I take them from him, balance the mount on my palm.

'Do you take them out of the case?'

'Sometimes.' I realise then, why he is looking at me like that, I've done something wrong, I've ruined them, devalued them. Behind me, Mama is thinking the same thing, she squeezes my shoulder, she is saying, *You didn't know, it's all right.* But it isn't.

'Ever off their pins?'

'No.'

'Why not?'

'Because they're fragile.' Instinctively, I draw it to myself.

'They're special to you, aren't they?'

I don't want to admit it, I don't want to seem childish or make Mama feel bad. But before the intensity of his gaze, I confess it, nod. The butterflies, like my plants, are life suspended and, in the theatre of my mind, only I have the ticket, only I can visit them again and again.

'It's okay. They are special.'

'Really?'

'Well, I think so. I'm a lepidopterist, butterflies are my life's work. You've kept them well, I hope you know that.'

Mama releases my shoulder.

'I wonder if you can help me with something. You've spent a great deal of time with them, more than I have. Could you tell me the difference between these two butterflies?'

'The black on the tips of the left one's wings are wider, the grey and yellow markings are bigger. The one on the right, the grey is bluer.'

He smiles at me then, a real smile, the way Mama does after she's played a violin concerto perfectly, the flying scales, the wild note runs, all the double-stops. 'Spot on. The butterfly on the left is male, the one on the right is female. The male and female of this species exhibit different characteristics.'

'They're rare, aren't they?'

'More than rare. They're extinct. The last sightings were in Singapore and Malaysia in 1990.'

I do the maths. Sixteen years ago.

'But my suspicion is these are older than that. Ms Tan, you said these were your grandfather's?'

Mama nods.

'Do you remember seeing him with these butterflies?'

'No, but I remember my father with them. I was probably five when he inherited them from my grandfather.'

'This is indelicate but I have to ask – how old are you now?'

Mama blinks, 'Thirty-three.'

'Which means these were pinned latest in 1978. To have a pair in this condition, this old, is so, so rare. Not even the Natural History Museum has this.'

'They're valuable.' Mama exhales. I didn't realise she was holding her breath.

'Extremely. Museums, private collectors would pay a great deal for these.'

'How much are we talking?'

'Ten thousand pounds. More, if we can get a few bidders, drum up an auction.'

'Ten thousand pounds?' Her hand covers her mouth. 'Mr Prior, can you handle the sale, is that something you can do?'

'I'd be happy to.'

Mama stands up, he does too, they are talking about buyers in Japan, contacts at American universities, German museums. I fall back in the armchair listening to them and then I slip the mount back into the case, spread my fingers over the glass one last time. I'll never see them again.

Mama hands him the case and announces that she's walking him downstairs. She is waiting in the corridor when I whisper to him, 'Mr Prior?'

He looks up.

Later, he will tell me how small I looked on the chair, knees drawn up to my chin, fierce and desperate, unafraid to beg. But I don't remember it like that. I remember thinking I couldn't bear to let them go without saying something, without impressing upon him how precious they are. 'Don't sell them to someone who won't look after them,' I say, haltingly. 'Sell them to someone who loves them like we do.'

He nods.

'Promise.'

He crosses the room, crouches down in front of me. He is so close I can see the flecks in his eyes – dark gold, sharded amber. 'I promise.'

*

From: Kit McDermott   **22:43**

The police station was madness. Men flying at the receptionist's window, women barely conscious. Thank God Cass came to stay with Millie. She would have been terrified. I was terrified.

The policewoman asked what were you wearing and I didn't know, you weren't dressed when I went to work, so I guessed and then I had to admit I was guessing. I sounded like a total idiot. They asked for medical information, any reasons you might have left, if you were vulnerable. I broke down when they asked me that.

They said the majority of people return within forty-eight hours, which is Sunday. I'm counting down the minutes, hopeful and terrified because every second is taking me closer to you coming back and never returning.

7

Blood Red

Now

Sunlight on my cheek, a breeze across my shoulders. I blink at the clock on the bedside table – 07:43. I'm struggling to make out why everything feels so wrong – the time, the clock, the towel round myself. Realisation is a knife sliding between my ribs. I've been woken by the weather, not the patter of feet across the floorboards, the warm, wriggly body that pushes its way up through the covers and says, 'Cuddle, Mummy.'

I almost walk out. It's unbearable, I can't do this, I'll find my phone, call Kit, he'll drive up immediately, park on the double-yellow lines and then my girl will be in my arms. She will hug me so tightly, nothing will hurt anymore, I will hold her hand in the car, I'll go home, back to my room at the top of The Wedge, and then I remember what I've been doing since I lost Faye, the futon in the greenhouse damp and unchanged beneath me, the crying that went on for so long, it didn't as much occur in intervals but was instead one single cry. Only a few days ago,

Millie came into the bathroom while I lay curled up on the floor of the shower, the heat turned up to the max.

'What you doing, Mama?'

Through the glass, her features were blurred in condensation and then suddenly sharp as she squashed her nose against the screen. 'Taking long time.'

She put her hands on the glass. I saw the three lines on her palms – life, head, heart.

'Why are you lying down, Mama? Are you sleeping?'

I can't go on like that.

I put down my phone. *This is fine*, I tell myself, looking around the room, *you need to do this*. I get slowly out of bed. It's still uncomfortable, although nowhere near as painful as it was three weeks ago, when I could only use my arms and legs to slide to the edge of the bed. Kit would wait patiently for my snail-crawl arrival, lifting my legs slowly to the floor to take the weight from my non-existent abs, and then, I am breathless with how much I miss my husband, how he insists on kissing me goodbye, how he always charges my toothbrush, how, after I lost Faye, he stocked the fridge with all my favourite foods: giant olives stuffed with chillies; lasagnes; a cheeseboard like it was Christmas. He must be going mad. I have driven him mad. I press my hand against my mouth. I cannot think of him now.

I tie the hotel dressing gown round myself and start unpacking. The desk is the perfect place to set up, a good, clear surface, away from the light. I wipe it down and then set out the contents of my old make-up bag, dropping tweezers and paintbrushes into water glasses, lining the back with test tubes and specimen jars, the blender, which, last minute, I pulled out from the kitchen cabinet.

I lay out the small, Ziploc plastic wallets, my little miniature library. I don't need to label them, I know them by sight – wolfsbane; giant hogweed; ragwort; cuckoo pints; bromelia – roots, leaves, prickles all dried, preserved, ground down to the smallest possible usable size. Then, I turn to the angel's trumpets. Gently, I remove the bag.

She's survived. The leaves, the woody stem are fine – no scratches or bruising. The flowers are intact too, that brilliant blood-red shade.

I turn each head of the flower towards me, peer inside. The tight buds of anthers are deep down the neck – it's fertilised by hummingbirds in the Andes foothills, all those long, slim beaks – but I can see them, they look good, the pollen bright and fluffy on the filaments. I tape up the petals. I don't want to lose a single grain.

After that, I get myself ready. I swallow some painkillers, pull on a fresh T-shirt, ease myself into my maternity jeans. Clothed, I brave the mirror. Before him, I used to hate how I looked, my hair and eyes most of all because they identified me as indefinable – not quite white, not quite Chinese. Beside the sleek dark of Mama, my smoky-brown hair, my swampy eyes looked rinsed, the right colour bleached out. But he made me see myself differently. He loved my eyes, so I loved them. Should I be grateful for this now?

I ring my eyes with black kohl, redden my lips.

I am an exaggerated version of myself.

The opposite of who he wants.

*

Dear Darling

From: Kit McDermott 05:02

I'm lying on the floor next to Millie. By the time I came back, she'd fallen asleep in front of *Peppa Pig*. I put her in bed but she kept waking up, calling for you — three, four times, I've lost count. So now, I'm beside her.

I know how devastated you are about Faye, I'm devastated too. But Millie doesn't. All she knows is that her mother isn't there. How could you do this to her?

8

RAT

Now

There was a study I once read about rats. A rat that witnesses the killing of another will return to the crime scene and scream for the equivalent of a human month. I think about that as the lifts open at Queensway Station, as I adjust to the light, the distant sound of drilling, the familiarity of the street. I am a rat. Returning to the place I was killed. If I stay here long enough, scream long enough, grief might become a location. A place I can finally leave.

Queensway is both the same as I remember and different. At the top end of the road, the buildings are being remodelled into luxury apartments with views over Kensington Gardens, at the other end, the old Whiteleys mall is being converted into unaffordable flats, a Six Senses Spa. Between these points of construction, the area remains a Middle-Eastern and Asian enclave. Shisha lounges and souvlaki grills are sandwiched between souvenir and bubble tea shops and, unbelievably, the old Chinese restaurants are still standing – Mandarin Kitchen, Four Seasons, rows of headless ducks hanging in the windows, their skins browned and crisp.

Even Oriental Supermarket is still here, although it is smaller than in my memory. The heated display in the window is the same, dripping with condensation from the BBQ roast pork buns and, outside, there are boxes of white onions and tomatoes mixed in with trays of Indian mangoes, bright globes of Japanese pears. I pick one up: £4.20. They were always ridiculously expensive. Mama would buy one to celebrate small victories, cut it into thin slices, arrange them artfully round a saucer for me. I peer through the doorway. I want to go in, grip the edge of the counter, say, *It's me, do you remember? I lived above here*, though the shop assistant isn't the kind, elderly Cantonese woman of my memory but a nineteen-year-old watching make-up tutorials. I study her, try to trace the lineage of her features until she senses my presence, glares. I step away.

Our old flat is above the shop, on the first floor. My eyes trail up slowly, but then my hand flies over my mouth, I don't want to see it, I don't want to be here, I want to see Millie. I turn on my phone. I know I'm scared, I know I'm stalling, but I can't help it. I open the Nanny app. Millie's bedroom is empty, Kit and Millie aren't there, they're probably downstairs, having breakfast. Still, I can tell what they've been doing. There's a pile of books to the side of her cot bed: they've had 'a snuggy read', when one of us gets in beside her and reads the books she brings over. I started it, I used to read to her for hours on Fridays when there's no rush to get to nursery, and on the weekends, when I woke up beside her. Even after I lost Faye, I'd drag myself out of the greenhouse to read to her. It was the one thing I could manage.

A bald man shuffles out of the building with a trolley bag – I should take this chance; I might not get another. I slip through. The stairwell reeks of weed, I press my elbow to my nose like I never did when I lived here. Over the wall, I see my old balcony. Mama gave it over to me for my plants. Salvager, interior design master, make-do extraordinaire, she picked up plastic crates tossed out by Oriental Supermarket, drilled holes in them for flower beds so I could plant the seedlings I'd liberated from Kensington Gardens into equally liberated soil. This balcony once bloomed with camellias, delphiniums, rose bushes. Now, it's empty. No evidence we were ever there.

I crane my neck over the stairwell, angling for a glimpse of the living room, my heart hammering. It's breathtakingly small, half the size of the living room in The Wedge, low ceilings, laminate floors, I'd balk at living there with Millie, though this is an adult thought, as a child, I never minded. I follow the windows – there is my room, where I draped pine cones from windowpanes, where I tacked maple leaves to the glass, there is the doorway where I watched him pick up the display case – and then, I hear myself whimper, make the sound of a small, wounded creature, because there is Mama's room, where her music stand used to be, her bed. I press my back to the wall as the slab of my grief, which I didn't know was there, cracks.

Did I believe I could outrun this? Sometimes. When Kit looked at me on our wedding day, when I held Millie in my arms, in my pristine glass office at Dulwich & Sullivan, I believed I could. But the memories would always return in retinal flashes: an iridescent blue wing; a butterfly net; a row of jars.

Dear Darling

What if before Millie, before Kit, I did what I am doing now? What if I'd braved these old places, broke their terrible power? I might have exhausted grief, exhausted rage, prevented their knotweed spread. Now, I risk so much being here.

I shut my eyes. Behind them, a star explodes, a bright burst of fear, why must I look at everything I've left behind? But I don't move. I am testing myself. If I cannot stand to be here, what will happen in a few hours when I see him again? I force myself to look at where I used to live, who I used to be. Let the memories ricochet.

9

Natural History

Then

Mama has been dating him for weeks now. 'He's different,' she says, although she doesn't have to – I see it. He isn't the third violinist with the slicked-back hair who tried to move in after the second date, or the conductor with the broad belly who pleaded with Mama at two a.m. to be let in then slammed his fleshy palms against the door when she wouldn't. Immaculately dressed, punctual, he takes Mama to places she has to wear heels for. They travel in black cabs. He leaves money for me to order take-away. A crisp £20 note.

Mama is also different with Daniel. With her other boyfriends, I didn't get a single detail, even if I begged to hear about her dates. 'When it's serious, I'll tell you,' she'd say, her way of protecting me. Now she cannot stop telling me about the concerts Daniel takes her to, the restaurants they eat at. Every day, she circles back to the moment he asked her out, the story of their beginning embellished each time she tells it: the drizzle outside our flat becomes torrents of rain; the hush after he asks her to dinner grows deeper. She weaves in details she's learnt about him – he grew up in an army barracks in the Philippines, he lives twenty minutes' walk away in the exclusive Holland Park, he's the senior curator of Lepidoptera at the Natural History Museum. I know more about him than my own father.

One day, after they've been dating for a few months, Mama tells me Daniel's asked if I'd like to go to the museum to see his butterflies. The invitation thrills her. 'He's trying to get to know you. It's a good sign.'

He meets us at the bottom of the steps of Hintze Hall, arms outstretched, as if the diplodocus, the arches belong to him, as if he is a king showing us his palace. In a way, he is. Volunteers nod to him, curators from other departments congratulate him on his latest publication. Mama beams and then, when it's just the three of us, she says, 'There's a photography exhibition I want to check out.' She squeezes my arm. 'Have a good time.'

I follow him up to the balconies. It's been years since I've visited the museum, I dimly recall the diplodocus, that there's a dinosaur exhibition, but I don't remember coming up here, where the museum's geological treasures are on show, or recall that the museum itself is a work of art – the mosaic tiles on the floor, the carved pillars, the vaulted ceiling inlaid with gold illustrated panels.

'I've seen your drawings,' he says. Colours dance on his cheek from the stained-glass windows. 'You're talented. The way you look at things, there's a rare detail to it.'

I blink. We've spoken in the flat while he waits for Mama; he asks me the usual questions, *how am I, how's school?* I give him brief, factual responses. But he's never said anything like this before. I hadn't realised he'd even seen the artwork on the fridge or on the walls of my bedroom. I turn his words over in my mouth, savour the taste of them. *Talented. Rare.*

'Your mother told me about your collection. Your botany—'

'—It's just a hobby.'

'Don't.' His abruptness jars against the rhythm of our walk, the easy smile he gives the security guards. 'Don't do that, not for anyone. Enough people will undermine what you're doing without you doing it yourself.'

I dare to look at him. Mama has always encouraged me to follow my passions, our lives are testimony to this, she left Singapore to focus on her violin, she went to the Royal Academy of Music to perfect her art. But while she approves of me giving myself over to something greater, she doesn't appreciate botany any more than I appreciate the violin, and of course, there is no one at school who understands. Once, in junior school, I brought in a perfect specimen of a steak fungus still attached to a piece of bark for show and tell. The boys called me 'fungus freak' for months. Since then, I've kept my discoveries hidden, botany something I do at home, when it's just Mama and me. But now, there's Daniel, a professional, who thinks my collection is worth something. It is thrilling. Having an ally against my doubting self.

'Will you tell me about it?'

I start slowly, studying his features for the slightest hint that he is indulging me, but when it becomes clear he is really listening, I can't stop. I tell him I am watching to see if the bluebells in Kensington Gardens are native or Spanish, that I will distinguish them by sight, by scent. I tell him I'm looking forward to spring so I can collect plants from root to flower and to summer because I love grasses – meadow foxtail, tufts of cocksfoot, the spiky heads of timothy.

'What do you do with them?'

'Press them, put them in my scrapbook, try to figure out what they are. But lately, it doesn't seem enough. My flower press squeezes the water out, the colours dull. I can't capture them as they are, not like this.' I gesture at the display of scarlet macaws suspended in flight. 'I started drawing them a few years ago to record the exact pigments.'

'I'd love to see more of them.'

'They're not very good.'

'They're astonishing.'

His praise settles deeply in the flush of my cheeks. I've never heard that word used about me before.

'Your mother said you were upset when the butterflies sold.' I feel a stab of rage against Mama, or perhaps the turn in conversation. How I sound like I sulk. How I sound like a child.

'You kept them in impeccable condition, they sold for an incredible price.'

I shrug.

'You don't care?'

I shake my head.

'You could buy whatever you wanted, clothes, a new flower press even, your mother wouldn't say no.'

'They wouldn't replace my butterflies. Aren't some things valuable just because?' I look away, confused at my outburst, ashamed at my disloyalty.

He is silent. He swipes a key card on the side of a door, holds it open.

The room is completely different from the rest of the museum. Gone are the honey-hued bricks, the intricate columns, the soaring arches. The floor is a practical grey linoleum and the temperature has dropped, the backs of my hands are suddenly cool. Before me are rows and rows of cabinets, most of which are pale grey and uniform and labelled, but to the left are cabinets that look antique – polished wood, leonine legs, ebonised knobs.

'Welcome to Lepidoptery. Take a look.'

I slide open the drawer closest to me. The sheer number of butterflies is shocking – I am accustomed to seeing just two but before me are eight rows of eight, sixty-four brown butterflies with white markings.

I crouch down, the ends of my hair skimming the glass. The differences are slight, some are greyer, redder, more dusty than brown, but that is the extent of my observation. How insufficient the human eye is. I know what 'lepidoptera' means, *lepido* scales, *ptera* wings, but I am hungry for a different kind of knowledge, I want to feast on them with sight, I want to see the scales in microscopic detail – their shape, their edges, the exact point the rust changes white.

'Let me show you another.' He pushes the drawer back, heads to the middle of the room, turns down a row. The drawer pulls out completely. This time, there are only eight butterflies behind the glass because they are breathtakingly large, each the span of my waist.

'What are they?'

'Queen Alexandra's Birdwings from Papua New Guinea. Walter Rothschild discovered the first but he didn't net her. He blasted her out of the sky with a gun.'

'Her'. Never 'it'. Always masculine and feminine, male and female.

'She's here somewhere, the holotype.'

'Holotype?'

'The very first specimen.'

Is this natural history? Not out there, under the grand arches of the museum, behind glass display cabinets smudged with a thousand fingerprints, but here, in this unimpressive labyrinth of corridors and rooms, here where species are being discovered. Beyond the mammoth, the colossal, the easy crowd-pleasers, history is quietly being made.

'Are they extinct?'

'Almost. They're endangered.' He shakes his head. 'Their habitat is forty square miles of coastal rainforest. But New Guinea is also the ideal climate for palm oil production so their forests have been cleared.'

'Palm oil?'

'It's in half the items you'll find in the supermarket – toothpaste, chocolate, cleaning products. The Convention on International Trade in Endangered Species has banned international trade in butterflies like Queen Alexandra's Birdwings but, frankly, it's not collectors bringing them to the edge of extinction, it's consumers.' There is a tremor in his voice, I watch him push it down. 'Sorry. I try not to get so riled up about this.'

'Please.' My mouth is dry but I don't want him to stop. He makes me feel new things all at once – sheltered, rebellious, rageful. 'Don't say sorry.'

'I might make a lepidopterist out of you yet. But this isn't what I want to show you.'

Beyond the cabinets is another room. It is a kind of lab, laptops, microscopes, equipment that looks like enormous printers set on long desks and, everywhere, there are trays of wings. Among them is an enormous volume covered in heavy green leather, the spine embossed with gold. It looks like a volume of fairy tales.

'You got this for me?' I say, not daring to touch it.

'It's a Hans Sloane herbarium - Sloane travelled to the West Indies in 1687, collected thousands of botanical specimens, so, it's pretty old. Here, take these.' He hands me a pair of gloves. I slip them on. Opening the cover, I feel like I'm touching something sacred.

The pages are aged, browned at the edges, undulated like they've been dropped in water but, even so, the plants and illustrations are still intact. I leaf through it too quickly and then go back to the beginning, start again. I stop at a spray of crisp brown leaves still on their stem, a broken shard of husk, a bean. I try to decipher the tight, faded calligraphy but cannot.

'It's from a cacao tree,' he says.

I didn't realise he was looking over my shoulder.

'Here, look at this.' He brings up a photo of the leaves and the cacao pod on his laptop, twists it to face me.

I check the leaves. He's right. 'I didn't know you knew plants.'

He laughs, shakes his head. 'I read a paper on the pollination of cacao by midges. But don't ask me another one, I won't be able to impress you.'

Impress me? All I want to do is impress him. I watch him walk back to his seat, pick up the journal and, before the sixteenth-century cacao plant, I decide. I want to be him. I want to be part of this, always. 'Daniel? Can I come here again?'

'Any time you want.'

*

Dear Darling

A few days later, Mama receives a wooden crate, outrageously large, packed with fruit I know only from browsing Oriental Supermarket with her – spiky red lychees, aubergine mangosteens, an almost ripe papaya, the skin still green. Mama is ecstatic, she tells me again that Daniel has grown up in the Philippines, how he knows all the Asian fruit she misses. She presses a starfruit to her cheek. 'This is my favourite,' she says and then she calls Daniel to thank him while scooping armfuls of fruit into the kitchen. She pushes a knife through the starfruit, the blade slick with translucent flesh, holds out a slice to me. But I am moving away from her. I've glimpsed something in the wooden crate.

I roll away a pineapple and four lime-green guavas. There. A cacao pod. Monstrous and ugly, it is the shape of a deflated rugby ball, the husk a deep rust. I cradle it with one hand, with the other, I press my fingers over my mouth, trying to stop repeating the same words my mother has just said. *This is my favourite. This.*

*

From: Kit McDermott   **07:41**
She's still asleep. I'm looking at her perfect face, her eyelashes, her hair and you know what, Laurie, you need to stop. If you want to leave me, you could've just told me, rip my heart out, I can take it.

But not her. You can't mess with her. Did you think about what this would do to her? She's already lost her sister. I didn't know you could be so selfish.

10

Tess

Then

He tells Mama I can go to the museum any time I want. I want to go every Saturday.

He says come when the museum is closed. 'It's different when everyone's gone, you'll see,' he says. He's right, I feel it standing behind him on the long escalator up through the centre of the giant metal earth sculpture, not just that the museum is mine but that the world is, the constellations on the walls, the rings of planetary orbit. He feels it too. Inside the earth's core, he looks at me and smiles.

He is different with me than he is with Mama. I listen to them whisper when they come home from their dates, bickering happily about whether the performance they've just heard is technically flawed, whether the cellist transitioned smoothly into the last movement – and I think he is perfectly suited to Mama. He is exactly how I imagine my father would be – intelligent, musical, unawed by Mama's beauty, equal to it. But when he's with me, I don't think of him like that at all.

He feeds my hunger for the secret insides of things, he buys me botany books, orders up illustrations from the museum's collections, he even introduces me to a pimply PhD student who teaches me the correct way to preserve plants.

'You're talented,' he repeats. He never mentions music. Only butterflies and botany.

One week later, he puts a wooden drawer in front of me. 'This one was hard to get,' he says. 'It's from Sloane's vegetable substances collection.'

He has been talking to me about Hans Sloane for weeks now. How his herbarium, while not the oldest or the largest, is unparalleled in scope and geographical range. How Sloane wasn't just a doctor, he was an apothecary, interested in the use of plants for medicinal purposes. Daniel requested specimens from the herbarium weeks ago, but apparently, the plants department is terse and uncooperative, unconvinced that his requests have anything to do with lepidoptery. Now, it seems as if they've relented. He pushes a drawer across the counter.

It holds about a hundred tiny boxes, each covered in marbled decorative paper with glass lids and backs. Inside are seeds, beans, skeletonised leaves, dried hard and brittle over the centuries. I pull on my gloves. What is it like to have such a collection? To have it outlive you?

'You shouldn't get too attached to Sloane.' He is watching me lay the boxes out on the desk.

'Why?'

'How do you think he amassed all of this?'

'I've never thought about it.'

'Think about it now.'

'I don't know.'

'He was extremely wealthy and, in the 1700s, only one industry guaranteed profits.'

'What?'

'Slavery.' He leans back in his chair. 'He married the rich widow of a plantation owner who was one of Jamaica's leading slavers. Slavery funded all of this.' He gestures at the museum around us. 'He wasn't collecting specimens himself, didn't venture out to net butterflies. He sent slaves.'

I put the box down.

'When you understand the scale of his collection, the voraciousness of it, it's disturbing. He didn't limit himself to plants and butterflies. He collected clothes worn by slaves. Among other things.'

My skin crawls. 'What does that mean? Should I not look at it? Should the museum not have his collection?'

'What do you think?'

I push the drawer gently away. 'I don't want anything to do with them.'

He shakes his head. 'Without his collection and the collections of so many others, there would be no way of tracking the evolution of species, the destruction of habitats.'

'So, you're saying the museum should keep it?'

'Keep it but know where it's from. Use it but recognise that it is born from cruelty. Hold together that one of the greatest collectors of all time profited from slavery. A man can be both.'

Decades later, I will read that the British Museum has removed the statue of Hans Sloane from its pedestal, imprisoned him in a glass case dedicated to his relationship to slavery, and I will recall this conversation, my eyes filling suddenly at how a man who confronted slavery years before the museum did could have wrought such damage. And it will occur to me that perhaps Daniel wasn't warning me off Sloane at all, but himself. The insatiableness of his collecting. The contradiction that existed inside him. His ability to love and hurt. But I didn't see it back then. I didn't listen.

Daniel tells me about himself. He has a special interest in Asian butterflies because he grew up in the Philippines, his father was a soldier posted to Fort Magsaysay. His passion for butterflies started in the forests of the military base. He is a curator, a conservationist, a taxonomist. 'I like to name nature. I want to name, describe, categorise.'

He teaches me basic lepidoptery, but over time, I find I am observing less the trays of butterflies or the volumes of herbaria but him. How he only wears glasses when he looks through the microscope. The shallow curve of his lower back. The line of buttons on his dove-grey shirt.

He has discovered a new genus of Nymphalidae ('nymphets' he calls them), he has identified two new species.

'Have you decided what you're going to call them?' I ask.

'Not yet. Paul wants to name it after Harry Potter characters – Harry, Hermione, Ron—'

'Ron!'

He makes a face. 'I know. But the goal is to get the public interested in butterflies, in conservation.'

'What do you want to call them?'

'Tess,' he says without hesitation.

'Is that biblical?'

He laughs. 'Almost. Thomas Hardy. He wrote *Tess of the d'Urbervilles*.'

'Never read it.'

'It's about a tragic woman who's failed by the men in her life – her father, her cousin, her husband. By the standards of Victorian England, she's fallen. But not for Hardy. He called her pure. Sometimes I think he must have known a real Tess, had strong feelings for her.' His mind seems to wander for a second, disappear beyond the walls of the lab and then return. 'I think about her when I look at these butterflies.'

He returns to the microscope, adjusts a shard of wing. The cuff of his shirt rides up his wrist.

I want my story to be different. But it isn't. It is this: I am jealous of the slide between his fingers, of the wing that holds him rapt. I want to be under his lens, I want his pupils to be wide and dilated above me. What is it to be the object of a man's obsession? For him to devote his life to the study of you? 'Can I look?'

'Sure.'

He bends down, straightens the slide.

Behind him, I lean forward. Breathe him in. His scent pulses through me: cotton, herbs and something else, sharp and astringent, like pure alcohol.

You see now why I've never told Kit.

Because everything Daniel is going to say about me is true.

It was my fault.

I started it.

11

BLUE WHALE

Now

When Kit and I moved to London for law school, he asked me to show him where I'd grown up because that's what normal people do, visit the landmarks of their childhood, point out homes and parks, trace for their partners how they came to be the people before them. My reaction must have had a profound impact on him because he recalled it afterwards as the first time he understood the effect of Mama's death. 'A stillness came over you,' he said, 'like watching ice form.' I remember struggling to display the right amount of emotion, to set off a controlled explosion – enough to shut him down but without unveiling the panic he'd detonated.

Occasionally, Kit would bring up West London with a tourist's enthusiasm, he wanted to take Millie to the Beatrix Potter exhibition at the V&A, the sensory play centre in the basement of the Science Museum, the pirate ship at the Diana Memorial Playground. Once, he suggested that we take Millie to the Natural History Museum for the day and my mind went white; for a few seconds, I was speechless. Finally, I said, 'I can't go anywhere I used to go with Mama. Not the South Ken museums, not West London. It's just not something I can do.' That stopped him. Even though it wasn't true.

Now, outside the Natural History Museum, I wish Millie was here, her dark blonde hair curling at her shoulders, a hair slide dangling by a strand, she'd be running ahead of the queue, excited to get in. My want for her is so keen, I grasp the iron railings.

I step into the museum. It's busy, I hold my arms around my middle to protect my stomach from the streams of visiting students, parents tugging their children. But even the busyness cannot distract from the museum's Romanesque façade, the gargoyle drainpipes, the soft hue of the terracotta.

The hall inside is cool and tiled and I think Kit was right, I should have brought Millie here, how could I have let her miss out? Because like everyone else, I am gasping at the skeleton of the blue whale suspended from the cathedral arches by invisible wires. My eyes follow the length of it, the hollow of its open jaw, the smooth plane of its nose, the vertebra that trails off into a tail. I can almost see it. Flesh flown back, heart returned, it dives suddenly for a shimmer of krill.

'I could watch you for hours.'

I turn.

There he is. The man I've escaped from and wanted to see for eighteen years.

'Lolly,' he says.

*

Dear Darling

I want his cheeks to have sunken, for his middle to be soft and doughy. But it's not true. He still has an electricity about him, he's more magnetic at forty-eight than he was at thirty. His hair isn't that rich brown anymore but it's still full and professionally silvered and he's clean-shaven, revealing that rakish scar to the left of his chin. Age has claimed him only around the eyes, deep folds where once his skin was smooth, but it hasn't touched the colour, still that brilliant navy.

He takes me in slowly, his eyes holding mine before running over my hair, falling across my body; under his gaze, I'm ashamed of my appearance – the fine lines around my eyes, the heaviness of my breasts, the pouch of my stomach. I call forth feminist slogans, mantras, Instagram posts – *I don't owe you pretty, I owe you nothing, Why should I care what you think of me, all that matters is what I think of you* – but they slide off me, someone else's words, I thought I believed them but I don't. After all this time, I can't help it. I still want him to want me.

'You came,' he says.

'You wrote me a letter.'

'I've written you hundreds. You never replied.'

'No.'

'It doesn't matter. You read the most important one.'

His shirt is unbuttoned at the top, exposing the hollows of his throat. His familiar musk is dizzying. Once, I would have found it irresistible, pressed my nose deep into his skin. I dig my nails into my palm. 'Why did you ask me to come?'

'You know why.'

'I really don't.' I stare at him, uncertain how to proceed. Eighteen years ago, I knew the taste of his lips. Now, I don't know anything about him. I'm not sure I want to. What words can bridge intimacy and strangeness, all the sharp and gleaming things between us?

He is struggling too, his mouth opens, shuts. Perhaps he's also practised what he'd say, perhaps he is finding, as I am, that everything he's prepared makes no sense. But then, he seems to settle on something; I'm not sure if it's appalling or perfect. 'Shall we walk?'

It's such an innocent suggestion – two adults walking through a museum, friends perhaps. But it isn't innocent and we are not friends. It's an invitation back. Because every Saturday, we'd take a slow walk from the staff entrance all the way to Lepidoptery. And then, suddenly, this moment is precious, the clutch of seconds before everything changes.

I turn away from him, back to the whale, I force myself to read every word of the display. Her name is Hope. Caught at low tide, on a sandbar outside the harbour town of Wexton, she struggled for two days before a lifeboat pilot harpooned her out of pity. Her carcass was auctioned off, her body butchered, the blubber boiled down, her skeleton sold.

Now, scientists have uncovered why she was in Ireland. She was a mother. She was travelling from the subtropical waters of the Atlantic after birthing her calf. They discovered it in her baleen, the molecules of her chemistry. Her child written in her bones.

'Lolly?' he says.

My eyes linger on her. I am crossing oceans for my family, Hope, I am braving treacherous waters. See me. Hear me. Give me strength.

Dear Darling

*

From: Kit McDermott   10:44

She's screaming for you.

    She fell over in the playground and now her chin is bleeding and she wants Hello Kitty plasters, which I do not have, because I do not carry them around with me like you do.

    Do you hear me, Laurie? Are you reading this? Your daughter is screaming for you.

    I will not protect you from this. I will not.

12

Ichthyosaur

Now

We walk out of Hintze Hall, under a pair of giraffes, past the watchful eye of a marlin. He is wearing what he's always worn, navy cotton-twill trousers, chocolate loafers. The precise shade of his shirt squeezes my throat – the lightest dove grey – in all my recollections, he is wearing that colour. He swerves to avoid an onslaught of students and I think there's a new strength through his shoulders; he is leaner, wirier than I remember. If I saw him in the street, I might not recognise him from behind. A lie. I'd recognise him anywhere.

We take a short-cut through the shop, I watch him smile at a rubber in the shape of a T-rex, cup his hand briefly over a seed bomb, run his fingers under key rings, strange behaviour he never did before, until I realise he hasn't been to a shop like this in almost two decades. At the shelves, he pauses, his eyes scanning the books before sliding away. His used to be there, *The Complete Guide to Butterflies*, a Common Jezebel on its cover. Not anymore.

'I've been waiting for you for days,' he says.

Dear Darling

He's been counting down the days, when for me, the recent past is a blur. I try to recall distinct details – what I did, what I said – but only snatches of yesterday are vivid: the bold, cursive, 'Dear Darling' at the start of his letter; Kit shaking his head at finding me sleeping in the greenhouse; Millie asking me where the baby is. I spread my fingers over the base of my throat.

'I came here straight after I sent it. It's silly. I'd only just posted the letter; there was no way it would get to you that quickly. But I couldn't help it.'

I look away, pretend I have no idea what he means, but I do. What exists between us is cyclone, tornado, funnelled wind ripping up everything in its path, we know this and yet we're both here. And I wonder. Have I really come for release? Or have I simply been waiting eighteen years to step into the sweet calm of its centre?

'You're a lawyer now?'

I nod. He knows I am; he sent that letter to the firm who redirected it to my home address. I think of him reading my online profile. He despises the corporate world, he'd skip over what I do, my deal list, my awards, but he would have lingered over the photo, the cursor blinking on my lips.

'I could never have predicted that.'

'What did you think I'd become?'

'A botanist, a scientist. I could never picture you anywhere but here.'

'I haven't come back here since—' Since what? I'm thrashing to find the right words, I've built a career on finding the right words, yet about this, I'm inarticulate, pre-verbal, savage.

'But your collection. Those sketches.'

'I don't do that anymore. Now, I'm just a lawyer.'

He's silent; I've disappointed him. A stab of pleasure flares in me. I am nothing like he thought. Nothing.

We turn into the Fossil Marine Reptile Gallery. Daniel seems relieved. He leans against the wall, breathes deeply in and out – he isn't used to being in a crowd. After eighteen years in prison, Saturday morning in the Natural History Museum must feel like being crushed. For a few seconds, I'm relieved too – it's quieter here, fewer people to protect my stomach against – until it occurs to me that there is too much space between us now, too much opportunity to observe each other without interruption.

'Are you married?' he asks, putting his palms on the brick as if to take in their coolness. 'Tell me about your family.'

'No.' There are lines I can't cross, though he and I have crossed so many together. I will not speak to him about Millie or Faye or Kit, not now, when everything is so raw. 'Tell me about prison.'

'No.'

Between us, the air sparks with all the things we won't say – the metal of his car against that boy's legs, the wail of a police siren, the softness of his prison jumpsuit, the trail of my wedding dress, a baby in my arms, so many unspeakable memories – and then I'm grateful to be in this museum, among the roar of children, the pound of palms against glass. In the quiet, this intensity would be intolerable.

He peels away from the wall, crosses the gallery to a pair of ichthyosaurs. No one is looking at them. In this gallery of petrified monsters, they are far from impressive. But for us, the shale of their skulls, the rattlesnake lengths of their vertebrae are bruise-tender.

'It's a lot, isn't it?' he says. 'Being here again.'
I don't reply.
'Do you remember?'
'I remember everything,' I say.

He takes me, one afternoon, to the Fossil Marine Reptile Gallery.

The lights in the main hall are dim, but here they are completely off. Ahead of me, he searches for the switch and then gives up, illuminating our way with the pale light of his phone. I wrap my arms around myself, willing myself not to shiver at the lithic phalanges of fins, the sharp points of teeth. His phone comes to rest on an enormous eye. The iris is the size of a pineapple slice.

'What is it?' I whisper.

'An ichthyosaur. There are a few in here but this was the very first. It was discovered not by a man but by a child, Mary Anning. She was twelve. Two years younger than you.'

He passes the light along the length of its snout. Swirls are imprinted on its knife-sharp ribs. Ammonites. I imagine them falling over the seabed like snowflakes.

'She was self-taught like you, barely educated, she never went to university but, when she was older, she was a better palaeontologist than any of the male scientists of the day. Her illustrations rivalled the technical drawings in scientific journals.'

I think of my own sketchbook.

'She'd go out at every tide, after every storm. She kept going, kept trying.'

'I'm not Mary Anning.'

'No. You're someone else entirely. You could do anything. Be anything.'

That evening, he tells Mama he wants to take us on holiday over Christmas. Mama looks like she is about to burst, she doesn't trust herself to say anything, unwilling to appear too desperate, too thankful, she nudges me to react. I do. I let out a peal of joy because I cannot remember a time when we've gone on a real holiday. School holidays are spent in the park or in front of the TV – Mama can't afford for me to go to the cinema or drink Black Forest hot chocolates or go shopping, which is what the girls in my class talk about doing together. Even if we had the money, they'd never invite me. I am too awkward, too quiet, too absorbed in my own world.

But as I hear Daniel talk to Mama, I realise it's more than just a Christmas holiday. Because he is speaking about going to Dorset, the Jurassic Coast, he is talking about fossils. The holiday is, at least in part, for me.

It's December. The hotel is a stately home – wooden floors, four-poster beds, fairy lights. An enormous Christmas tree stands in the hallway decorated with silver and pink baubles, garlands of spruce are draped over the stairs, in every room, there is the crackle of burning logs. Mama is not interested in Mary Anning country, she doesn't want to go outside, not when the weather's so bad, not when there's a private cinema, an indoor pool, a spa. So, it is Daniel who goes out with me at low tide.

The beaches are deserted, no one wants to brave the winter storms, but Daniel says it's the best time for collecting, the sea batters the cliffs, exposes fresh fossils in the clay. On the shore, it's too loud to speak, the crash of the waves, the wind lashes away any words but we fall in step with each other; he waits as I sift through shale, I pause as he empties sand from his boot.

He presses the ribbed stem of a sea lily into my palm. I excavate a hunk of pyrite, it has another name, 'fool's gold', luring immigrants to America with glitter and false promises. But although it's the size of my fist, it's not what I am searching for. I want an ammonite like the ones I saw on the ichthyosaur at the museum, they're common here, not even on the cliff face but loose, among the pebbles.

When I see one, shining darkly with sea water, joy shoots through me. I call out something, his name perhaps, he is beside me as I pluck it from the beach. I brush off the sand, hold it out to him, millions of years coiled and perfect between my fingers, 'I found one!'

The sky around us is grey and dim but the smile on his face is sunlight. 'Didn't I say?' I hear him shout over the wind, the rain. 'You can do anything.'

I blink at the display case. He knows what he's doing. There's a reason he's taken me to this ichthyosaur. Here, in the museum, on those Dorset beaches, he gave me something – self-belief; I've used it at school, at university, at Dulwich & Sullivan, its power inside me as definite and tangible as a pebble. He really did love me before he destroyed me.

The glass whispers against my wrists. I could smash through, let its jagged edges slice through my skin, the lilac of my veins, but not even that will separate him from me. How do I sever what he's given me from what he's taken? He is in the whirr of my brain, the flutter of my heart.

There is only one way.

13

Under the Arches

Now

'Are you okay? You seem—'

I don't reply. I am taking the lead now, turning out of the Fossil Marine Gallery, making my slow, painful way against the pull of visitors. I don't care that I'm plunging him back into crowds. My mind is clear apart from a thin line of static. The crackle before a radio station comes on.

'They've built a whole new Entomology building since I've been gone,' he says. 'It's called the Cocoon.'

'We're not going to the Cocoon.'

He understands then where we're going, he surrenders to it. We're back at Hintze Hall now, Hope's skeleton suspended above us as we cross to the central steps. I take each one carefully, if I'm too abrupt, my abdomen twinges. At the top, I pause to watch him. He blinks at the sight of the old route laid out before us as if he's come out of a darkened room, taking in geological treasures on the left, birds on the right, and then I know in the days he's been waiting for me, he hasn't dared come up here. I wonder if he dreams about these long stretches of balcony like I do, if he fears them. Their quiet, transgressive power. Falling captive again.

The door to Lepidoptery is the same – utilitarian, nondescript – we cannot get in without a pass but there's no need, just this small section of balcony is electric with memory. Pillars soar up to the vaulted arches of the ceiling, I lift my hand to one. The stone, carved to resemble the bark of fossilised trees, is as much a part of the first time I touched him as the touch itself, and then all my pretending falls away, the stupid games I play to erase what happened. Under my fingertips, truth is bulletproof.

He is seconds behind me on the highway of memory, his face a reflection of my own, a collapsing building, the jolt of bricks before the floors fall through. He steadies himself against the wall, a hunched, broken posture, and it occurs to me that I've never witnessed the damage on him; right to the end, he was always so sure, so certain. But he is blown apart too. He presses the back of his hand to his mouth.

I turn away. I thought I wanted him hurt. But I don't have the stomach for his grief.

After a few minutes, he joins me at the balcony. We look out over the hall together. Below us, the visitors are liquid under the cage of Hope's ribs, water forming and reforming.

'Did you think about this place?' he asks.

I nod. 'You?'

'Every day.'

'We never really talked about it when we went away,' I say. 'What happened here.'

'No.'

'So many questions I never asked.'

'We didn't think it would end.' His elbows lean against the railings; he presses his fingertips together. 'But now, we have all the time in the world.'

Or none. Fresh out of prison, he has no obligations – no family, no career. But for me, time is the one thing I don't have. Even standing here now, I'm a thief; I've stolen minutes, hours, days away from my husband and daughter, each second ticking down an already negative balance.

A laugh echoes from the opposite balcony, a couple in their twenties, meandering through the displays, his arm slung languidly around her shoulder, her arm around his waist. They are pointing at the pheasants. Simple Saturday activity.

'Ask me,' he says, his eyes on them.

'What?'

'You said there were so many questions you never asked. Ask me. Whatever you want.'

How much time have I squandered thinking about him? Is it even calculable? I've tried and failed to stop myself but my mind has always been ungovernable, sliding back and forth like a finger across a frosted pane. 'Where do you go?' Kit would ask when we first started dating because the smallest thing – a flash of blue, a shirt collar – would send me reeling back. Later, it became an inside joke, that I was a daydreamer, one of my little idiosyncrasies. But I am not a daydreamer. *Where do you go?* I am on this balcony, in a mews house, on a beach, desperately trying to find answers in facts I've already sifted, memory I've already dissected.

But in a relationship, there are two bodies, two minds, two memories. This is the chance I've been waiting for. To test if my version of events is true.

'When I touched you—' I start, then stop because it is impossible to carry on, I have a daughter, a husband, how can I say these words out loud? But there is something else here too: relief. The expression of our intimacy after almost two decades of silence is a bloodletting. 'Why didn't you stop things?'

He turns to stare at the door to Lepidoptery. He imagines himself back, as I do too.

I'd been feeling it for months. Each Saturday I saw him, every time I heard Mama talk about their dates, their future, a tightness would fill my chest, a balloon expanding. One afternoon, as we're leaving to go home, he holds the door open and I'm seized by the fact that there are only a handful of seconds when I am standing in front of him, this moment, a grain of sand trickling through the narrow neck of an hourglass. Surely, he can see it, everything between us – wings and watercolours and ammonites – and then I cannot bear it anymore. In front of the pillar, I touch my finger to the pulse of his throat.

There is a single beat of silence.

'Lauren,' he says quietly and I know I've made a terrible mistake because the way he says my name is the way he's always said it in the lab, nothing more. I run through the dark of the balcony, tears smarting my face, trainers smashing against the museum tiles.

'You should have done something,' I say.

'What should I have done?'

'Something. Anything. You should have told my mother.'

'What would I have told her?'

'The truth. That I was attracted to you.'

'Based on that?' He shakes his head. 'Nothing happened.'

'But then it did.'

'Months later.' He meets my eyes, blue on brown. A family passes us with a little boy and girl wearing dinosaur tails from the museum shop. I want to shove them out of the way, shield them from the unfurling carnage, keep them safe from the scene of this car crash. My voice is an awful half sound. 'I was fourteen. You were thirty.'

'I'm aware of the maths.'

'Maths?' A terrible laugh escapes from me. 'It's called something else now.'

'Don't.' He puts a hand out to stop the word but it's too late, though neither of us says it, it flaps manically around us, a caged bird finding sudden, stuttered flight.

That's what it was, I almost say, but the words fade on my lips, it seems implausible that this man – who still has the most beautiful shoulders I've ever seen – could be *that*.

He steps towards me. He is so close, his scent is almost overpowering. 'I loved you.'

Old words. Overused, meaningless, if they were a currency, their value has long depreciated, but these warnings play in my head like a podcast, background noise, incapable of reaching me here under these museum arches, powerless to prevent my dismantling. My heart beats so hard, I'm afraid he'll see my pulse through my skin.

'Stop,' I say, more to myself than him but I can't help it. Despite everything I've schooled myself in these past eighteen years – grooming, power dynamics, #MeToo – he has turned something in me to honey, dark and sweet and liquid. My tailbone slams against the railing, the one solid thing in my astonishing loss of control. 'I have to go.'

    He calls after me from the balcony, shouts that name he's always loved, but I am at the top of the stone staircase, under the skeleton of the blue whale, out of the museum, away.

14

Gift

Then

I am in the museum a week after I touched him. I've said nothing to him, not a word, I told Mama I didn't want to go anymore but she insisted, she said it was important, this week more than any other, unless something was wrong, unless something has happened. What could I say?

He watches me from the other side of the lab, he has brought me a Wardian case, a type of early terrarium used to protect foreign plants on their journeys to England. A few months ago, I'd have pored over it, the glazed glass, the iron swirls, worked hard to capture it in my sketchbook. But his offerings hold no interest to me anymore. I am dropping beads of paint into water. Turning them to rolling clouds, stormed skies, thunderstorms.

'I have something else for you,' he says.

I don't look up. I am tired of museums, of discoveries, the endless stream of the living and the extinct, what is the point of dissecting a thing to its constituent parts, of understanding the inside of things when I can't understand myself? Knowledge is a futile project. Everything is closed and secret.

But he insists. He pushes something within my line of sight. The knots in the mahogany make me catch my breath. 'It can't be,' I whisper but it is. Those pitch-black markings, the striking ochre of the hindwings. Until I hold the display case again, I didn't realise how much I missed it. 'I thought you sold it?'

'I did.'

'The museum bought it?'

'They were one of the bidders, along with Harvard and two private collectors.'

'You said there were only three bidders.'

'I didn't realise you listened so closely.'

'I listen to everything you say.' I stare at him. He looks away.

'There was another bidder,' he says. 'Last minute.'

'You?'

He nods.

'But Mama said they sold for eleven thousand pounds.'

'Yes.'

'Why would you pay that? That's an insane amount of money.'

'I guess I believe what someone once told me. Some things are valuable just because.'

Then, despite the shame, the snarling coil of humiliation, I am lit up inside, I am buzzing. He's done this because he understands. He's done this *for me*. The need to touch him is overwhelming. It is such an easy thing. To cross the space between us.

'Lauren, what happened last week—'

I shake my head, I don't want to go back there, I want to stay in this moment, holding his gift in my hands. But he carries on in his low, gentle voice. 'It's okay, nothing's wrong. It was just a mistake.'

'Was it?'

For what seems like an age, he says nothing. Then, he backs slowly away. 'I'm with your mother.'

I don't reply.

'You're her daughter.'

I don't move.

'She's going to tell you tonight but it's important I tell you now. We're getting married.'

His words come to me from a distance, I understand what he's saying and I also do not. When Mama talks about him, he is someone who knows about property in Kensington and Chelsea, chamber music, French wine, but when he and I are together, he is butterflies and terrariums and colour. So, I am struggling to connect the Daniel in front of me with my mother's Daniel. Yet I know what he's saying must be true. This is why Mama wanted me to see him. So he could give me the display case, show me he cares. In the opposite way I want.

The butterflies glitter beneath the glass, poppy red, sunflower yellow, I've wanted them back for so long. But now, I understand that they are nothing more than a consolation prize. A stand-in for something else.

After I get home and Mama tells me she's engaged, after she and Daniel leave to celebrate (she begs me to come, I tell her I don't feel well), I go to Mama's room. The spritz of her perfume lingers in the air – patchouli, vanilla – but it is her wardrobe that holds the distillation of her, her distinctive musk.

I open the doors. Her wardrobe is neat like mine; 'You must look after your things,' she drilled into me. Which is fine, neither of us have much, just clothes from charity shops, although every single piece is good quality. Mama, with her eye for style, is adept at picking out clothes, she doesn't wear tracksuits like the other mums, she wears shirts with lace collars, silk trousers, woollen car coats. I grab a fistful of her concert dress, press it to my nose. Then, I start yanking things out, whatever catches my eye, a silver lamé dress, a black robe, a patterned shirt. The wrench of cloth quells the fury inside, the noise a relief against the terrible silence of the lab, the quiet way he backed away. I try them on, one after the other, all the clothes I've seen her wear for him – a violet dress with lace panels, a peach silk wrap, a gold sequin halter, the heels growing higher as I grow more desperate because it is painfully clear that I look nothing like my mother. These dresses, which she has tailored exactly to reach her knees or ankles, cut awkwardly across my thighs or calves, I cannot fill them, the material sags over my flat chest, my boyish hips. I thought the dresses would make a difference. But it isn't the dresses at all. Mama is attractive in them, shapely, because *she* is attractive and shapely. I have never felt uglier in my life.

I stumble to her dressing table. I've never tried on anything but mascara but I've watched Mama so many times, I think, foolishly, that observation is a substitute for practice. Her foundation on my skin is shockingly dark, her lipstick too red, her eyeliner, drawn by my inexpert hand, is thick and jagged. I look at my reflection. I am something from a horror movie. A pageant girl who's applied her own make-up.

No wonder he doesn't want you, I think. *No wonder.*

From: Kit McDermott   **13:29**
I've just found the pasta you made Mills. I can't stop crying.

15

Prodigals

Now

I'm shaking so hard when I reach the tube, I can't hold my Oyster card steady, I swipe twice before the gate swings open. I think of one of my trainees who had obsessive-compulsive disorder, she'd disappear into the toilets every hour of the day, when she returned, her hands were wet and raw. Now, I think I understand. I'd do it all the time if it worked, plunge my hands into the burn of hot water, the enveloping cloud of soap. I'd wash hundreds of times for the certainty of being purged.

I loved you.

'Stop being so easy,' I say out loud to the open tracks, and then I know what will turn the traitorous tide of my thoughts, the untamed part of me that still hasn't learnt. I get onto the tube, take four stops to Hammersmith.

The church is open, through an extension that wasn't here eighteen years ago. I step inside. I'm greeted by an eager volunteer in a red T-shirt who asks if I'm here for the debt advice centre. I glance round. Opposite the bookshop is a café where people are being paired up with volunteers. I shake my head. My voice trembles. 'I just wanted to visit the church.'

The volunteer nods, this is, apparently, completely normal. She waves me through the double doors. It's cool inside. Light filters down from the stained-glass windows. I cast around, vigilant for memory, but the grey, stone walls, the high arches, the navy ceiling don't ring any bells. So, when I finally see the triptych at the front, it is a double blow. 'They haven't finished it,' Daniel whispered to me all those years ago, as the vicar showed us round. Only two of the panels were painted – a blacked-out cross in the centre, an old man flinging his arms round a skeletal prodigal son on the right – but the left was blank, just gold leaf. Later, while Mama and Daniel exchanged their vows, I stared at that panel, trying to feel nothing, trying to feel as blank as it was.

I don't make it to the triptych. I crawl into the nearest pew, press my head to the polished wood. I held a bouquet of tulips as I walked down this aisle. Daniel beamed. I willed him to give me something, something that felt like our museum afternoons: herbariums and cacao pods, stormed beaches and butterfly cabinets. But as the congregation rose for Mama, he lifted his eyes to her. His expression changed for her.

What would she say if she were here, if she knew everything that happened after? I stare at the panel of the old man pressing his lips into the matted hair of his wayward son and think that's how Mama used to hold me. Everything else falls away.

You were a child. Just a child.

A child who prayed he'd see me not you.

You had a crush.

Crush, crush, a squeeze of juice poured over ice, a summer drink. When people say it, they don't mean it can crush you. That it can blow you apart.

You've suffered enough.

My eyes are stinging. In quiet of the church, I feel everything, the sharp sear of stitches, the contractions of my stomach, the fullness of my breasts. When I was little, I was scared of needles, I would scream when I had to go for vaccinations. Mama would push up her sleeves and hold out her wrists. 'Squeeze,' she'd say. 'Give it to me.' I squeezed until her wrists turned white, until I felt no pain, only her insides, her bones. She would never have wanted this for me. She would have taken it herself.

The day after she announced her engagement, she tried to draw me into her arms, she said she wanted me to come on their honeymoon. 'We've always been together. Nothing needs to change.'

I pushed her away. 'I can't think of anything worse.' The hurt in her eyes made me feel good and sick all at once. 'I don't want to tag along!'

She looked at me like I was a stranger. The engagement sent a fault line between us, I started more fights with her than I'd ever done in my life, needlessly difficult if she asked me for my opinion on her dress, moody when we visited wedding venues, argumentative when she tried to involve me in the flower arrangements. When she shouted at me, I felt relief. I wanted her to hate me as much as I hated myself.

'What's going on with you?' she'd ask over and over. 'Are you worried things are going to change? Don't you like Daniel?' I put my hands over my ears so I wouldn't hear his name. When he came to the apartment, I'd go to my room, shut the door.

It was Daniel who found the Easter camp at Wyatt. I'd never been to camp before, we couldn't afford anything like that, but Daniel opened up an entire world. 'It's a boarding school, one of the best girls' schools in the country, and you could go for the holidays.' Mama showed me the website. The school was a sprawling Victorian manor set between Chiltern hills, acres of grounds with a lake, gardens. I shrugged, pretended not to be impressed, even though it was the only thing that kept me sane during wedding preparations, its possibilities tinkling inside me like bells. I could become someone else, I wasn't sure what, but definitely not awkward or quiet or fungus freak. And when I got back to St Matthews, I'd finally have something to say about my holidays, I wouldn't have to endure the humiliation of confessing I'd done nothing, spoken to no one.

The only fly in the ointment was Mama. She let me sign up, politely accepted Daniel's offer to pay the fee, but she wouldn't stop talking about what had happened between us. 'When I get back this needs to change.' She gestured at the space between us. 'This needs to get better. We have to make this better.'

She called me every day from Lake Garda on the mobile she bought me specifically for that purpose. I watched it ring, didn't pick up. I didn't want anything to do with them. I wanted to be here, where the light fell clearer, greener than in London, sparkling on the lake before I broke the surface with the new dive I'd learnt, or glancing off the white stone walls of the hall where there was more food than I could ever imagine – roasts, a salad bar, five types of dessert.

The girls at Wyatt were a different breed. At St Matthews, I was one of two Asians; Christine was the other and I hated her because she was exactly who I thought I should be – petite, black fringe, Grade 6 on the piano – she called Mama 'Auntie' when she saw her and spoke in perfect Mandarin. But at Wyatt, almost a quarter of the girls were Asian and, like me, they didn't play musical instruments, they understood but couldn't read the language of their parents. At Wyatt, I felt normal, sometimes, even special. The first lunch at camp, a girl called Jennie slammed her lunch tray down next to mine and cupped a handful of my hair. 'Oh my God, you're so lucky. Your hair colour is *exactly* the shade I've been looking for!'

It was easy to let Jennie and her friend Lisa adopt me, to let their dramas overpower my own. Lisa's father was some kind of Hong Kong property magnate; her main topic of conversation was her horse, Toffee, and her on-off boyfriend from the neighbouring boarding school. Jennie, from Seoul, was obsessed with beauty – make-up, skincare, hair – and determined to educate me in K-pop. I never touched my sketchbook. There was no time with horse-riding and make-overs and movie nights. I was almost too distracted to think about my butterflies, the warmth of Daniel's body behind me, the pulse of his throat. Almost.

Mama left me long voicemails, where she pretended she didn't know I was ignoring her. '*Ciao, bella*' she'd start, sunshine in her voice. She'd tell me about the boat trips and the linguine, the hotel and the cobblestone streets, sometimes I listened all the way to the end, other times, it gave me unbelievable satisfaction to press 'delete' while she was still talking, just cut her off.

The messages stopped after six days. *Finally*, I thought, *she's got the message*. But as the days rolled into a week, eight days, nine, I started to worry, it was fair that I didn't want to speak to her but not that she didn't want to speak to me. I called Daniel. His voice was flat and strange, he sounded like he was on a motorway. He said he was already on his way to Wyatt; he'd be there within the hour.

When he arrived, one of the camp leaders led us sombrely to an empty classroom. I stared at the clean whiteboard while he told me Mama had left the hotel early to go to a flea market, I pictured her at the crack of dawn, leafing through antique lace, staring into the curve of a silver spoon, appraising a jug carved with lemons. He'd wanted a swim so hadn't gone with her. He said he'd regret it forever.

The police weren't sure how it happened, just that she lost control of the car. It crashed into a protective wall. The fuel tank exploded. I covered my face. He pulled me into his arms.

Light arrows over the church pew in front of me, it's so bright where it's shining that, for a second, I pretend she is just beyond it, about to step towards me, and then I am crying because after so many years, I still want my mother. She would have wept over Faye. She would have loved Millie. She'd be horrified that I've left.

This needs to change, she'd said. *This needs to get better.*

I stand up.

I will go back to him. To the man who made me lose everything. And I will change things. I will make things better.

*

From: Kit McDermott   **13:47**
I'm sorry for saying you were selfish, I didn't mean it. You're the least selfish person I've ever met.

Dear Darling

It's me, isn't it? This is all my fault. A few months ago, I watched you climb the stairs, you had to haul yourself up, one hand after the other, your beautiful stomach sticking out from under your T-shirt, and I thought this is too much for you.

It was so much worse this time round. Not just the nausea, all those hospital visits, the extra scans but the tiredness – you could barely talk at the end of the day. Sometimes, I'd watch you plaster a smile on your face for Millie when she showed you another toilet-roll creation and I thought you can't do this again. Now, I wish I could turn back time, I wish I'd never asked you for a second child.

If anyone's selfish, it's me.

16

Park

Now

Less than an hour later, I'm outside his house. Seeing it in the afternoon enrages me more than it did last night; in the day, the house doesn't just look tidy – it's pristine. There are no cobwebs at the corners of the stable door, the cream-painted brick looks recently washed, even the drainpipe looks like it's been wiped. He belongs here. Fresh out of prison and, instantly, he belongs.

He rubs his eyes when he opens the door, he can't quite believe I'm here. Behind him, the house isn't the pale grey of my memory – the walls are a sumptuous indigo. It reminds me of a private members' club, the inside of a yacht, so different from stained prison walls, strip lighting, metal grates. He wants no reminder of the place he was in just a week ago.

He follows my gaze. 'Do you like the colour?'

I raise my eyebrows.

'It was the name that sold it to me, they called it "Mazarine Blue", after—'

'—I know what a Mazarine Blue is.' It's a blue butterfly, extinct in the British Isles. As well as Asian butterflies, Daniel specialised in Blues.

'I taught you well.'

I will not react to this. To all the things he should and shouldn't have taught me. 'How have you done all this? I thought you got out last week.'

He shrugs. 'I knew what I wanted, I had eighteen years to plan it. As soon as I got my release date, I contacted some builders, an interior designer, I gave them very detailed instructions. So last week, when I came home, everything was ready, everything was perfect.'

He'll have made them visit him in prison; he's always disliked talking on the phone. Behind smudgy glass, they'll have shown him mood boards, fabric swatches, pressed a grey telephone receiver to their ears. What did they think when he explained the paint was named after an extinct British butterfly? Did they know he'd been given the maximum sentence for a hit and run, for running a man over and never going back? Or did they simply ask for proof of funds? A deposit with enough zeros after the digit?

'Do you want to come in?' he asks carefully.

I shake my head. 'Let's go to Holland Park.'

It's a cop-out and he knows it, two humiliated spots bloom on his cheeks – he thinks I don't want to be in the house of a criminal. But the truth is, I am less frightened of him than myself. Butterflies, empty nets, the twist of his bedsheets – dangerous evocations. I'm not ready to see those. I don't think I'll ever be ready.

He is still for a second; he is debating if he should confront me. But he decides against it. He unhooks his blazer and pulls the door shut.

We walk to the top of the mews then left along Abbotsbury Road, he toys with the collar of his shirt because it's so warm. I loved the area when Mama brought us to visit even before he pointed out the Beckhams' house, Richard Branson's, Michael Jackson's, because it wasn't the white Italianate mansions or the private gardens that captivated me but the trees, the height of them, how they canopied the pavements in sap-green light.

'I'm sorry about earlier, at the museum,' he says. The park gate squeaks as he pushes it open. A girl and boy are playing on the bronze sculptures of tortoises. 'I scared you off.'

We take the oak-lined path to the right. The air swarms with the shouts of children, over the low fence is a playground. A wooden boardwalk snakes through the trees, there's a silver slide, a zip line. I smile at the sandpit. Sand is Millie's favourite, if she was here, she'd ignore the impressive equipment and head straight for it, commandeer a discarded spade, form a girl gang to dig a hole.

A baby is crying. It's a girl, I can see her white frilled socks and pink shoes. Her mum pushes the pram back and forth, she's distracted, she's talking to her older son, and I am seized by the urge to walk over, unbuckle the baby and take her to the hotel. She'd sleep on the bed next to me, on me, whatever she wants, let us be marsupials, pouched and animally close, breathing the warmth of each other's skin. I could call Kit, he'd come and I'd uncover a corner of the warm blanket, say, 'Look. I didn't lose her at all, it's Faye, right here.'

'Lolly?'

I blink back tears. I can't be here anymore. Too many buggies. Too many children.

'Are you okay?'

Dear Darling

My breasts are swelling. I took medication to stop my milk coming through but that hasn't stopped the sensation, real or imaginary, that they are filling every time I think too much about Faye. I cross my arms over my chest and pull ahead of Daniel.

He catches up at the Dutch Garden. Geometric beds display cheerful alstroemeria and showy dahlias, too pretty for me, too pretty for everything that's happened. We don't speak as we walk past the giant chessboard but I can feel him taking me in, his sly, sideways glances.

'Are you unwell?'

'I'm fine.'

We fall in step with each other, easily, too easily. Kit is tall, lanky even, it's a joke between us, the difference between our heights, he has to deliberately slow himself down to keep pace with me. With Daniel, there is a rhythm to our bodies, instinctive. I hang back, let him walk ahead.

When we pass the copper fountain, something changes in him, an electric current amped up. Under the orangery arches, he squeezes through a slim gap between a group of tourists and then, he rushes along the path in front of Holland House. I don't call after him. I know where he is going. I find him at the bench opposite the football pitches. It's the bench he took me to see the primroses.

After he tells me about Mama, he gives me a choice, I can stay at Wyatt or go back to London with him. I go with him. I am frightened. Something is coming, I can feel it, tremoring at the back of my mind, distant at first but picking up speed. I don't want to be with new people, pretending everything's okay.

It is not the funeral that brings me really low, because there isn't one. Daniel says he can't bear the thought of people he doesn't know – her pupils, members of orchestras and quartets – he doesn't want them to offer him hugs or shake his hand or tell them their memories of her, but if I want a big funeral, of course he'll organise one. I shake my head, struck by the fact that, in my grief, I am not alone, that there are things he cannot bear either.

It is the arrival of her things that pushes me over the edge – our flat, which he is renting out, needs to be emptied for new tenants. Daniel hires movers to pack up the contents, they carry boxes into his house in pairs, build walls of them around his study, and though he is careful to shut the door, it weighs on my mind. The bulwark fact of it, the entire room of our things that I must pass every day, punctures all my pretending that Mama is still in Italy, travelling for a season, about to walk through the front door.

I stop speaking. There is a place inside me where I feel nothing at all; if I lie on the bed which isn't mine, in a house which isn't mine, and stare at one single thing for a long time, I can get to it. I hear Daniel speaking to me sometimes, cajoling me to eat, watch television, go for a walk, but it is very distant. He seems more like the flicker of my own thoughts, the electrical impulses between the neurons of my brain.

Slowly, though, his voice grows louder, his presence more real. When I tune in, I realise he is talking not about Mama and what will happen to me, but about flowers.

'There's a patch under the horse chestnuts.' He sets a single flower down on my bedside table. A primrose. I stare at the lemon petals, the succulent crinkle-edged leaves.

'Look at these,' he says a few days later. This time, he's brought a pair. 'They're different. This one has this greenish disc at its centre but this one—' he separates the petals to show me its heart, 'has a cluster of anthers.'

Primroses are heterostylous, I think. One is *pin* the other is *thrum*.

He tells me that when he walked in the park, he'd been lifting up the furry undersides of the leaves to check for brimstone eggs. 'They're great butterfly nurseries,' he says, pressing a jar into my palm, 'the colour's a perfect camouflage.' The eggs are pale green and luminous. The casing is ridged like the inside of a shell.

So, when he tells me that primroses have appeared along the banks of the North Lawn, the single patch turned to drift, when he says, 'Let's go see them,' he's already spent weeks tilling my mind, planting seeds. I get up.

He walks his palms over the bench as if to test its solidity. He searches the ground for the primroses but there are only bluebells, pushing through the alkanet. 'I've thought about this place a thousand times.'

'Did you think about what would happen if we met again?'

'Always. That and the summer I had with you. Nothing else seemed real, not my life before, or the trial, or . . .' He breaks off. That silence again around prison. 'And you? Did you think of this place?' He doesn't dare look at me. His dream of us is so fragile, I could kill it or give it life.

I nod.

He takes a long drag of air in and out. My admission has quelled something in him. He straightens up. 'What you were saying at the museum . . .' his words are hesitant, he is gesturing, 'about our ages . . .' He stops. How strange. For a taxonomist obsessed with naming, describing, categorising, he hasn't realised that his refusal to name something gives it power.

'What I'm trying to say is, at the museum, I was worried you'd changed how you saw our time together.' He pauses. 'That you're seeing things differently now to how they really were.'

A seam of rage unravels. I force myself to watch the junior football club practising on the lawn, follow the ball's jagged route from boot to boot until I'm certain my voice is level. 'Hindsight is twenty-twenty.'

'What does that mean?'

'It means things are clearer now as a thirty-two-year-old woman than as a fourteen-year-old girl.'

'I don't know if that's true.'

'You think the judgement of a fourteen-year-old girl isn't impaired by her age, her understanding?'

'I don't know anything about fourteen-year-old girls. I'm not talking about them. I'm talking about you.' He steps towards me. 'Why are you doing this?'

'Things have changed.' A striker takes aim, misses. The ball catapults off the goal post, the boys roar chasing it down the pitch. 'So many scandals. We know so much more about people like you—'

'—People like me?' he repeats slowly.

'—There's a playbook.' The words come out with a lightness I don't feel. Under my clothes, I'm trembling.

'How does that go?'

'You choose a vulnerable girl—'

'—*You* chose me.'

'You turn her from her friends—'

'—You never had any friends.'
'Her family—'
'—Your mother was dead!'
'You shower her with gifts—'
'—I provided for you; I bought you everything you wanted.'
'You tell her you love her—'
'—Because it was true.'
'You fuck her—'
'—Stop!' He rears back, as if I've pulled the pin out of a grenade and rolled it towards him. 'That was never what it was! You know that wasn't what it was!'

A fleck of his spit lands on the corner of my mouth. I wipe it off. 'Then, you leave.'

'I never left you! I was in a car accident—'

A car accident? Is that what he's calling it?

'—And after that, I was arrested!' He runs his hand angrily through his hair. 'I sent you hundreds of letters, you never replied!'

A cheer rises from the lawn. Someone has scored a goal.

'This playbook you think I've used, I haven't. It doesn't apply to us, it isn't real. You're twisting everything that happened.'

'Or you are.'

We're both breathless. The air between us is snakes, tails lashing, tongues flicking.

He gives in first. The set of his jaw softens. 'Lolly—'

'Don't call me that. Don't you *ever* call me that again.'

'Lauren, then,' he says carefully, his hands open, no weapons. 'How do we move past this? There must be a way.'

My stomach spasms. I wrap my arms around myself.

He registers the flicker of pain. 'Sit down, please.'

Reluctantly, I lever myself onto the bench.

He stays at the other end, doesn't come any closer, but I feel his eyes running over my body just like he used to, as openly as if it's his own. 'Something's really wrong, isn't it? You're walking strangely, you can't stand up straight, you keep clutching your middle.' His voice is low and tender. 'Are you hurt? Has someone hurt you?'

You've hurt me, I want to say. *This is all because of you*, and then I remember the doctor saying, 'We have to go,' the piercing coldness of the anaesthetic, the blue curtain.

I shut my eyes, listen to the club disband, the congratulations from the coach, reminders of next week's match and then the boys are being collected by their parents, there is talk of pasta and movies. I want to collect Millie, I want to make her pasta. I'll let her watch as much *Peppa Pig* as she likes. I turn away so he won't see me cry.

'Listen to me, listen,' he says. 'The second I was released, I sent you a letter, I wanted to see you.' His voice trembles. 'You think I wanted to come back here, to all these memories? I could have gone anywhere – the Philippines, Columbia, Peru – somewhere with a decent number of butterfly species, I could have resurrected my career, I was a damn good lepidopterist. But I didn't do any of those things. I stayed in London for you. I'm here for you.'

There's a word pilots say before their plane crashes, what is it?

'I know I haven't been in your life; I've missed so many things.'

Brace. Brace.

'But I loved you then. I love you still.'

'I love you still' doesn't unravel me like 'I loved you.' Perhaps it's because, eighteen years ago, I loved him too; there are times – breastfeeding Millie in the unholy hours of the night, pushing her buggy in the driving rain – when I can still feel the fire of it. But 'I love you' in the present tense doesn't land. Because it's ludicrous. Absurd. 'You can't mean that.'

'I do.'

'It's been almost two decades.'

'Does that matter?'

'Everything's changed.'

'Some things change. Others stay the same.' He traces the outline of my face in the air before me and it is enough; my lips remember the press of his thumb; my scalp remembers his fingers through my hair. A flash of heat shoots up my spine.

I clamp my jaws together. 'You don't know me. Do you know how much muscle it takes to make it through the day? To get out of bed, to go to work . . .' *To be with Kit, to play with Millie.* 'I'm not a very good . . . I haven't been a very good . . .' *Wife, mother.* '—You don't know anything about me.'

'Then, tell me.'

'—Not a single thing.'

'Then show me.'

Can it be this easy? I've watched countless YouTube videos of abusers being confronted by survivors – aged Catholic priests, doctors, film producers – watched their faces fall in as their victims bared their rage. None of them *wanted* to be there. They wouldn't look up, wouldn't even respond, who wants to be confronted with what they've done? I was certain Daniel would be the same, that's why I started my garden beyond the brambles, the pots in my greenhouse, I would make him listen. I never anticipated he'd just *ask* to hear it. And I wonder. How certain am I that he is wrong and I am right?

'You really want to do this?'

'Yes.'

'You won't like it.'

'I want it. All of it.' He holds my eyes for an excruciating length of time. Once, I wouldn't have been able to meet his gaze, bewildered by its intensity, the flame in my cheeks. Now, I raise my chin higher and higher, my eyes defiant and unblinking, and as the moment unspools, it settles on me, the risk I'm taking, the bargain I'm striking. He is going to prove he loved me. I am going to prove he ruined me.

My stomach twinges, I need a painkiller. I rifle through my backpack. He watches me pop them out.

'Lauren,' he says. 'Start by telling me what's wrong.'

'It'll make sense later.' I stand up, start walking.

'Later?' he says, still at the bench.

'Tomorrow,' I say. 'I'll pick you up tomorrow.'

I make my way slowly out of the park. I think of nooses around necks, lambs led to slaughter. But who is lamb and who is butcher?

PART II

Sunday

17

Ivy

Now

01:49. I can't sleep. The hotel room is sunk in darkness. I could be anywhere. I thought I heard Millie, she gets up round this time, calling for me from her cot bed. By the time I stumble downstairs, she'll be sitting up, trying to push back her own bed-head hair. 'Mop-a-top', Kit calls her. He says she doesn't need me to get in beside her, on nights when she's on his watch, he kisses her, tells her he loves her and leaves. But even though her cot blanket is the size of three tea towels and I end up with a backache, I can't resist the warm bun of her body, her heavy, sleepy limbs. A few months ago, she started saying, 'snuggy'. 'Get into my snuggy bed, Mummy,' she'd whisper when she spotted me sleepy at her door. When I told Kit, he put his hand over his heart, like it was breaking. 'Yeah, all right. She wins.'

But I'm not at home. And it isn't Millie. Only the gurgle of pipes, the thud of a suitcase against the wall. I reach for my phone, I have to see her, my heart is thundering because she might actually be awake, it's the right time, she might be calling for me, and though seeing her will split me in two, I'm desperate.

The screensaver of the three of us appears, we're on the heath, eating Mr Whippy ice creams, Kit's head tilted almost ninety degrees so he can squeeze into the selfie, his blond hair lighter in the sun, his green eyes creased at the edges from the broadness of his smile. On the bar at the bottom, my messages total fifty-eight. Kit. My husband who washed the rug after I dripped blood onto it, who checked my scar for infection because I was too frightened to look myself, who fitted those mammoth maternity pads into my equally mammoth knickers because I couldn't bend down. 'Let's get this bad boy in,' he'd joked, and though the pain was breathtaking, I smiled. One tender, funny word from him and I'll go straight home. Leaving would have been for nothing.

I don't click on the messages.

I click on the Nanny app.

Millie is asleep. The shadowy curl of her body rises and falls with her breath; she's kicked off her blanket. I start pushing back my own covers, my brain on automatic – I'll get an Uber across London, it'll be quick at this time of night. I won't wake them when I get to The Wedge, I'll be quiet up the stairs, tuck her back in, kiss her cheek. I'm already standing up when I see Kit pulling her blanket over her. He smooths the hair back from her face and then lies on the carpet beside her. He hasn't brought a pillow or blanket. He's always like this. He doesn't eat breakfast unless I make him, won't wear a new coat unless I put one over his shoulders, he's the second of four siblings, he's used to getting by without much. I used to worry what he'd do if something happened to me. I know he'd look after Millie; he'd read her books, tie her hair up in bunches, play unicorns with her. But who will look after him?

Dear Darling

*

I've been metres from his house for the last three hours, pacing the high street, circling the mews. The sky is marbled with dawn; there's only runners and dog-walkers this early. I watch a collie chase a labradoodle with a pink clip on her fringe across the football pitch. Kit always spoke about getting a dog; I should have encouraged him. There would be someone there for him when I wasn't.

He is smiling when he opens the door, he is too pleased that I am here. 'Are you coming in this time?' he says lightly, as if my refusal to enter his house is an in-joke between us, as if we are friends capable of having in-jokes.

I stare at him coldly, until his smile fades. 'Are you ready?' I ask.

'Where are we going?'

I don't reply.

'You don't want to tell me.' I feel him appraising me, all the things I say, everything I don't. 'What are you worried about? That I won't go with you?'

Is it my mouth that gives me away, my eyes? How can he still read what I think and feel?

'Listen,' he says, so gently, I'm reminded of him lifting a butterfly from a twist of nets, how tenderly he used to untangle them. 'You can tell me the plan.' His scent rushes over me - cotton, herbs, ethyl acetate. 'I'd go anywhere with you.'

I step back, try to stay in control. My voice is pitchy and forced. 'I wanted to take you to my old law school.'

'Why?'

'Things happened there.'

His eyes narrow, then he nods slowly. 'Okay. Give me five.'

I don't wait for him on the balcony. I rush down the steps, eager to return to the person I was two days ago, standing outside his house, clutching my angel's trumpets in the dark. Revenge felt easy then, I was bolder, dangerous, not this tired sog of a mess. I scratch the cream brick of his house. Paint fills my nails; stupid, I've hurt myself more than him. I cast around for greenery – moss blooming on his wall, herb pots on the step, dandelion shoots – but the only hint of the wild and untamed are the tendrils of ivy creeping over from his neighbour's wall.

It's enough.

I examine the leaves. *Hedera helix*, English ivy, not poison ivy although all of it is poisonous. In the winter, the berries will look like blueberries, Millie's favourite. We got a call from nursery once, we had to collect her immediately because her poo was black, a sign of internal bleeding. Children's A&E was miserable, the mural with the bright sun a pointed contrast to the exhausted parents, the terrifying low whine from a girl in her mother's arms. After a seven-hour wait, the results came in. No internal bleeding. Just too many blueberries. Kit laughed with relief but I couldn't stop thinking how different this could have been. A handful of ivy berries can fell a horse.

I pluck three perfectly glossy leaves. Slip them into the back pocket of my jeans.

He locks the door behind him. He is remarkably spry down the steps, for a second, I forget that he's forty-eight, not thirty, his body still holds so much energy. I squeeze my fingers into fists. I will not think about his body. The power it possesses.

'Where's your law school?' he asks.

'Moorgate.'

'Let's get a cab then,' he says, like he used to when we'd finish at the museum. He always despised public transport. I'd walk everywhere – school, Hyde Park – or get the bus to the Natural History Museum, swinging onto the open rear of a Routemaster, grinning at the conductor, but Daniel only drove or travelled in black cabs. But now, black cabs are rare, he can't find one and I'm almost certain he doesn't have Uber. He leans into the road, scanning for the orange light of a black cab. A cyclist catches his shoulder. He staggers back. For a second, I glimpse the elderly man he'll become – prone to falls, baffled by bikes, phones, apps.

'The underground might be quicker,' I say gently.

He blinks at me, nods. Leading him to the station, I'm electric at his bewilderment. Old orders have been overturned. London is mine.

It's busy on the tube, we're standing by the doors when we get on but, as we draw closer to Oxford Street, we're pushed into the middle. He removes his rucksack, I unsling my black one, and then I realise how stupid I've been, I haven't thought this through. Without the shield of our bags, I can smell the detergent of his shirt, the complex scent of his skin underneath. The last time we were this close, we were crying, pleading, kissing. I shut my eyes.

'This is some kind of trip, isn't it?' he asks. 'A journey through your life.' The tube shudders through the black mouth of a tunnel. I want to put my hands over my ears against the sudden jerks, the howl of the wind. 'Am I close?'

Does he think I'm playing a game?

'You've planned this, haven't you?'

I've hatched plans within plans, a Russian doll of schemes, inside, there is something always smaller, more intricate.

He cocks his head, studying me. The tube lights flicker off, on. 'You're different to how I imagined.'

He means I'm not naïve. Not fourteen and all over him.

'You're stronger, sharper.'

The train brakes suddenly, everyone is thrown forwards then back, and though all around, there is shouting, swearing, the clutching of shopping bags, my senses are honed on one single thing – his body against mine. I feel the jut of his knee, the line of his shin, the slab of his shoulder. I am feeling him, as he is feeling me.

I take one deliberate step back. Doesn't matter that the student behind rolls his eyes or the posh woman with her coiffured hair asks me what on earth I think I'm doing. I don't talk to any of them, only him. 'You're wrong,' I say, feeling for the shape of the ivy leaves in the back pocket of my jeans. 'I was always strong. Sharp.'

*

From: Kit McDermott   **09:29**

The police told me to make a list of what you'd taken, so, one of the first things I did was pull open your bedside table drawer. And there they were, in plain sight: a strip of tablets. I've looked them up. You're on antidepressants?

18

Colour

Then

I do not speak in his house. When I wake up each morning, there is a moment of confusion – where am I, what's happened, where's Mama – before the fug descends. During the day, I'll crave those moments, I'll pray that tomorrow, they'll last longer, save me, even for a few seconds, from the bludgeon of grief.

He doesn't badger me about speaking. He is patient. Sometimes, he sees I am on the brink of it, the words are there, blooming on my tongue but I can't get them out, my mouth is pulp, the sticky sugar of spun candy. When that happens, he waits until he is certain the moment has passed and then he pats me on my arm. 'Don't worry. It will come.'

He is working from home so he can look after me, he hasn't been to the museum in weeks. The fact that it's just him and me adds to the strangeness of what's happened, everything feels wrong, upside down. I've never spent so much time alone with him, never seen him do chores or wear anything but grey shirts and blazers. But now, he is folding my laundry, chopping vegetables, wiping down surfaces, I've seen him in his pyjamas (a simple dark T-shirt, checked bottoms). I am knocked off course, in an alternative universe. If Mama walked in right now and said it was all a mistake, I wouldn't even be surprised, I'm so bewildered.

When I finally speak, it is because he gives me something. He lays it at the foot of my bed, it looks like a sleek wooden briefcase but then, I see the brand emblazoned in silver and hold my breath as I push it open. It is a box of a hundred and twenty-two oil core colour pencils presented in two shelves, the top, a rainbow constellation. But it is the bottom shelf that astonishes me – twenty-two greens, thirteen browns. I put one perfectly sharp pencil to paper. The line is so fine, faithfully translating each doubt and tremor of my hand, but when I angle it to the side, press harder, the pigment is vibrant, the texture, butter.

He turns to leave. I catch hold of his sleeve, push words out, 'Thank you.' Not just for the gift but because, if only for this moment, he has gifted me myself.

He smiles. 'Draw.'

Flowers help with words, colour helps with words, a new vocabulary flooding in where guilt and grief has run the ground arid. I choose light yellow glaze over ivory to capture the primrose petals, cadmium yellow for the darker heart. The pin head of the stigma, I shade may green, edge it in lime. Then, as he gifts me more botany books, as he starts taking me for walks in the park and I find flowers again, I break into other colours: delft blue; manganese violet; burnt carmine.

He talks to me constantly about butterflies – he is working on a country-by-country count of butterfly species to track population growth and decline, he's made a new discovery about the mating habits of nymphets, he tells me about each rare butterfly in his private collection. My mind fills with markings and wings, it is better than thinking about all the cruel things I said to Mama, her car exploding. At night, when my imagination unfurls in cinematic reel, I shove it aside with lists, reciting the rarest butterflies in the world, the biggest, the smallest.

He has been speaking to some researchers about a British butterfly, the Cornish Blue. I imagine an astonishing creature like the Queen Alexandra's Birdwing he showed me at the museum, shimmering turquoise, a wingspan the width of my waist, but it is small by comparison, the colour a gas flame cobalt. One night, over dinner, he tells me it is going extinct.

He has made steak; he is slicing through it. Daniel can cook, something I never realised until I lived with him. He makes sea bass, salmon, chicken cacciatore with simple vegetables, no carbs, no drinks apart from water or fresh fruit smoothies, he makes me take daily vitamins: cod liver oil, vitamin C, vitamin D. He is also fastidious. Maria comes every Tuesday to clean the bathrooms and hoover but between her visits, he wipes down the surfaces, empties the dishwasher. My laundry comes back in folded squares. At home, Mama just dumped the laundry on my bed. It was my job to fold it, hang it, put it away.

I make a gesture with my chin, to ask him why the Cornish Blues are going extinct. I am not speaking much, a few words, a few gestures, if I don't he might stop talking and I don't want him to. I like watching him, how relaying a fact can change his expression, his whole body straining with the excitement of it.

'That's the interesting part.' He widens the collar of his shirt, it's warm. 'After the colonies dropped to four, a connection was discovered between the Cornish Blue and a type of red ant.' He chews. 'The only way the Blues survive between caterpillar and chrysalis is by pretending to be the ants' own larvae, they emit a chemical pheromone, almost a honey that makes the ants believe the caterpillar is theirs. The ants, sweetly deceived, carry the caterpillar back to their nest. They look after them, feed them, even sing to them.'

I raise my eyebrows.

He laughs. 'You didn't think humans are the only species to sing lullabies to their young?'

Mama always played me lullabies from the living room, she'd start off with a classic – 'Silent Night', 'Somewhere Over the Rainbow' – then morph it into something else, a pop song or a piece of her own invention. I dig my nails into my palm.

'But this social parasitism is fragile. Which brings me to something I wanted to talk to you about.' He puts down his fork. 'They've asked me to lead a project to halt the extinction of the Blues. I need to take a trip.'

Lost in violin lullabies, trails of marching ants, I am not following what he is saying.

'So, I was thinking, this might be a good time for you to think about going to Wyatt.' After the funeral, we decided together that I should transfer to the boarding school I went to during the Easter holidays. I half listened to his reasons (he might be away on research trips, Wyatt was light-years ahead of St Matthews, one of the best schools in the country, he wanted me to have the best). My reasons were different. When I thought of St Matthews, I remembered Mama warming my uniform on the radiator in the winter so I wouldn't be cold, how she hung two ends of a washing line over the kitchen table to clip on all my artwork, how proud she was of me when I came back with a report card full of As. There was no chance I'd go back there without her.

But the decision to transfer to Wyatt was not without consequences. The school was one of the top girls' schools in the country; while they were sympathetic about 'this difficult period,' they were keen to keep up my grades. They started sending me brown envelopes, one for each subject. The first was a friendly note from my English teacher asking me to write my own version of *Romeo & Juliet*'s prologue. I re-sealed the envelope and dropped it on the floor.

'I know you haven't taken things well.'

How does a daughter take her mother's death well?

'I've been struggling too.'

I haven't thought once about how he is; he seems completely himself. Perhaps that's my fault. How can he grieve when he is looking after me?

'But I'm worried about you missing so much school.'

Until this moment, Wyatt seemed faraway and distant, I hadn't put together it might be here, now. Desperation electrifies language; where I'd managed before only single words, fragments, I am jolted into whole sentences. My voice is a hoarse, broken thing. 'I'll catch up. I promise.'

He blinks, surprised at my reaction. 'Of course you will. I have no doubt you'll get up to speed. I just wonder if it's better to be back at school, around people your own age—'

'I'm better with you.'

'I'm worried—'

'Please.'

His resolve falters, my need for him loosens it. I cannot abide parks, butterflies, drawing being replaced by the clamour of Wyatt, all its bright new faces.

'All right,' he says. 'I'll write to the school, tell them you need more time. You can come to Cornwall. As long as you don't mind.'

How could I mind? There's no one else I'd rather be with.

*

From: Kit McDermott   **09:32**

I'm really freaking out here, Laurie, I don't know what's going on. Why the hell are you on antidepressants?

I get it if you got them a few weeks ago, we lost a child, we're both grieving. But there are prescriptions here from six years ago. Which makes no sense. That's before Millie. Before we were even married.

I'm going insane. I'm properly going insane.

19

Producer

Now

I know the exact date the seed took root. It was Friday 20 October 2017, eight years ago. Project Mozart had just ended, it was the third failing European bank I'd helped carve up and sell off and although the deal had been signed the night before, my body didn't believe it was over. The adrenaline of the past eight months was impossible to switch off, it trilled through me, making me jump at the ping of someone else's phone, their ringtone.

It was lunch time, I'd bought a turkey wrap, I stared at the brown paper bag and it struck me that this was the first time in months when I could eat without my emails open, without Bruce flying into my office to discuss the letter from the European Central Bank or an impromptu meeting with Finance. Tentatively, I minimised my inbox, reached for my sandwich and opened BBC News to a story breaking across America.

The women I recognised instantly, they were the faces of my childhood. The youngest sister in the TV series about three sister witches – I watched it on Saturday nights when Daniel and

Mama were on their dates, wishing I had a sister witch to battle demons and monsters. The lead actress in the movie I watched in the common room with Lisa and Jennie a year after Mama died. Beautiful, beautiful women, they were stars, Mama wanted to be them, we all wanted to be them.

I didn't recognise the name of the movie producer, but it was clear from the way he held himself that he was a Hollywood mogul. He wasn't remarkable in any way – small eyes, greying stubble, a layer of fat under his chin – if he was dressed in a plaid shirt and jeans, you'd pass him on the street without a second glance. But he was never photographed in plaid. Always in an expensive black suit, a bow tie at his throat, flashing an LA-white smile.

I pored over hundreds of images of him after I read the article. I watched his hands. Mama always said it's our hands that give us away. She showed me hers, how the fingertips of her left were hardened from decades pressed against the strings, the soft indent on her right from holding her bow, she would unfurl mine, pointing out streaks of chlorophyll. 'The violinist and the botanist,' she'd laughed.

In a few photos, the brute fleshiness of his paw was visible as he waved to fans on the red carpet or halted the intrusion of a camera lens when he was talking to the First Lady. But by far, the majority of stills pictured him pulling a starlet close, half his age, four fingers flat under the line of a bodice, thumb on bare skin, and then I blinked stupidly at my reflection in the glass wall of my office – my nude heels, silk shirt, the lip gloss winking on my lips, my mind seemed to take it all in as it crashed towards something immense and unnameable.

Half his age.
Thumb on bare skin.
I threw up in the wastepaper bin.

It consumed me, the scandal. My browser became a library of refreshed news tabs, I couldn't go anywhere without my headphones, losing myself in interviews from actresses and American daytime TV hosts, cursing whenever I lost signal between train stations, pulling an earphone discreetly out of my ear whenever Bruce looked like he was reaching for the handle of my office door. When one of Mama's favourite actresses was interviewed, I locked myself in the toilets, my throat constricting as she described the floor plan of the hotel room freezing in her mind, how he'd badgered her over and over again to go further, the oral she promised to get out. Afterwards, the words she said about why she'd spoken out now circled in my head, a constant loop, a washing cycle with no end: 'This is the moment.'

For what?

'Are you all right?' Kit asked one evening, sliding under the duvet.

'Just tired.' I'd been staying late at work, it was easier than pulling myself away from the stories, easier than talking to Kit. I'd get the last tube home and slip quietly into bed beside him.

'I thought Project Mozart was over.' Smart, quick-thinking Kit, it was hard to get away with the smallest white lie when he was a corporate lawyer too. He was well aware that weeks of downtime followed the frenzy of a deal; I wasn't leaving until past eleven. 'Have they staffed you on something else?'

'There's a lot of loose ends.'

'What are you reading?' He tapped the outside of my phone. 'You seem glued to the news. Anything interesting?' He pulled closer, put his hand on my hip, the gesture asking for more than I could give, not then, not for months to come.

I rolled to the left, turned off the light. 'True crime.'

Later, when I'd think about my twenty-four-year-old self, sitting alone in her glass office researching the producer, the absolute stillness of the department, the hum of a distant vacuum, the smell of the sour cream pooling from my unfinished burrito, I'd want desperately to travel back in time. Not really to change anything. But to push open the door and pull up a chair beside myself. Because it was lonely and tortuous. The education of my predation.

The language I learnt quickly from journalists, twitterati, the slogans scrawled on placards outside court buildings – #MeToo; believe women; break the silence; time's up; power imbalance; grooming. That wasn't hard. It was the other kind of learning that was hard. I kept it at bay as long as I could but it was impossible against the deluge of stories. Or perhaps I wasn't trying to stop it, perhaps that was why I read so much, part of me wanted, needed to be brought to breaking point, for that singular moment when something in me snapped and the treacherous thoughts would flutter out of the locked box I'd kept them in.

His hand drifting up my back.

His thumb at the edge of my vest.

Vest. Skin. Vest. Skin.

Then everything I'd told myself would rise up in me, my inner voice coldly reasonable, like it was interrogating a witness too emotional to think straight. *It was completely different. Yes, there was an age gap, a hotel, his thumb on your back, but he wasn't flabby, disgusting, he was beautiful, don't you remember the animal leanness of his body, he never pushed you down, never forced himself on you, you started it, you wanted him first, you loved him and he loved you, it's different, utterly different* and then I'd shut the box, stop reading, go home.

But it never lasted long. Soon, I'd be reading, listening again. The stories were a drug I was addicted to, I was searching for something, although I didn't know what.

Then, a few weeks later, I knew what. I found what I'd been looking for.

Twitter was ablaze with the latest story about the producer, another model had come forward, this time with a rape allegation. I read the article in *Vanity Fair* and then settled down to read the comments on Twitter, which had already climbed to five hundred and twenty-six. Towards the last third, the tweets seemed to drift away from the model, turn to the issue of rape in relationships. That's where I read it. It was a single tweet by @vplnskl243. Afterwards, I tried to find her but she was a person without a face, without followers, she'd posted no other tweets, she'd created an account just to say this, to set her own treacherous thought free: *I was 14. He was 30 #MeToo.*

Finally, I saw. What had happened to me.

20

Cottage

Then

He chooses the tiny fishing village at the foot of the valley because it is sandwiched between two gardens, a National Trust garden on one side, a private garden on the other. 'I'll get you passes to both. Then you can visit them as much as you like,' he says as we drive down to the foot of the valley. 'It'll be just like London.' He is worried that the change of scene will destabilise me, I am cracked glass on the brink of fracture. Perhaps I am. Because when Daniel gets out to ask for directions, I get out too, make my way towards the sea.

It's the water. An aquamarine so astonishing that the desire to feel it is physical. Colour is fragile, anything can change it, the clouds rolling in, the sun dipping towards the horizon; if I want to savour it, it must be in the body, now. I pull off my trainers, my socks, leave them at the sea wall. Underfoot, I feel crushed shell, a cigarette butt, the crackle of dried seaweed – and then the shock of water, so cold everything falls away. I am knee-deep when Daniel calls my name. He is as close to angry as I have ever seen him.

'How far would you have gone if I hadn't called you?' he asks when I reach him.

I don't know.

He's asked for directions; our cottage isn't in the village but a two-minute drive away. He drives back up the road, takes the dirt track into a woodland of oaks. The cottage is a simple timber cabin with a thatched roof, something from a fairy tale, a woodcutter's cottage perhaps, a gingerbread house without the gingerbread. A porch hugs the front with a picnic table that looks out to sea. Under the window is a generous pile of chopped logs.

He unlocks the front door. A pink sofa faces the fireplace, there is a desk with a lamp and a vase of wild bluebells. 'Not what you're used to, I'm afraid,' he says and I think he has forgotten I do not live in his mews house or in Wyatt's stained-glass windowed dormitories but in the flat above Oriental Supermarket, no log fires or sea views in sight. The cottage, to me, is beyond lovely.

'Choose any room you want,' he says. I drift upstairs. The master with its quilt folded at the end of the double bed and expansive dresser seems impossible, as is the twin bedroom – I don't want to sleep in a place where there would be space for Mama. I choose the smallest; it reminds me of my box room at home. The wallpaper is yellow with cream roses and there is just space for a narrow bed, a chest of drawers. When he brings my bag up, puts it on the floor, there is almost no standing room. 'This one? Are you sure?'

I nod. Give me suffocating spaces, freezing seas. Stop me feeling, missing, remembering.

Ella King

*

From: Kit McDermott   **09:36**

I've even seen you take the pills, every morning with the glass of water I bring you. You told me they were vitamins. My God, Laurie. You didn't hide them. You just lied about them.

21

Doctor

Now

After I read, 'I was 14, he was 30 *#MeToo*', that anonymous tweet, that collision of hashtag and the fact, I sank into a depression. I was a ship cut loose, quietly unmoored, all bearings lost. I kept reading the stories, more and more every day, more actresses coming forward, more confessions of hundreds of women without status, without followers. How can the internet bear the weight of all their stories? They were like waves crashing on a beach, no end, no relief. I'd fall asleep reading another headline, find my phone in the morning, the battery dead.

At first, the doctor was like so many others, another predator taking advantage of his status, another complicit industry. That he pretended the abuse was medical, that he conducted his 'treatments' on girls while their parents were in the room, no longer shocked me. Nor did his victims – Olympians with their crystal-studded leotards, the outstretched musculature of their arms. They were like the actresses. Another category of women brought low.

Still, I followed the story when it broke in the UK, more out of habit than anything else, doggedly tracking back to the original story in the local American paper and then following the developments in the federal and state cases. It was the start of a new year; the first snow was falling heavily outside my office window when I read something startling. As part of the doctor's plea bargain, he'd agreed to let each survivor speak to him in court.

I called in sick. I hid it from Kit. Usually, in the mornings, we'd get on the train to Cannon Street together, get some wedding admin done (he'd proposed a few months earlier). But every day that week and into the next, when he walked to Moorgate, I headed a few streets over as if I was going to work, before circling home. In our bedroom, under a cave of covers, I watched the televised trial. At the start of the week, the numbers of survivors due to speak numbered eighty-eight. By the end, the number bloomed to a hundred and fifty-six.

I cried as they described the shame and the nightmares, the eating disorders and the ways they'd tried to kill themselves. But it was smaller things that destroyed me – how gentle he was when he taped up their shins, how they needed him to put them back together, how they believed if anyone could fix them, it was him – because they mapped so faithfully onto how I felt about Daniel. And then their thoughts, which were my own, started to make sense. How in a meeting, I'd suddenly think, *I'm not real*. How when Kit talked to me about wedding venues, dinner options, a drinks reception, I'd feel a plunging terror. How twice a day, when a train pulled into the station, there was a split second when I found the chatter of the tracks utterly captivating. *One step,* they promised, *one step and this will be over.* These were not shameful, disconnected incidents. They were burning stars in the constellation of my trauma.

The girls smashed me up, broke me apart. But carved open, something I'd never felt before remained: rage. The girls simmered hate, spitting out words through peach-glossed lips, the ends of their hair flashing like knife blades. *My hate towards you is uncontrollable,* they said. *Little girls don't stay little forever. They return to destroy your world. I hope you burn.*

A father asked the judge to grant him five minutes in a locked room with the doctor. The judge declined. The dad launched himself across the courtroom. He was fast for a man of that size, that bulk, a heavy six foot three, he was nearly at the doctor before he was tackled by three guards. 'Let me have him, I want that son of a bitch, I want that fucker!' he shouted as he bear-reared against them, they had to twist his neck into a lock and force him to the ground. When they finally pulled him off the ground in handcuffs, he looked at the guards, bewildered. 'What if this happened to you?' he asked. He had three daughters, all victims. One was called Lauren. My heart almost burst.

'I'm not a hero,' he said at a press conference.

You are.

'I lost control.'

Someone should.

'I cannot condone vigilantism,' said the judge.

Can't you?

I watched the doctor carefully. I'd seen mugshots of him but hadn't seen him live, shuffling into the courtroom, unshaven in his faded navy jumpsuit and gold-framed glasses. His facial expression didn't vary as the girls spoke. Usually, he sat with his head in his hands or stared into the middle distance, sometimes, he'd shake his head, as if this whole thing was a mistake and he was astonished things had got this far. The girls would ask him question after question and he wouldn't react, wouldn't even look up.

Until day four.

He broke down as soon as she stepped to the podium, he had to pull his glasses off to wipe away the onslaught of tears. Sobs convulsed through his body before she even spoke. Her first five words seemed to unravel him completely. 'Wow,' she said. 'What have you done?' I watched him weep and a thought slithered through me: if Daniel was in that box instead of the doctor, would I be the girl he wept for? *Of course you would, he killed for you* and then I hated myself, twisted thoughts, twisted heart, hated that I had consumed this terrible mass of suffering when, ultimately, it didn't really matter. Because it hadn't touched my innermost self, it hadn't changed the sick, simple fact that I was, and probably always would be, proud that he loved me.

She said she'd known him nearly all of her life, before he was even a doctor – he was a family friend. He treated her in his apartment, she remembered the light in the kitchen, the egg timer on the toilet, the bathtub. She said they loved him like family. She thought he loved them back.

She told him that based on the time frame that she knew him, her specific injuries and frequency with which she saw him, it was estimated she'd been abused about eight hundred times. My mind reeled from the mathematics of it, the axioms of trauma, the calculations of damage. She thought she was lucky. She thought his wife was lucky. She wished she'd find a man like him.

She was tender to him, she called him 'my old friend', but her questions were appalling, to listen to her was to hear the hideousness of my own thoughts: *Was I the first? Is that when you went wrong? Or was it always wrong?*

She stole glances at him after she'd finished, willing him to answer. But he never did. *How can this be the end?* I thought. *How is this justice?* I wanted to march into that courtroom, right up to the movie producer/the doctor/Daniel, drag them into a car and drive away, let it be just us, a gun in my bag, nowhere and anywhere to go.

The thought, when it came, was piercingly clear: *I will have this for myself.* No judges. No jury. I will take him on a trip. I will draw out the truth from its dark, coiled places, I will extract every terrible detail until my haunting ceases, until there are no more questions, everything is answered. Then, I will tell him my truth. All that's happened. All I've done. All I'm going to do.

When Kit came home that evening, he thought something was wrong because I hadn't messaged him for a few hours; even at work, we'd send each other regular one-liners: 'Bruce just walked in with a Kim Jong Un haircut'; 'My trainee just cried on a call'; 'Am I a David Brent-esque middle manager?' But when I wasn't in our bedroom, he'd flicked on all the lights, searched every level of The Wedge. He found me outside, in the January cold of the garden, relief breaking through the worry of his voice: 'I've looked everywhere for you. I thought something had happened.'

Something has happened.

'What are you doing?' he asked, glancing at the snow I'd shovelled away, the overgrown thicket exposed beneath.

'Just some gardening.'

'Gardening?' There was a second when he came close to asking me more, when I almost told him, but then he left it, lifted the hair from my shoulder, made a joke into my neck. 'Do you have green fingers?'

I kissed his cheek. *I have green fingers. I can make all things grow.*

*

From: Kit McDermott   **10:01**

I've checked the date of the oldest prescription against our messages, our photos, I'm wracking my brains to figure out if we had a fight, if I was working too hard, if I was stressed, if there was some plausible, rational reason why you never told me you were depressed. I've come up with nothing. All I've worked out is that we were engaged when the oldest prescription was issued, on the date itself, you asked me what I thought about hydrangeas for your bouquet. You've had so much time, so many opportunities to tell me what was going on. What the fuck.

22

Net

Then

I keep my promise to him. In the mornings, while he meets with researchers at the university or in the field, I do my schoolwork at the desk downstairs in the cottage, diligently writing *Romeo and Juliet* essays, filling the squares of my maths book. The schoolwork doesn't come to me as easily as it did at St Matthews, my attention drifts, it's the sea view, the higher standards, the Easter break, the breakdown. I have to keep bringing myself back to the page, telling myself to focus. My mind feels muffled and woolly.

In the afternoons, he takes me to the field. It is the only time I feel like my old self. The outdoors unzips my carapace and the girl who used to be me steps out. Except now, I've traded the slow walk through the museum for a coastal path, exchanged extinct exhibits for wild hedgerows. Daniel's lab has become the dense crop of wild thyme, no microscopes or lenses or slides here. Nothing comes between our eyes and their object.

While I sketch plants, he is tracking the Blues; he nets them and puts them in the cooler. After each batch of ten, he takes them out, sexes, tags and releases them; I watch them shake off the cold and flutter back to the thyme. It is the first time I realise the image I have of him in the Natural History Museum isn't really him. This is who he is, the focus in his eyes, the quick snap of his wrist. How gently he untangles the butterflies from the net.

'You've been observant these last few days,' he says.

I look up from my sketchbook. Heat flushes through my cheeks. I try not to touch them.

'I could really do with some help. What do you say? Could you take a break from your drawing?'

He speaks to me all the time about the Blues, he shows me the males' low flight pattern, points out lumpy nests of ants, but not once has he asked me to help. The invitation, then, is a sort of initiation; if I do this right, I might graduate to assistant, protégée. I nod.

He passes me the net. It is different to what I expect, it is light, the frame aluminium, and it's big, in my hands, the black net bag touches the ground, the opening large enough to catch a bird. I swish it through the air.

He smiles. 'Butterflies are deaf but they have compound eyes, they can see thousands of versions of you holding that net. So, no sudden movements. You have to sneak up on them.'

I hold it still against my shoulder. Together, we look out over the thyme.

'There,' he says, pointing to a flash of skittering blue. It is a patrolling male, dipping in and out of the purple haze of flowers.

'Wait.'

It stops on a cluster, hesitates and then flies to another.

'Let it settle.'

Dear Darling

It walks over the flower three times; I think it will fly off. But then it opens and shuts its wings slowly and starts to nectar.

'Now.'

I swing down. Comical when still, the net is suddenly not comical at all, it slices through the air, a perfect aerodynamic weapon. There is a flash of cobalt and, inside me, a rush of elation, a clear, pure high. My heart pounds as I push back the gauze. But when I reach the butterfly, it isn't moving. 'I think I killed it.'

I hand him the net. He works quickly, closing the wings, drawing it carefully out. He sets it on his palm, strokes its legs to see if it revives. It doesn't. From a distance it could be a leaf; with its wings shut, the bright blue isn't visible, only the muted silver beneath. But up close, I can see the zebra stripe of its antennae, the black rounds of its eyes, the inky markings ringed in white. A lump grows in my throat.

'The first time is always hard,' he says.

'I did it too fast.'

'No.'

'Too much follow-through.'

'It happens,' he says and I think he is either very kind or he really doesn't see the brutal pointlessness of it. How a single mistake is the difference between life and death.

23

MOORGATE

Now

The University of Law looks like any other building on Bunhill Row, the ground floor painted a dark grey, the rest an exposed sandy brick. Beside it is Fleet, one of Dulwich & Sullivan's main clients, it can't be more than a few weeks ago that I crossed their marble reception, swiped my visitor pass at the gates, headed up to the third floor for a meeting. At the time, it felt so mundane, asking their legal team how they wanted to proceed, sending out clarificatory emails. But now, walking past it, I want to make impossible trades. Rewind the reel. Go back to when my baby was taut and proud in front of me. When I confidently said how many weeks I was.

The campus has been refurbished, it used to be white walls, grey linoleum floors, blue sofas. Now, there are pops of colour – orange bookshelves displaying the latest legal journals, a pair of low-slung lime sofas, red bar stools. The café is in the same place though; Emma and I have sat there hundreds of times. I met her on the Dulwich & Sullivan vacation scheme. As soon as I saw her pearly silk shirt, her diamond pendant, how she held out her arms in greeting, I knew she was exactly my kind of person, someone whose outsized drama would overwhelm my own. It was Emma who introduced me to Kit – they read economics together. I liked how obvious it was that he liked me, how he blushed whenever I looked at him, how he already knew Pepe's, my favourite £1 pizza place behind the station. How, even after he said, 'Well, if this isn't a date, I don't know what is,' he was still too nervous to kiss me.

Daniel heads to the café. He buys a bottle of water, asks me what I want. I refuse, I can pay for my own drink, but it's getting awkward so I ask for a tea. The waitress beams at him, she thinks him handsome. He could be a lecturer here, company or trust law, something that means he's made his money elsewhere, something that explains the sharp cut of his blazer, those unblemished leather loafers. She doesn't think criminal.

I choose a table in the middle. There are only two students at the café tables - it's July, exams are finished - but a few weeks ago, this place must have been rammed with students chanting cases while mainlining espresso. I remember Emma bounding up to Kit and me at the vending machine in the corner just before our contract law exam. 'Tell me a case, any case,' she said, wild-eyed, and then, the reversal confuses me: Daniel and me here, Kit at home.

'This is where you read law?' Daniel asks, removing his blazer.

I nod.

'I can't see you here, studying law, being a lawyer,' he says, unscrewing the cap of his water. 'It's the complete opposite of botany, of conservation. So corporate and mercenary. No discovery or beauty.'

'You realise I'm a lawyer, not a banker?' I say, hackles rising. 'I'm not destroying the worth of the Indian rupee or taking positions in South American debt.'

'It's all the same though, isn't it?' He swallows half his bottle of water in a single mouthful. 'Keeping rich corporations rich.'

It is the first time I realise that our history, however earth-shattering, is only one moment in time, a point I've travelled very far from. Now, Daniel is the type of person Kit and I would warn each other about at a dinner party, whose eyes glaze over when we say, 'We're lawyers,' no idea of what this entails, no interest in finding out. He doesn't see that law is like botany, like lepidoptery. That it has its own ecosystem where there is mystery, discovery, beauty.

'You should have studied biology.'

'I did that at undergraduate, at Oxford.'

His face lights up, he looks like he's about to hug me. 'That's all I wanted for you. That's exactly what I would have chosen.'

I want to slap the smugness off his face; watch it roll to the floor. What *I* would have chosen? Possessing my body wasn't enough. He must imagine making my choices too.

'Why did you stop?'

I don't tell him he ruined botany for me. That the labs reminded me of lepidoptery. That I would shiver whenever I looked down a microscope. I will not give him the satisfaction. Instead, I say, 'There's no money in biology.'

'Money isn't everything.'

'It is when you don't have it.' In my second year of university, I was mercenary about which law firms I applied to, comparing salaries, maintenance grants, whether they paid course fees, ruthlessly applying to firms with the most generous offerings. They were all American. Henry, a friend on my corridor who was reading law, laughed when I told him, 'You know they're going to beast you, right?' I didn't care. Beast me. Until I become a beast too.

'You could have used the trust fund. I set it up for you.'

'I didn't want to depend on you more than I already had.'

'You say it like it's such a hateful thing.'

I let that hang in the air.

The waitress arrives, she smiles at Daniel, her dark hair falling over her face. He ignores her. She hands me my tea. On her wrist is a tattoo of a dove. I want to press my thumb into the spray of its wings, hold her there. *You're lucky*, I want to say to her. *You're too old.*

He leans in when she leaves. 'Did you like studying law?'

'I loved it actually.' I press my tea bag against the side of the mug. 'I liked criminal law best.'

He takes his bottle of water, squeezes the base.

'I liked the clarity of it, how everything divided into neat categories. Offences against property, offences against the person. Fatal offences against the person, non-fatal.'

'Nothing is ever that neat.'

My eyes flick towards the ceiling, was it in one of the classrooms above us where I first read the Sexual Offences Act 2003? The words stole the air from my lungs; I had to grip Emma's arm to steady the ratcheting of my heart. She took me to the toilets and then back to the flat we shared; I shut my bedroom door, pretended I was dehydrated, exhausted, when really, I was sitting at my desk, wondering if I was brave enough, strong enough to open my textbook and turn the analysis on myself. I was not. I didn't get through copying out a single offence before I set my lined paper on fire over one of Emma's scented candles, watched it burn. Later, when Kit dropped by with two Hawaiians from Pepe's, he asked me why I smelt of burning.

'Did you realise it was wrong?'

'What?'

'You and me.'

'No.'

'You never thought about our ages?'

His eyes fix on me while he shakes his head, that startling navy blue. 'You were always so self-possessed, so intelligent, all I could think of was—' He breaks off. When he starts again, his voice is hoarse. '—I'd found the one.'

I struggle to keep my features steady. 'So, you didn't think about the legal definitions?'

'Legal definitions?'

In my fantasy of this moment, I am iron, I am steel. I've practised the three words I want to say thousands of times, watched myself mouth them in bathroom mirrors, changing rooms, the matte black of my computer screen. But now, when the moment presents itself, something in me gives way. Could he have done this, this man with his razor-sharp blazer and navy eyes? I look at him and the jury of my mind is still out.

Yet, this is also why I'm here. To show him, to show myself, that however absurd it seems, however unlikely, there is only one answer to what he did, what that makes him, what that makes me. *Nothing is ever that neat*, he said. This is. It's clean-cut. Black and white. I push out the words, though my fingers are twisting round and round themselves: 'You raped me.'

He is still for the longest time. Then, he caves in. His eyes close first, he covers them with his hands but nothing can hide the collapse of his body, which folds over his knees. And although I have done this, the sight of him devastates me. I squeeze my own throat.

'How can you think that?' he whispers.

'That's what it was,' I say, although my strength for this has disappeared, I'm not even here, I'm over there, by the orange bookshelves, watching a woman parrot words to a man who looks like he's reeling from a blow. 'It's the intentional penetration of the vagina with your penis when the other person doesn't consent—'

'You consented, you consented!' His hands slide from his face. 'You did more than consent! You started it, remember? Months before I did anything back. In the museum!'

The memories detonate. Carved pillars. The balcony. The pulse of his throat.

He reaches for my hand. I jerk back. But if he tried again, I'm not sure I wouldn't let him, I am tempted, badly, I'm so frightened of everything he's saying. 'There's no need for this. I wanted you and you wanted me. It's all right.'

A jar of fluttering Blues. His lips on my arm. I wanted to, I wanted to and then, I understand this is less a fight with Daniel than a fight with myself, because it takes every ounce of me to blink back the romance of a seaside cottage and see instead the man sitting across from me, trying to pin me silent.

My vision clears. Back then, I had no words to describe what happened except, 'I started it,' so that became memory, slick and sticky with my shame. But I've acquired a new language now, I have different memories. I didn't seduce him, I was groomed. I wanted him. But wanting isn't the same as consent. 'You can't consent when you're under sixteen.'

I watch him, anticipate another blasting apart. But it doesn't happen. He doesn't seem to register the importance of what I'm saying. 'You didn't want to?' he says, slowly.

'It doesn't matter if I wanted to.'

'Your feelings are irrelevant?' he says.

'Yes.'

'Not to me.' His eyes are wide and unrelenting. 'To me, your feelings matter more than anything in the world.'

I don't understand. If the law is axiomatic, incontrovertible, why doesn't truth feel true? Why does my assailant feel like my biggest defender? I fall back to the lines I've practised, not because I believe them like I did seconds before, but because there is nothing else to cling onto, they're cliff face, they're rope when I am derailed, blown off course. 'This isn't about me. It's about you. You committed a crime. It's not a defence that I came on to you.'

'It should be.' He looks at me like he loves me. 'Anyone confronted with the astonishment of you wouldn't have been able to resist.'

Lamplight.

My wrist in his hand.

'You're utterly rare,' he said. 'Astonishing.'

He pushes back his chair, stands up. His voice is very soft. 'Besides, there is a defence.'

Dear Darling

I shake my head, the only movement I can summon when I am barely treading water, I am drowning in the treacherous shallows of memory.

He leans across the table. His breath is so warm against my face. 'Insanity.'

24

THE BLUE

Then

Over the next few days, he asks me to try netting again and again, he says I am too hard on myself, I just need practice. But I can't muster up the courage. The Blues are too fragile, too delicate; they deserve him not me.

This afternoon feels different, though. The sun has been blazing on the hillside for hours and now, as it sets, it turns the sky rose, the sea violet. The scent of thyme has deepened with the heat and, above the flowers, there are so many Blues.

'Come on,' he says, 'botanists can catch butterflies too,' and despite my reluctance, I want even less to spoil the sultry beauty of this afternoon. I take the net.

'Swing firmly so it doesn't fly out but not so hard that it jams in the back.'

My first few attempts are half-hearted, he knows it, he watches me in silence. But the fourth time, it is so easy, I catch one against the ground.

'That's it!' he shouts. He is beside me in the thyme. 'Press the whole ring down. Good. Now, lift the net bag.'

I do as he says. The butterfly flies instinctively up. In one deft movement, he twists the net around it, flips the frame and hands it back to me. 'Are you going to get her out?' he asks.

I stare at the Blue darting manically in the black.

'You can do it. She's safe with you.'

I shake my head.

'Grasp the forewings together above the head, that's where they're the thickest.'

'I'll rub off her scales.'

'Not if you're gentle. I'll hold the frame.'

My heart is pounding. With one hand, from the outside, I locate the section of the bag where she is, with the other, I make my way into the net. I am touching her.

'Astonishing, isn't it?'

I cannot speak. He has converted me, him and the warm air and the life fluttering against my fingers, he has baptised me in this little Blue's flight.

'Now, ease her out.'

I know what to do, I've seen him do it hundreds of times, I wait for her to still before I take hold of her wings but whenever I move, she starts flapping, one wrong move and I will squash her head, snap her antennae. 'I'm going to hurt her.'

'You won't.'

'I can't.'

'You can.'

'Help me.'

He puts his hand into the net. As he does so, his knuckles skim the length of my arm.

Later, I will think there were many reasons I felt the way I felt. I'd never been touched by a man. I'd wanted him for months. Or perhaps it was simpler than all of that – a question of anatomy, the science of skin against skin. But in this moment, I do not think any of these things. There is no thinking at all, only feeling. And the feeling is electric.

I shiver against him.

He freezes.

'Lauren.' He says my name so quietly, it is barely audible above the buzz of the thyme. 'This cannot be.'

Except, it is. Because he doesn't move. And his indulgence of this moment, the seconds he lets it tick on, is everything. Around us, the Blues are nectaring, the insects hum in the hedgerow, waves crash on the beach, somewhere, in the distance, a tractor rumbles to life, but none of that compares to the absolute stillness between us, stillness in which his arm is pressing into mine. The Blue, sensing the disruption, darts along my arm into the open dusk.

'It's impossible,' he says. His breath on my cheek is so sweet. 'This cannot be what you want.'

My reply comes to me fully formed and clear. I say it even though this moment is fragile, I say it because I am less afraid of ruining this than not knowing his answer. I should have said it months ago, in the balcony outside Lepidoptery, in the lab after he gave me back my display case. Because it has never been about me. It has always been about him. 'What do you want?'

His hand slips away. He jogs through the thyme, then he breaks into a run.

Dear Darling

*

From: Kit McDermott   10:23

Is it me? What have I done wrong? Have I made you feel you couldn't tell me? I thought we had the best relationship, the best marriage, when friends complain about their partners, ask for my advice, I don't know what to say, I have no wisdom to impart because we never fight, we never argue. I thought it was because we were happy. Now, I wonder if I'm just an idiot. If all your secrets are hidden in the fights we've never had.

    Come back, Laurie, shout and scream and cry. I will listen to it all, I will hear it all.

25

PRICKLES

Now

It's too ordinary in the café – the clink of teaspoons against crockery, the waitress stacking mugs, a student watching a tutorial on his laptop – when, watching Daniel make his way to the toilet, I want to hurl cappuccinos, make steaming liquid arch through the air, hear the smash of ceramic.

I knew this was going to be hard, I anticipated his denial, deflection, resistance. But not my own. I am quicksand towing myself under, I am cannibalising myself. *Insanity.* It's absurd, no lawyer would put that forward as a defence, yet none of that clinical logic can stop what he said from flooring me. Because it was insanity, wasn't it? An insanity I've never felt again.

I cast round the café, searching for anything that reminds me of Kit, his quick smile, his intelligent hazel eyes, but I can't find him, my head is rushing with Daniel. I came for a reckoning. Instead, I'm slipping back. He is a black hole pulling everything in, collapsing stars, sinking gravity. I'm never going to get out.

No.

My stomach spasms, the pain blasting away memories of Daniel, detonating other ones. 'Where's baby, where's baby?' Millie said, running up to the empty car seat Kit brought in, searching for Faye in the blankets. Kit drew her into his arms, buried his mouth in her hair. 'The baby's gone, my love,' he whispered. 'I'm sorry.' But no matter how many times Kit told Millie, she wouldn't stop asking me, she grabbed me the day I left, 'Where's baby? I want to see her. Where did you put her?'

My mouth tastes metal. I glare at the closed door of the toilet. *You've done this. You.* His blazer is slung over the chair; I drag it onto my lap. Then, I pull on a pair of disposable gloves and tear up the ivy leaves I picked earlier. Juice bleeds from the slashes, I rub it all over his collar. I want some for his sleeves, anywhere the fabric touches his skin, but there isn't enough. I leaf through the Ziploc bags I've brought, choose. The bromelia prickles. In the light of the café, the flocking on the spines is silver. I sprinkle a few on the inside of his cuffs. Not too many. As if a bush has caught his sleeve, as if it's circled his wrist in a crowd. Quick, uninvited intimacy.

The toilet door is opening; I return his blazer. I take a sip of tea to quiet the drum of my heart – it's stewed. I scoop out the bag. This is what it's like with Daniel. All appetites gone until you realise you're famished.

He pulls out his chair.

I start before he sits down. 'Is this real to you or just a game?'

'Lauren—'

'Because I've left my entire life to see you.'

'I'm sorry—'

'My husband—'

'You're married?'

The look he fixes me with is terrible and vulnerable, like I've betrayed him. Part of me is astounded that this is the scythe that carves him open but then I remember that merely the thought of me with another man was what broke us in the end. I want him broken now. 'Yes. Kit's a lawyer, like me. We met here.'

He blinks at the coffee bar, the lilies in their ceramic pots, the posters inviting training contract applications. He sees it now. This is the place where another man's history with me begins.

'I have a daughter too. She's three.'

He puts his hand over his mouth.

'I left them to see you. But now, after everything you've just said—' Pain overtakes me, I grasp the table. '—I don't think you're worth a second away from them.'

'Wait a minute, wait—'

'—For what? For you to deny everything? I don't need that.'

Two students enter the building; a gust of air blows in with them. He slides on his blazer. Excitement flutters high in my ribs. This is going to work.

'You know, because of what I felt for you once . . .' I pause to let him feel the blade of that, 'I came to see you when I got your letter, I thought this is the chance I've been waiting for, speak to him, confront him, show him what he's done, find out once and for all if he's different from the others.'

'The others?'

'Other men who do this to children.'

'Lauren—'

'—But you're not.'

He rubs the back of his neck slowly, then stares at his fingers, trying to figure out why his skin is on fire.

'There's a hobby I have, harmless really.' A lie. None of my hobbies are harmless. 'I follow news stories, read articles, listen to podcasts, watch documentaries, there are so many scandals now in every industry. You know what's interesting?' I pat the flat of my spoon against the tea bag. 'They sound exactly like you. It wasn't rape, I didn't force her or trick her, she wanted it, she asked for it, she started it.'

He breaks off touching his neck to glare at me. Distantly, the waitress takes another order, the coffee machine blasts steam, two more students settle down to work but he and I are completely still, rapt by the other's next move.

'Are you finished?' he asks.

I clench my jaw. I'm confronting him, poisoning him, hurting him, and still, he can make me feel simple and fourteen, walking into the Natural History Museum with a sketchbook under my arm. 'Depends,' I say in my iciest voice. 'Are you going to say anything new?'

'You've made that impossible.'

'I haven't made anything impossible. I didn't write the law.'

'The law isn't the only measure of what happened.'

'It's the only measure of whether you're a criminal.'

'I'm not particularly interested in whether I'm a criminal,' he says, and I glimpse, for a second, the insanity of the story he is telling himself – *he thinks he didn't deserve to go to prison*. Doesn't matter that he killed a boy or that the jury convicted him of gross negligence manslaughter or that the judge gave him the maximum sentence. To him, only his conscience matters. A chill runs up my arm.

'But *your* feelings, whether *you* think I'm like those men, that matters to me more than anything else in the world.'

Elation jolts through me – it's only me that matters – but the shame that follows is swift and tidal. How has his flattery worked on me, even for a second? The thought makes me cruel. 'Those men,' I say slowly, 'they're monsters?'

'Yes.'

'Deviants?'

'The worst of the worst.'

'You realise the only reason you even know about them is because you were in *prison* with them.'

'That's different, that's—'

'—Did you share a cell with one of them? Did they whisper to you over food trays? In the shower—'

'—Stop it, stop!' He slams his palm against the table. Teaspoons jump, cups clatter, students stop their conversations to stare at him but I don't care. Because finally, we can all see him. Scratch beneath the confident, thirty-year-old lepidopterist he's pretending to be and this is the real Daniel – a forty-eight-year-old ex-con who's lived almost half his life behind bars, who's spent more time studying inmates than butterflies.

'Sorry, sorry.' His voice is trembling. 'I just can't—' He grasps the edge of the table. He is barely holding it together. One wrong move and he might shatter. 'I *am* different from them,' he says quietly. 'You know I am.'

I am silent.

'You *know*.'

'I don't know that at all.'

He squeezes his wrists. The prickles. 'You do. Because you're here.' He drags his eyes up to meet mine. 'If you really believed I was a monster you would have ignored my letter or gone straight to the police. But you didn't.' His voice grows steadier, more confident. 'You came to meet me because you *don't* believe it.'

I think a hundred things. He is a fine dissector of motives. The ruthless beauty of his logic. But also, that his obsession with this particular version of us blinds him to the delicate science of our relationship, causes him, always, to underestimate the only variable beyond his control: me. He's never seen I have the power to hurt him. That I might want to. That I'm doing it now.

'And I'm here too. Isn't that proof?'

'Proof?'

'I'm not like them. If I was what you're accusing me of, why would I be here, why would I come back to you?' He is rubbing his wrists now, raising ugly bracelets of hives. 'I'll go anywhere with you, I'll listen to whatever you want to say, I'll work this through with you until you realise.'

'Realise what?' My heart is beating very fast, a sick crush of rage and fear and hope.

'It was real,' he says. 'What we had was real.'

*

From: Kit McDermott   **10:48**

I've just pulled everything out of your wardrobe. Wrenched your skirts off hangers, your silk work shirts, pulled down your blazers. I must have been very loud because Cass has come in three times to check on me, do I want to go to the park, do I need a drink, should I get some rest? I can't tell her I am searching for your secrets. That I am going to find all the things you've hidden.

26

SHEETS

Then

After that moment on the field, he doesn't take me with him again, he leaves before I wake up. I don't see him in the evenings; he returns when I am in bed. Late at night, I hear him cooking in the kitchen downstairs, the flicker of gas, the slide of the skillet. In the morning, there's a small pot of vitamins on the table, a fresh fruit smoothie in the fridge, a Tupperware with that evening's dinner in it with a message on Natural History Museum notepad paper laid on top: *Tuesday – chicken with spinach*. I throw out the vitamins, pour the smoothie down the drain, eat no more than a few bites.

There is something wrong with me, a defect in my genetics, if a scientist cut me open, they'd see the flaw in my double helix. *There*, they'll say, *this is why*. I try out my own brand of electrotherapy, I tell myself, *He is your mother's husband, he is your stepfather*, I say it many times a day, quickly, slowly, out loud. Sometimes, I add, 'dead'; *He is your dead mother's husband*, as if Mama is watching me from heaven, disgusted. On those days, I feel very bad, like a swamp has pooled at the deepest part of myself, I am waterlogged with algae, dead bracken, decaying rushes. Even that doesn't work. My mind drifts back to the thicket of thyme. How big his arm was. How warm.

I obsess about the length of time his skin pressed against mine, perform mathematical calculations. Instinctively, I believe we spent an entire minute there, sixty whole, perfect seconds but when I test my hypothesis by timing the words he said to me (*It's impossible, this cannot be what you want*) it's pushing no more than four seconds, ten if I add in pauses, looks, butterflies, and then I am frightened it is just my desperation rushing in to make up the extra fifty seconds. I need it to have been longer than ten seconds. Because it means it wasn't just me.

The days become impossible. I can survive the mornings, I eat a bowl of cereal, keep up my schoolwork. When lunch time draws near, I make myself a sandwich, alert for the tread of his footsteps on the path; each day, there is an inextinguishable flicker that today is different, today he will come and take me to the field. He doesn't. The next hour, minute, second gapes wide and open ahead of me until his absence in the cottage is so strong, I have to break it. After three days of resisting, I give myself free rein: I go through his things.

My afternoon schedule becomes this: I search the study first and then his room. He has turned the twin room between us into a study, he asked the cottage owner if he could replace the beds with tables. The owner, who has an antique store in Falmouth, has brought in two long trestle tables stained with turpentine and paint on which Daniel has arranged a lamp and his butterfly things. Some of this I recognise from the field – glassine envelopes, tweezers, identity stickers – some, I don't. Jars with white foam at the bottom. Packets of pins. Foam boards. Strips of tracing paper. There is an unlabelled bottle of liquid, the first time I flicked open the lid, it burnt the back of my throat, like nail polish remover only stronger. Beyond that, there is very little of interest. He has taken anything of fascination with him; the Blues, like him, are absent. In the corner of the room, two nets of different sizes rest against the wall. I wave them madly like he told me not to do, hoping he'll materialise and tell me about compound eyes.

But the study is just a prelude to his bedroom. It is always tidy, he doesn't leave clothes over the chair; his dove-grey shirts are hanging in the wardrobe, his loafers set straight at the bottom of the wardrobe. His bed is made, the sheets tucked in under the mattress, the quilt folded at the end of the bed, just as it was when we arrived. Still, there are traces of him here more intimate than anywhere else. Creases on the pillow. Sheets holding his musk.

In the beginning, it is enough just to check nothing has changed from the day before, occasionally, I might bring his pillow to my nose, imagine myself back in the thyme. But as it becomes clear that his absence is less of a mistake than a decision, a weight descends over the cottage, inside me. I start getting into his bed. I pretend that the sheets, warmed by the afternoon sun, are really warmed by his body, I pull them over my face, let my breath lift them up and down, I wind them between my legs. One time, I remember a game Mama taught me, 'horsey', she'd called it, we'd lie on our backs on her bed and kick up our legs, *There's a ditch, jump, a broken bridge, jump*, our abdomens sore with laughter. I do it on his bed once, flail my legs like a newborn colt, but there is something wrong with playing games here, childish games I played with Mama. I don't do it again.

Afterwards, I never make his bed. Sometimes, I leave the nest of where I was as it is, other times, I throw the sheets on the floor, the quilt. I want him to say something to me, to wake me up with angry knocks, to push into my small, dark room, say, 'This needs to stop, you've gone too far.' He doesn't. Each afternoon, the room is spotless again. I feel like I'm going mad. Perhaps I was never in his room. Perhaps he *lets* me mess it up, he understands it is a necessary outlet for the terrible unrequitedness of my want. The thought infuriates me. I turn out drawers. Pull clothes from the wardrobe. Throw his loafers against the wall.

At night, if I wake up, I don't let myself go back to sleep, I force myself up. Things are clearer when I am half awake, acts that in the morning seem crazy, are suddenly vital in the dark. I grow bold. I pull back my sheets, walk down the corridor, push the door to his room open.

He sleeps with abandon, his arms flung out above him. He doesn't wear a T-shirt; his chest is bare. I hover my hand over the velvet fan of his lashes, the ridge of his Adam's apple, feel his breath against my palm. I want to peel him like an orange. Release the secrets within.

27

Doorway

Now

'It's going to rain,' he says, when we're outside the university.

He's right. Clouds gather beyond buildings, thunder tremors through the air. But I don't care. I can't sit across from him anymore, staring at his shoulder blades beneath his shirt, the wide spread of his hands. Even with him scratching like a dog, he's still magnetic. I pull up the hood of my parka.

'Should you be walking so much with your—' he gestures at my middle.

'I'm fine,' I say, though he knows I'm not, he winced watching me stand up, he reached out to help but I batted him away. This is the most I've walked since the postnatal ward, they wouldn't discharge me until I could cross its length, so I did, I forced myself through each excruciating step; I'd have rather split my stiches than watch Kit flinch every time a baby cried. But at home, I lay down on the floor of my greenhouse, I didn't get up. What for? I had no baby to feed, no one who needed my heartbeat to fall asleep. Millie snuck downstairs a few times to visit me. 'What are you doing, Mama?' she'd ask, tossing Acorn across me so she could use both hands to scramble onto my dirty futon. 'Play ice cream with me, read to me, colour with me.' I'd cry, put my hands on her plump cheeks, inhale the sweet gloss of her hair. Then I'd hand Acorn back to her. 'Go inside, baby.' To your father, Aunt Cassie, any one of those good, whole people who haven't killed your sister.

'Let's get a taxi,' he says.

'I'll be fine,' I insist. I find my painkillers, swallow two dry. 'I want to walk.' Walking reminds me of Kit. Before we had Millie, Kit and I used to meet outside one of our firms and just walk the streets of the City, before getting on the nearest underground. 'No destinations, no maps,' Kit said the first time, taking my phone out of my hand and slipping it into my coat pocket. 'Not until the end.' I would have gone with him just because he asked. But after he explained it was a family tradition, how his entire family would set out together on the weekends, I understood he was trying to create a family with me, a family I'd never had. I wanted it too, a mother who was alive, a father with a name, siblings. I took it for the sparkler of a promise it was.

'You didn't reply to what I said in the café.'

'I'm not sure what to say.'

A drop of rain skims the back of his hand. 'Say anything you want.'

We're on Moorgate now, empty except for the rumble of an occasional van. Kit's firm, Williams & Pierce, is off to the right on Ropemaker Street, the rounded glass, the closed Costa beneath; if I go right up to it, I can see his office on the fourth floor, he might be right there, finishing an email.

He's not.

It's a Sunday. His wife is missing. He's with Millie, where I should be, and then I'm so scared of what I'm putting them through, it's not worth it, I haven't made it worth it. Years of preparation have amounted to nothing more than accusations about crime and consent, when none of these have moved Daniel. Now, walking past Williams & Pierce, places I've been to with clients and colleagues and Kit, I realise my mistake. I've been appealing to Daniel like I would to Kit, who'd turn back to pay for a packet of sweets Millie stuffed into her buggy or balks at running a red light. But Daniel isn't Kit. He said, *I'm not particularly interested in whether I'm a criminal*, because he isn't frightened of being one. He already is.

But watching Daniel in reflections of shop windows, how close to me he walks, how tenderly he looks at me, it is suddenly so clear what will convince him. He thinks I'm the rarest butterfly in the world, copper dashed with cobalt. He thinks he's pushed back the tangle of nets, cupped me gently in his hands. He thinks he's saved me. But that's not true at all. I need to show him how he's ripped my head from my body, torn my wings to rags. He's not a conservationist. He's a killer.

'You said it was real,' I say. Rain glistens on the silver of his temples, darkening the wool of his blazer. It's going to wash all the poison away. 'You said it wasn't wrong. Because you never saw the harm.'

'You can't be serious,' he says, his pace slowing. 'I went to *prison*.' As soon as he says the word, something in him collapses. Everything flooding out. 'You have no idea what it was like. How many people killed themselves. The blood. The fights. I'd be walking to dinner and, a second later, the alarm would blare, everyone flying out of their cells, pulling flick knives from their socks, razors from their waistbands. There are things I wish I didn't know. Like what Spice smells like. Like how to sharpen a chicken bone into a blade.' He drags his hand across his mouth. 'So don't tell me I never saw the harm. I wasted the best part of my life with *animals*. I wasted it slowly. I watched it trickle away.'

I try to imagine the slippage of weeks into months into years but I can't. The last eighteen years for me have been so full – Wyatt, Oxford, law school, Dulwich & Sullivan, Kit, Millie and Faye. So many things have happened to me against the nothing that has happened to him. Pity rushes in at the pointlessness of it, and then, as quick as it comes, it turns sour inside me. I will not feel sorry for him.

'You didn't go to prison for me.' My voice is a low hiss. 'You went to prison for *killing* that boy.' I didn't realise, until I said it, how much I want to keep that day in the past, how much it hurts to talk about in daylight. The day I disappeared. The day he hurt someone else. 'How could you have done something like that?'

'It was an accident!'

'Did you know him?'

'Course not.'

'But why were you driving so fast? Why did you leave him to die?'

'To get to you!' His eyes on me are tunnels. 'I was driving that fast to get to you! I left him there to get to you!'

I shut my eyes. I've spent so much time trying to separate my decision to run away from Daniel, from the death of that boy. *It's not my fault*, I've repeated a thousand times, *he ran him over, he didn't stop, he didn't get out and help.* But eighteen years on, my guilt still astounds me; in the unfurling consequences, I cannot see where my responsibility ends. Because it's true, isn't it? If I hadn't run away, Daniel wouldn't have come after me. That boy would still be alive.

'I'm sorry,' he says. His neck and wrists are inflamed, but he's trying not to scratch, he just presses his fingers to them. 'I'm not saying it's your fault.' He pulls up the collar of his blazer against the rain. 'I just think I've done my time.'

He says it flatly, no remorse. I'm so jealous of the easy way he's put down his guilt, his complete absolution. There are weeks I can't shut my eyes without seeing car crashes. 'What about me?' I ask.

'You?'

'I'm the only person who's served time for *us*.'

His laugh cuts through the muffling of the rain. I ball up my hands. 'You haven't suffered! You're thirty-two, utterly beautiful, you have a career, a husband, a family, you have everything you could want!'

'You don't get it, do you?' I pound my fist against my chest; it makes a dead sound. 'You split me open, you slit my throat!'

'What are you talking about?'

'I can't have normal relationships! I have no real friends!'

'That's my fault?'

'It's completely your fault!'

A group of men spill out of a pub, their laughter grows louder when they think they've walked into a domestic. 'Calm down, love,' one laughs at me.

'Keep it at home,' another guffaws, his arm slung over his friend's shoulder.

'He's not my husband!' I want to say, but that's far worse, isn't it, to be shouting in the street at a man who isn't my husband, and suddenly, Daniel has stepped between the men and me. He is bristling, shoulders raised, fists clenched, he's a split second from launching at them, and I can't help it – I put my hand on his arm. He stands down instantly. They turn the corner. Abruptly, I remove my hand.

He blinks at the imprint of my palm on his sleeve. 'You were saying?' he asks and I am astounded at his snap from inmate to lepidopterist, from the man he was in prison to the man he is with me, but also at my instinct to calm him, the power I still wield.

I take a deep breath, try to calm down, to sort through the rush of thoughts. I will speak coolly, rationally. I am a grown woman. Not a child. 'It is your fault I have no friends. Because at some point in a friendship, someone will say something awful and true . . .' Jennie at Wyatt, who told me she'd rather stay at school during holidays than hear her mother unscrewing her bottle of gin; stick-thin Evangeline at Oxford, who once told me her father pulled a chip out from her mouth and called her a greedy cow; Emma, who said she clubbed all night because she was so fucking lonely. 'When they do that, they're inviting you to do the same, to go deeper, if they give you their secret and you give them yours, you're friends for life. But I never say anything back.'

'Why not?'

'Because if I do, they'll see you.'

He stops suddenly under the covered doorway of an investment bank. The quiet here, the rain falling beyond makes me feel like the world has drawn a circle round us and abandoned us in it, everything hushed and dangerous, and then I know he is about to shatter the ground beneath my feet, tilt my axis, because he gives me a look, long and penetrating, the same look he gave me the first time he saw me in my living room, when he took my wrist between his fingers. 'You haven't told him, have you?'

'Who?'

'Kit.'

I blink. Knowing this buys me only seconds from the car crash of my life. Wanting them anyway. Through the window, the lobby is lit with chandeliers, the receptionist is straightening newspapers – I could walk right up to her, say, *Help me, please. I need to get away.* But I don't. I stare at the man staring silently back at me, willing me to have kept our secret, terrified I might have told, and the enormity of my mistake breaks over me. Because if I had told Kit, Daniel's hold over me would be broken – Daniel knows it, I know it. But I never told him. I feel, then, the cool needle of my own complicity sliding into my side.

'He doesn't know you exist,' I whisper. 'He only knows that Mama died, that I went to boarding school. I never told him that you married Mama or that she died on her honeymoon or where you've been for the past eighteen years.' I'm not sure how I've done it. Kept this entire world of a person a secret. 'I came close to telling him a few times.' Those lazy, weekend mornings, nothing separating us except skin, Kit would tell me all his secret fears – how he'd never felt as clever as Cassie or as fun as his younger brothers, and I tasted it then, my confession on my tongue. But I didn't. Just diverted him with more ordinary hurts – the strangeness of never knowing my father, how ugly I used to feel, the grief of losing Mama. Never the guilt. Never Daniel. It wasn't just shame. There was a ruthlessness about it also, I saw a chance for reinvention and I took it. I almost told him later, when he found me digging up the garden, but we'd just moved into The Wedge, we were engaged, we were talking wedding venues. I was so close to normal. I couldn't let it slip away.

'Do you love him?'

'What?'

'Do you love Kit?'

My mind goes white, I'm falling. I hear myself shouting things ('How dare you? Don't say his name! Don't you fucking say his name!') as if they might defy my terminal velocity, as if they are ripcords on a parachute. But there is no parachute.

'You can't love him if you don't trust him.'

'I've never said I don't trust him!'

'Then why have you kept so many things from him? Oh Lolly, this is why you're here, isn't it?' And then I know he's seen it, my swarming hive of secrets. I cross my arms over my body, a desperate, helpless gesture, because I am defenceless against him, powerless to make him stop. 'You don't love him and he doesn't love you. How can he when he has no idea who you are?'

'Stop!'

'And you had a child? With *this* man?'

'Don't you dare!'

'Did you ever feel for him what you felt for me?'

'Get away from me, get away!' I whisper, but he does the opposite, he pulls me into the cave of his blazer. *Scream*, I think but nothing comes out, because we're both stricken by his hands on my arms, both captive to it. I think a hundred crazy things. That his arms feel so much stronger after prison. How large and warm his chest is. How small I feel in his grasp.

'Do you think it's any different for me?' His whole body is trembling, or perhaps it's my vibrations pulsing through him. 'We're each other's secret. No one can change that.' Our ribs rise and fall together, our breathing synced. I don't know if he's going to punch me or kiss me. Do I want him to do neither or both? 'Don't you see, darling? We're the same. Cut me open and inside it's you.'

*

From: Kit McDermott   11:05
You took your favourite T-shirts with you, those black, linen ones that you wore for the whole of your pregnancy, the ones with holes in that you promised you'd throw away. Well, here's a secret for you, you who've kept so much from me. Two weeks ago, I ordered five new black ones, I had them delivered to my office so you wouldn't notice, I've been swapping the old ones out for the new. I think of you all the time. Are you thinking of me?

28

Swim

Then

When I eventually step out of the cottage, it is an act of rebellion, *You cannot leave me in here, it's not fair, I will not be stuck here*, and while I am aware it is a rebellion entirely of my own invention (he has never forbidden me to leave, God that he would), it feels good to have something to push against.

My heart is pounding when I am in the clearing with everything I will say if I see him; I march through the woods, my sketchbook tucked under my arm like a rifle. But, I don't see him. The disappointment fades. I slow down. The rush of blood in my head stops, I hear birds' song, waves. I hold out my palms, touch the waist-high blooms. They are clusters of lacy white flowers growing in umbrella shapes. I pick off a flower, crush it, smell its scent – a sharp aniseed. I take out my *Guide to British Plants*, which he bought me. It's cow parsley, native, common, it self-seeds, which is why the woodland is covered with it. I open my sketchbook.

Drawing has always been a state of dual consciousness for me: I am concentrating on capturing the simple five-petalled flowers, the ridged celery stem, but another part of me is set loose, drifts. It is this part that at first, is preoccupied with the thought of Daniel discovering me in the woods, I imagine entire conversations with him: *What are you drawing? Cow parsley. See, how it's almost identical to hemlock water dropwort but one you can eat, the other will kill you.* Sometimes, I resolve to say nothing to him, I will turn the silent treatment he has used so effectively against me, on him. But eventually, I am fatigued by these thoughts, there are limits to how long I will torture myself. I think of the flowers themselves. I walked past them many times on the way to the field, each time, I made a mental note to look them up but I never did. Why not? Why now? Because I am alone. Because he is not walking in front of me. Because I am not focused on the line of his belt, the tan deepening above the neckline of his shirt.

The sea draws me eventually, the sea that has, before, formed only the backdrop to my afternoons with Daniel. I have brought a swimsuit to Cornwall, my black school one, but the first time I enter the water, I have not brought it, I left the cottage with no intention of going in. The beach at the end of the slipway is not as stunning as it was the first day, the tide is out, revealing a flotsam of plastic bottles, crisp packets, sticks. But the low tide uncovers something else: another beach to the right of the one we drove up to. I walk over.

I hated swimming at St Matthews. There were lessons at the local sports centre where there were only four changing rooms; unless you were aggressive, pushed to the front, you had to change with all the other girls, keeping your skirt on as you edged your knickers off, pulling your swimsuit up and then facing the wall to unbutton your shirt, praying no one would see you, make a comment about your new breasts, your thighs, your toes. Now, I understand that I do not hate the water at all, only my self-consciousness. There is no one to be self-conscious with here.

I leave my sketchbook on the rocks, peel off my jeans, stand in my T-shirt and knickers at the water's edge, feeling the tow of shells and pebbles. I plunge in.

What I love about swimming:

The annihilation of it.

That it feels like being held.

That if I swim out far enough, away from the shallows, I come to a place where the water moves not in waves but in swells, where it is dark and misty with forest-green seaweed, where slick fronds wind around my wrists, circle my ankles. Tethered to the sea, I think there are mysteries here no one knows. Mysteries beyond myself. Mysteries beyond him.

29

RAIN

Now

I am shaking as I walk away from Daniel, my teeth are chattering. I look back to make sure he isn't following me and then pull my parka tight round myself. Pointless. It's not my body that's undefended.

You don't love him.

'I do,' I whisper furiously to empty pavements, empty streets. 'He's my soulmate, the love of my life,' but labelling Kit like that, in words I've never used about him and he's never used about me, only underlines their falsity. 'You're my best friend,' I've said to him a thousand times, 'the best husband, the best father.' But now, these sound like greeting card slogans, unable to withstand the landslide of *Cut me open and inside it's you.*

It's raining steadily now, I'm on Threadneedle Street. Across the road is the Bank of England, the long wall of pillars, the flag waving in the wind.

Did you ever feel for him what you felt for me?

I stop. Stand on the pavement, staring at the dark, slippery road. A bike whizzes past, traffic lights change from green to orange to red. A double-decker bus brakes at the crossing before me. The driver catches my eye, gestures at the green man. But I don't move. I'm at a different set of crossroads. Daring myself to answer Daniel's question. Wondering if it's an undetonated mine I need to explode. A brick wall I've come here to hit.

No.

I do not feel for Kit what I felt for you.

Voices roar in my head, so loud against the patter of rain. How could Kit compete with the voltage of first desire, the electric discovery of my own body? It is classic, playbook, that's why grooming is so manipulative. That's why it's so wrong.

But there is another voice too, it waits until all the others die down before whispering: *You set him up, right from the start.* And then, I am moving again, rushing away from the dead calm of the street, as if I can rush away from myself because it's absolutely true. The moment Kit lifted up his hand and gave me a shy wave, I knew instantly I wanted to be with him, more than any man I'd met at Wyatt or Oxford or Emma's house parties. Because he had green eyes not that intense navy; he was lean and wiry not powerfully set; he was witty and self-deprecating instead of charismatic and serious. Sometimes, I'd catch him putting gel in his blond hair or cracking a joke or clearing his throat before he spoke on a call and doubt would crawl over me like insects: have I ever wanted him for himself? Or only as a negative of Daniel?

My stomach is spasming; I've walked too fast. I unsling my backpack, swallow some water before shielding my eyes from the rain to get my bearings. I'm on King William Street. There is the rooftop restaurant where Kit and I celebrated becoming fully fledged associates, Snow + Rock where I tried on hiking boots for our honeymoon to South America, the Nespresso shop where I bought him the coffee machine before we had Millie, if he was here, he'd put his arm round my shoulders, say, 'Do you remember, babe?' I do. But I also know that for every pure memory of his, mine is tainted. Because each second with Kit, I'm comparing him to Daniel. Exultant that he is nothing like him. And devastated.

Do you love him?

He doesn't kiss like Daniel. He doesn't say my name into my mouth. He tells me I'm pretty but never that I'm beautiful, rare, astonishing. He doesn't linger over my body with that slow, penetrating gaze, like I'm a land he's charting, a sea he's navigating. Instead, he sends me emojis of mangoes when he's horny, we giggle when we take off each other's pyjamas, after we have sex, he brings me decaf coffees, I love him for all these things. But how can I trust how I feel when I've also felt their opposite?

The rain is growing stronger. People scatter for shelter, tourists because they wear plastic cagoules and enormous rucksacks, there are two groups under an Italian suit shop doorway, a cluster under the lip of a sandwich shop. I look at them and wonder if I am truly as alone as I feel or if any one of these marriages is like mine – built on flimsy foundations, deceptions, guilty trade-offs. Because I gave Kit everything. To make up for never being able to give him myself.

It isn't hard. Kit is a feminist and an economist, we've always talked about the gender pay gap, the disproportionate burden of emotional labour on women. When I decided to go back to work four days a week, he was the one who raised the impact it would have on my career, how it shouldn't mean I was Millie's main caretaker because he never wanted to be the kind of dad who wasn't involved. But there would always come a point when we needed to make a decision – wedding venues, holidays, houses, nurseries – when I'd just hand him the reins. Now, it's a struggle to express a different opinion. The muscle of surrender has grown very strong.

'Have you noticed?' Kit once said to me. 'We don't really fight?'

I cupped his cheek in my hand. 'I have nothing to fight with you about.'

He has no idea who you are.

I can feel the rain on my skin now. Under my parka, I'm dry but it's spattered my jeans, seeped into my trainers, it is running down my face. In front of me, there are no pedestrians apart from a man walking on the other side of the road, and I wonder if he is the same as me, if he doesn't care about the rain, if the wet makes absolutely no difference. Because he is crying too.

*

From: Kit McDermott   11:36
I've found your secret.

30

Boy

Then

There is a boy on my beach when I get out of the water one day. He wears black swim shorts. He has gel in his hair. He is comfortable in his body, something I am envious of, his palms are flat on the sand behind him, his feet are a man's, flung out and fleshy. A boat is moored up a few metres from the shore.

'You've been in there for ages,' he says. He looks at me frankly, and that old self-consciousness comes back to me, I am aware of the uncertain colour of my eyes, my flat chest, the blotches on my school swimsuit from a washing accident. I am probably the only mixed girl he's ever seen. The sand is suddenly itchy, a strap of seaweed is plastered to my leg from the fistful I've brought out of the water to sketch. I wrap a towel round myself, drop the seaweed on a rock.

'Are you at school?' he asks.

His question confuses me for a second and then it dawns on me that it is an obvious one, it isn't Easter holiday anymore,

Dear Darling

I should be at school, although I have lost my sense of what time it is, if it's a weekday or weekend. I shake my head, try and frame a response that wards off further questions. 'I'm off for a bit.'

'Oh.' He digs his toe into the shingle.

'What about you?' I ask.

'Finished at three. Although, I don't really see the point in school, I don't want to go to uni or anything like that. I'm going to fish, like my dad.'

I stare at him. That someone sees school as pointless, does not intend to go to university is beyond me. Mama was always adamant about running my botanical hobbies alongside traditional education, she never went to university, she went straight to the Royal Academy of Music. 'Don't be like me,' she'd said. It's only now, listening to this boy, that I think what a strange thing that was to say. Why would I not want to be like her? What was wrong with our life? I would do anything to go back.

'That's mine over there.' He points to the boat called *Forager*. The hull is painted sky blue; an orange buoy hangs over the side. It is moored at least ten metres out; he has swum to the beach; he must have passed me in the water.

'What do you fish for?'

'Dover sole, lemon, turbot, mackerel.'

I cannot picture what a mackerel looks like either alive or on a plate. It seems like something old men eat for breakfast in country hotels.

'Conger eels, sometimes; rays—'

'Rays? Like sting rays?'

He throws his head back and laughs, which I do not like, I do not like feeling stupid. 'Thornbacks mostly, cuckoo rays, spotted rays. Dad said there used to be common rays but now they're not common at all, they're only in Wales and Scotland.'

I stare back at the water I've come from. I've seen small shoals of fish when I swim, nothing more. But now I think the sea is like the woodlands, like the thyme on the grassy chalkland, it is worlds inside of worlds, under the surface, it is teeming with life. 'Tell me about it.'

'About what?'

'Fishing.'

He presses his lips together in a taut line. 'Are you having a laugh?'

'No.'

'You summer folk don't care about that.'

'What do you think I care about?'

'I don't know. Lip gloss. Clothes. Magazines.'

I shake my head.

He looks at me then as I am looking at him, as if we're different species, we're equally curious about each other.

'I just like learning about different things,' I explain. 'Plants mostly. But all kinds of things.'

I don't tell him that 'like' is an understatement. That what I feel is more like a thirst, a craving for prising open plants, creatures, language. I don't say that I am not strange at all, there are people like Daniel and me everywhere, tucked in the back rooms of museums, labs, in fields, hungry to discover nature's secrets. I don't say that I miss Daniel. Or that I am lonely.

Dear Darling

He waits for one beat, two, to see if I am serious. I stare back at him.

'I like diving for scallops best,' he starts. 'If you dive for them, you don't ruin the seabed—'

I listen.

31

RIVER

Now

London Bridge unfurls before me, empty, like I'm the only person in the world. The rain is deafening now, louder than the traffic streaming past, and the clouds are so low. At a different time, I might have been afraid of how dark and dense they are. Now, I think of all the rain they were carrying. How good it must feel to let it out.

You had a child? With this man?

I said yes when Kit said, 'Let's have a baby,' but I had no idea what it meant. I took NCT classes that made me worry about the wrong things – epidurals, formula, co-sleeping – when actually, it was pain and Millie's falling weight and breastfeeding that were the worst. Two secret fears never materialised – that my body would fail me and that I wouldn't love the baby – hadn't my body, my feelings always been untrustworthy, disloyal? But the birth had gone well and when the midwife laid Millie in my arms, tiny, perfect, beautiful, I thought *Finally, finally, I feel what I am supposed to feel.*

I make my way to the centre of the bridge. An open-top tour bus streams past, the destination sign broken, it flickers before spraying a wave over the pavement. I don't move out of the way. Water crests over my trainers. Breathtakingly cold.

Maternity leave unravelled me. The intense quiet between changing Millie, feeding her, reading her books, singing her songs, plunged me into my own thoughts; I'd never allowed myself to have this much time, I liked work because it never gave me any time. I'd make Millie fruit purees and think about the food Daniel used to make me. I'd take her to the sandpit and, suddenly, I was on the beach outside the cottage. I'd tickle Millie on our bed and I'd remember playing horsey in Daniel's bedroom, his shoes lined up neatly at the bottom of his wardrobe.

And then there were the times when I felt like I couldn't be a mother. When Millie would cry and I would try everything – feed her, burp her, check her nappy – but she would keep going, her face tightly scrunched with pain or anger, I didn't know, and the same thoughts would circle my head like a drain that never emptied – *I don't know what I'm doing, why don't I know what I'm doing? Because I'm a shit mum, of course I am, no matter how much I pretend or try to move on, I'll never get away from it, all the appalling things I've done.*

'I'm thinking about going back to work,' I said to Kit, five months in.

He looked at me, astounded. 'I thought you were enjoying it? Is anything wrong?'

I couldn't tell him how I longed for the marble lobby of Dulwich & Sullivan, the satisfaction of finalising a memo, no crying or failure or shame. Just the simplicity of work and reward. 'It's just a thought.'

I shiver against the wind, wrap my arms around myself. It's the rain soaking through my jeans, the wind is turning them chilly. But it doesn't matter, not now. I take my backpack off. Put my hands on the railing.

When I returned to work, I decided to go back to four days a week, *I want this*, I told myself, *I can manage a whole Friday with her.* I did for a while. Once I was officially back at Dulwich & Sullivan, there was always more work to do, no more swathes of time left to my own punishing thoughts. Then came the tantrums.

They were always on a Friday, always with me, never at nursery or the weekends or in front of Kit. Everything was a hair-trigger – books, fruit, TV, her coat. Nappy changes became brutal, those juicy thighs I adored leaving bruises on my arm. I did everything I could to help her through, I'd talk in a low, soft voice, empathise, make her feel understood, give her a healthy alternative to express her anger, I tried it all. Nothing worked except waiting it out. I'd sit mutely beside her as she smashed her heels against the floor, always thinking the same thought, a thought I fought with everything I'd read – *This is normal. The terrible twos. Just a developmental phase* – but they were only knives I'd brought to a gun fight and bullets were already firing, they pelted through me, they said, *There is only one reason she does this with you, just one: she knows.* My daughter, born from my ruined body, knew that part of me was absent, carved out, lost somewhere in a Cornwall cottage, on a beach, a field, and she wasn't satisfied with a halved me, the me in pieces. It didn't matter that I loved her beyond what I thought was possible; she was constantly testing me. Because no one else needed to be tested. Everyone else had passed.

I climb onto the ledge. There is a second of vertigo, just half a metre higher up, the water is suddenly that much closer. I tip my head back to the wind; feel it lash against my face.

You had a child? With this man?

The second time Kit said, 'Shall we have a baby?' I opened the fridge and wished it was an oven. He slipped his hands round my waist and in the seconds he took to ask me if I'd heard what he'd said, I made a decision. It was the same one I always did: to lie. Because to tell him the truth was to unravel all my deceptions, the hundreds and hundreds I'd strung together, leading back to the first time I met him in the university café. I couldn't tell him the person he loved wasn't real. I was scrabbling, always, to make her real.

Then, when I lost Faye, I realised my mistake. Faye was like Millie. She'd inhabited me, she knew all my secrets, read all my thoughts, and then, she granted my deepest, darkest wish. Just when I didn't wish it anymore.

You've kept so many things from him.

The river is dark and inviting. It would be so easy. The worst part would be the fall, losing my body to gravity, the explosion of fear. But then, the best part would come. The obliterating cold. Everything finally stopping. Water closing over it all.

A boat speeds under the bridge, sending a series of waves through the river: a Thames Clipper. I took that last summer with Millie from Greenwich all the way here, she sat on my knee eating snacks while I pointed out castles (the Tower of London), giant boats (HMS *Belfast*), the monster hedgehog spike (The Shard), and she'd turned to me, crumbs all over her mouth, and said, 'I'm happy, Mummy.' This keeps me above the water more than any life ring, drenches me deeper than the rain. Because that's what I want, isn't it? To have a million more moments like that with her. Moments when I'm whole and healed.

'Are you all right?' It's a woman. She is dressed in a black puffer jacket; rain is streaming down her nose but her eyes are wide on me. 'I saw you from across the road and I thought . . .' She doesn't finish.

I let the railings go. Climb down from the ledge. I will not give up now. There are too many things I need to do to get back to her, to Kit. The sky growls above me. I sling on my rucksack, pull up my hood. 'Thank you,' I say to her. 'I'm fine.'

*

From: Kit McDermott   11:38

I know they're secrets because you've wrapped them in so many layers – a scarf, a plastic bag, the rucksack you bought for our honeymoon to South America. I guess you thought the rucksack was a good place to hide them. You thought they were safe.

And you know what, you're right, your secrets are safe. Because even though I've found all eight of your sketchbooks, I have no idea what they mean. You've never once mentioned to me that you like art or that you can draw. Yet, I am staring at hundreds and hundreds of drawings – mostly plants but also butterflies, always blue.

Dear Darling

I'm losing my mind, I'm actually going mad, I'm certain this is important, then a second later, I think it's not. Maybe this is nothing, just a hobby you did when you were a child. But then why never tell me about it? Why were these more hidden than your pills?

32

END OF THE WORLD

Then

The boy, whose name is Alex and who starts to meet me on the beach after he finishes school, tells me that the sea I'm swimming in is not the sea at all, it's an estuary nestled between the western edge of Falmouth Bay and the eastern side of the Lizard Peninsula. That, if I take the coastal path from the cottage, in the opposite direction to the thyme field, I'll come to The Ferryboat Inn, the pub where his sister is working. That, as long as I hug the coastline, I can kayak all the way from the cottage to Port Navas where he lives.

I've never had a friend like him before. He is sixteen to my fourteen but our schools feel the same – teachers, cliques, bullies. We spend much of our afternoons caricaturing our enemies who make us feel inconsequential and separate – their big boobs and greasy skin, their blockhead stupidity. I confess that after Mama died, no one has tried to contact me from St Matthews. He says they're shits. I tell him about how I brought that fungus in for show and tell. He says he once took in a spider crab, which escaped and got stamped on by Bradley Wayne. Our sides sear from laughing.

I find myself talking a lot about my father. I tell Alex that he left my mother when she was pregnant with me, that I couldn't tell him Mama had died or that I am staying with Daniel because I do not know his address or even his name. Alex says, in his experience, it is better *not* to know these things. He tells me he knows all these details about his mother but it has made absolutely no difference; since she left their family, she has never called or visited. When he talks about her, he twists his thumb and forefinger around his wrist. If I lay my hand over his, he stops.

One time, we take *Forager* past her house, Alex points it out to me, a neat, whitewashed cottage with green shutters. He lifts his chin as we go past, daring her to come out, but when the boat slips away, so does his bravado. He slumps over the side. I put my hand on his shoulder but he doesn't get up. So, I use my St Matthews words, words Mama would never let me say. 'Wanker.'

He chuckles sadly but that's enough for me. I run to the end of *Forager*. 'Wanker!' I shout at his mother, give her the finger, 'I hate your shutters!' and then he is behind me, he is grinning and that grin is everything, we are calling everyone wankers, all the people who've abandoned us, the banal ways they've screwed us up, our rage reverberating across the water. It feels so good. To be young and rude and loud.

It is a relief to talk to Alex about Mama, I hadn't realised how much I'd been holding in. He listens as I comb through every fight I've ever had with her, repeat every hurtful word. 'I was a total bitch,' I say over and over. His response is indefatigably the same. He looks out onto the open water and says, 'It doesn't matter. She loved you,' and somehow, in that look, those words, I feel like her love is the sea, my twisted guilt tiny against the magnitude of it.

The one person I never speak to Alex about is Daniel. I don't tell Alex the real reason I fought with Mama or that Daniel hasn't spoken to me in days. If Alex asks about him, I pretend he is strict and boring, I parody him catching a butterfly, I mock his jars. But simmering under every conversation with Alex, the secrets we tell each other, the places we go, I am always thinking of Daniel, always assessing and reassessing everything in relation to him.

I am struck, for example, at how reliant I am on Daniel, how utterly incurious I've been about where exactly I am. In London, I walked to and from school, met Mama before her concerts, went to parks and museums; the city was as navigable to me as the estuary is to Alex. And I wonder if the intense focus on botany, which has fed me, comforted me, healed me, has robbed me of broader perspectives. I can tell the difference between the innocuous cow parsley and the poisonous hemlock water dropwort but I don't know where the nearest supermarket is or the name of the closest train station.

I start to imagine end-of-the-world scenarios where all human life is wiped out apart from Alex, Daniel and me. Who would survive? Alex is the clear winner. He drives his father's truck, he knows where to trig for cockles, he can cook shellfish in their own brine. Then, it would be me, I know that dandelions are complete proteins from root to tip, I can make my way round mushrooms and berries. Daniel, with his mews house and microscopic knowledge about butterflies, would be the first to go. The thought gives me a dirty rush of pleasure. Not all knowledge is equal. Some things are more worth knowing than others.

Dear Darling

For Alex, knowledge isn't something to pursue in and of itself, it's a means to an end. He isn't interested in the genetic differences between two mackerels or the Latin names for genus, species, sub-species but he knows where to fish for them and how much they sell for. I go on *Forager* with him, watch him unhook the mackerels from the line, their silver tails thrashing in the blue plastic crate. Once, he catches a cuttlefish, an awful-looking thing with a swarm of tentacles under its eyes. He lets me watch it for a few minutes and then he takes it from the box and cuts it up on the deck with a pair of scissors. His practicality disgusts me and awes me. The efficient way he spears the cuttlefish right back onto the hook he caught it on as bait for something else.

For this reason, he doesn't understand my interest in plants. 'Wow,' he says when I throw my arms round him after he tells me the names of the seaweed I've found – sea cabbage, dulse, bladderwrack. His attention drifts when I tell him my theory about how I think the different colours of seaweed are related to how close they are to the surface of the water, it doesn't connect with him, I make a mental note to tone it down. In these moments, I feel strange and unknowable and want Daniel.

Still, he tries, he is generous in a way that boys at St Matthews never were. He invites me out with his friends, Simon and James, both fishermen's sons. I always say no. For my sketching, he kayaks me up the creeks to muddy foreshores where ancient oaks grow, festooned with lichen. He fits me with his sister's snorkel and fins and another layer of the world is lifted up, peeled back – clutches of cuttlefish eggs clinging to blades of eelgrass, rocks thick with the glisten of mussels. My body changes as my sketchbook blooms: my calves grow shapely; my arms muscled with swimming and kayaking. Now, every afternoon, when I pull my swimsuit on, I look at the strength of my body in the mirror and think maybe, just maybe, I could do this without Daniel.

*

From: Kit McDermott   **12:06**
I've broken into your greenhouse. The door was padlocked, so I punched through. It felt good. All that smashed glass.

    Soon I'll start rifling through your things — seeds, pots, plants, soil — even though it makes me feel dirty, like a thief. But now, for this moment, I'm going to sit in the greenhouse I made you, in the deckchair you love, and pretend none of this is happening. Just watch the rain.

33

Sky Garden

Now

I'm walking but I don't know where to go. I can't go back to the hotel, I'm afraid of rectangles – that cold, clean square of room, of waiting for a glimpse of Millie and Kit on the screen of my phone. On the bridge, there are life rings, one every few metres, and then, the orange buoy on *Forager* flashes through my mind, what I'd give to be on a boat with Alex right now, the hum of the engine, the horizon of estuary. A gull flies overhead, swooping low over the Thames and then rearing up against the skyline, and I see the skyscraper, half shrouded in clouds: The Walkie Talkie. It is everything they say it is, a swollen pint glass bulging comically at the top and narrowing at the bottom. The only reason the council granted planning permission is for the precise reason my heart is lifting at the sight of it. It has the highest public roof garden in London – Sky Garden.

I've never visited before; I don't let myself go to gardens. I live within strict rules: no collecting outside The Wedge, no looking things up, I've contained that part of myself, in the soil beyond the brambles, in my greenhouse. But I'm not home anymore and I need this. Open the cage. Let out the beast that's lain drugged and dormant for so long.

There's almost no queue, it's still raining, the worst day for viewing London. But I'm not here for the views. Heat streams over me as I enter the lift lobby; until I feel it on my skin, I don't realise I'm shivering. I stay there for a few minutes, squeezing out my hair, wiping rain from my face. Then, I take the lift up thirty-five floors.

The doors open out onto what could easily be the lobby of a bank, a spotless stone floor, sofas and bistro tables, except that directly ahead is pure window. There are so few people here, a mistake, because seeing London in a storm is breathtaking, the gathered fists of shadow, the highest buildings covered in banks of clouds. Rumour had it that The Walkie Talkie was put forward as a potential new office for Dulwich & Sullivan. The partners voted it down. 'If something happens that far up,' Bruce told me with the kind of appetite for risk that makes him a lawyer and not a banker, 'you'd never get out.' Surely, that's the thrill of it, though. The insanity of working thirty-five floors up. The absurdity of a garden in the sky.

But, despite London laid out before me, the thunderous sky, the flashes of lightning, my eyes are drawn to a mother and her son. He looks about four, a little older than Millie. He holds out his arms. His mother swings him up onto her shoulders as she points to The Shard.

I fist back tears. She is the mother I can never be. I don't like to put Millie on my shoulders, throw her, catch her, when she was a baby, I refused to carry her round the house, I'd only ever

Dear Darling

hold her sitting down. 'You know you're not going to drop her, right?' Kit would say, but how would I know that? I don't trust my body – gullible, treacherous – I am unsafe inside it. Why would I trust it with my child?

The garden is a set of raised terraces on either side of the central restaurant; I take the stairs slowly to the top. Beyond the glass, a different side of London is visible, the swirl of the Gherkin, the white dome of St Paul's, but I'm more interested in what's in the soil. I reach out, examine the plants. They're mostly New Zealand black tree ferns with their ink-ribbed fronds – tough but edible. Not what I'm looking for. No matter. Almost every plant defends themselves. If you know what you're looking for, there are weapons everywhere.

The slope falls away to cycads; with their stout, woody trunks, their sprays of leaves, they look like small palms. I unsling my backpack, roll on a plastic glove. My heart races. I reach over the bed and grab a handful of seeds. No one stops me. No one is policing the plants.

I'm bold by the time I get to the foot of the slope; it's filled with seasonal crowd-pleasers – succulents, irises, blue lilies, silver lamb's ear spikes – so many saps and spines and bristles. I crouch down slowly, trying not to hurt my stomach, then gather as much as possible as I pretend to admire a leaf, tie my laces, take a photograph. Daniel's words circle in my head. *How can he love you when he has no idea who you are?*

'You love me,' I whisper. 'And you have no idea who I am. No idea at all.'

My backpack is heavy with what I've collected. I peer inside. It's beautiful, full of foliage, flowers, stems, if someone found it, they'd think I was one of those women who makes floral wreaths, who hang them up on their front doors with a length of silk ribbon, so creative, such a lovely hobby. Kit thinks that about my gardening. 'You grow such beautiful flowers,' he says if he finds me in the greenhouse, surrounded by Brugmansia, foxglove, laurel. In this, Kit and Daniel are alike, united in their profound misunderstanding. *My loves, don't you know? Beauty is the best cover for deadly.*

*

From: Kit McDermott 12:15

When I found out the greenhouse was locked, I was actually excited, I was convinced there was something up here, why else was there a padlock I'd never seen before? But I haven't found anything. I think you might have taken that trumpet flower with you, although I can't be sure. Do you remember dragging it out from the greenhouse and setting it outside in the summer? We'd sit on deckchairs, holding hands, watching the sun set, the intense scent of those flowers washing over us. Is that why you brought it with you? A reminder of this? I want those back too.

34

KILLING JARS

Then

I am in the field with Daniel. The setting sun flushes through the thyme, the scent of it penetrating my lungs, and there are butterflies, so many of them all around me, rising up from the purple haze. I shut my eyes, hold out my arms, feel their wings brush my skin, hear them flapping but there is something wrong, a stinging smell like alcohol. I open my eyes. The orange glow of the afternoon instantly disappears because I am not in the field, it is night. I am in my narrow room in the cottage. But still, that smell.

I know what it is. It is the fluid in the study, in that unlabelled bottle. I get out of bed, walk down the corridor. A bar of light shines from under the door. I push it open.

He's there, sitting at the trestle table, his laptop open. After living with only my thoughts of him and the traces he leaves in the cottage, that he is really here, in front of me, is almost too much. I am scared my presence will send him away, I want to stay like this, watching him from the doorway. But he hears me, turns.

'I smelt something,' I say stupidly. 'It woke me up.'

'I'm sorry.' He hasn't changed from the field; he wears a dove-grey shirt, cargo trousers. Behind him, the trestle table is not empty like it was when I checked it this afternoon. Instead, it has ten jars on it and a mesh cage filled with Blues.

'What are you doing?' I ask.

'Research,' he says. A few weeks ago, he would have volunteered what that research is, the complex, fascinating reasons he's selected each of the butterflies from the hundreds he has identified and released. Now, he does not.

'What's the smell?'

He hesitates, reluctant to enter into our old dynamic again, but the prospect of enforcing this now, in the middle of the night, seems to overwhelm him. He rubs his eyes. 'Ethyl acetate.'

'What does it do?'

'It's for the killing jars.'

'Killing jars?'

He nods. He has no energy to soften the blow, not this evening. He unscrews the lid of a nearby jar. The smell floods the room. He unzips the mesh cage, takes a butterfly and drops it in.

The fluidity of the action reminds me of Alex. He screws on the lid. I tell myself *I will not watch it die*, I am tired of the desperate pump of mackerel gills, the frantic grasp of cuttlefish tentacles, but, in the end, I do watch because the fumes work in seconds, not minutes. The butterfly flutters manically and then drops to the bottom. He studies it for a few seconds. I wish I was a thing in his jar. I pick it up, hold it to the light of the lamp. 'Does it hurt them?'

He shakes his head. 'Their neurological systems are simple; they don't have the same sensation of pain we do.'

'You're sure?'

'I'm sure,' he says. If we were speaking right now, he would tell me about the butterfly's brain, heart, pain receptors, what difference it makes that their nerve centres are in their thorax, not their heads, and then I have a cruel, heartless thought: what a poor stand-in Alex is for Daniel. I have been managing with him, surviving, but he is a bird feeding me pecks of seed when Daniel throws me meat. With Daniel, I don't have to pretend to be less weird, less excited, less hungry. It is suddenly urgent that I fix what is broken between us, if only to get back to this. I hold the jar out to him. 'Why can't they feel pain?'

But he won't be drawn. He takes the jar from me, sets it gently on the table. He presses the heels of his hands into his eyes. 'It's late.'

It is. The alarm clock that used to be on one of the bedside tables says it's just after two a.m. I stare at the row of empty jars, the butterflies fluttering in their mesh cage, his open laptop. 'Let me help.'

'You should go to bed.'

'I can drop butterflies into jars as well as the next person.'

'It isn't that. You know it isn't that.' He puts his hand to his forehead, squeezes his temples. The act, one of utter exhaustion, shames me. I have done this to him. If he's been working here late into the night and getting up early to avoid me, he must be sleeping only three, four hours.

'I'm sorry,' I say.

'Don't.'

'You're exhausted because of me—'

'—It's fine.'

'It's not.' I glance at the spreadsheet on his screen, the hundreds of entries he is trying to make sense of. 'I won't bother you anymore. You can come back to the cottage to work. I'll stay in my room until you go.' I think of the state I leave his room every afternoon, the clothes on the floor, the bed, how long it must take to put everything back together. 'And I won't mess up your room.'

He lets out a long sigh that saps all the energy in the room and I know I haven't gone far enough. It isn't about messing up his room, it's the incurable knot inside me that makes me want to cross the space between us. 'And that other thing . . .' my voice stumbles over itself, 'I won't do it again.'

'You didn't do anything.'

'I won't want to then.'

'Can we help what we want?'

Panic flares in me. These promises, after acting up for so long, aren't going to work: he is going to send me away. He will drive me to Wyatt or put me on a train and that will be it, no butterflies or woodland, eelgrass meadows or ancient oaks. The edge of the table grazes my hip, I press hard against it. 'It won't happen again.'

'How can you be sure?'

'I'll stop myself.'

'Can you?'

'Yes.'

'And what about me?'

'What about you?'

'What if I can't?'

There is a second of confusion when I'm not sure I've heard him, when I'm not sure what he means. But then he removes his hand from his face and there is no mistaking his meaning. The world shifts, turns liquid, I think I might faint. I grasp the edge of the desk. 'I don't understand.'

'I am not exhausted from working late or from avoiding you.' In the lamplight, his eyes on me are not navy at all but obsidian. 'I am exhausted because you are all I think of.'

My heart is hammering so loudly, I can barely hear myself speak. 'I thought it was just me.'

'How could it ever have been just you?'

'But, in the field, you ran—'

'—I was afraid.'

'And now?'

'I've tried to keep away, I transferred you to Wyatt, the last few weeks, I've thrown myself into work, I haven't come back to the cottage. I've told myself it is unforgivable, wrong, I might have convinced myself if I'd gone away, if you had. But being here with you, seeing you—' He looks at me then, he takes all of me in, my face, my breasts under my long-sleeved T-shirt, the hike of my shorts, my bare legs, and then I realise the hundreds of times he's looked at me are shadows of this look, only this is real because being looked at like this changes my entire body, every inch of me is searching for him, straining towards him. '—I think I was deluded. Because I can't stop myself.'

I close my eyes briefly. 'Then don't.'

'You don't know what you're saying.'

'Not all of it. But I know some things.'

'Like what?'

My throat is tight, I think I might cry. 'I know there is something between us. I knew it the first time we met. It's always been there, in the museum, on that beach in Devon, in your house, the thyme.' Behind me, butterfly wings brush against the mesh. 'I don't know what it is. Does everyone have it? Maybe it's like this with other people—'

'—No,' he says softly. 'It isn't like this with other people. Only with you.'

There is a burst of joy in me, something I didn't believe was there.

He takes my wrist, forms a circle round it with his thumb and forefinger. He draws the circle up, pushing back the cotton of my sleeve. At my elbow, he stops, slips his hand under my arm. He seems to examine it for a second, the smoothness of my skin, the eddy of my veins. 'Rare. Astonishing.' He bends his head and kisses it.

35

Apothecary

Now

Back at the hotel, I get to work. My mind is a happy hum as I pull on my gloves and empty out my haul. I feel like I am in my greenhouse again, Millie safe with Kit in The Wedge or at nursery. I sort through what I've collected into flowers, leaves and seeds, then, I boil a kettle of water to sterilise the jam jars, I want things to be perfect. I pour in scalding water. Mist rises. Condensation runs down the outside.

I start with the baby's breath, cutting the sprays of tiny white flowers to the same length, dividing them into bunches. The wardrobe is the best place to dry them, it's dark inside, away from the humidity of the bathroom or the windows. I string them up from the hangers. Pretty. Kit and I went to a wedding four years ago where the bride walked down the aisle with an entire bouquet of baby's breath, bound together with a silk bow. Kit looked at me, he was thinking about our wedding day, and I squeezed his hand as if I was too, but I wasn't. I was thinking how that bouquet was a skin irritant, that it can cause gastronomic and respiratory issues. Which was fine for her. No one was rubbing it into her skin. No one was making her eat it.

Botany was always women's work. Daniel might have started my botanical educational but I finished it. In the libraries at Wyatt, at Oxford, I discovered that way before those wealthy Natural History Museum collectors sailed to their West Indies plantations for specimens, the first botanists were women. They were called other names then – herbalists, healers, hedge witches – they bartered their services for eggs and honey, they distilled, purified and poured to make poultices for aching muscles or salves for wounds, to bud an empty womb or to stop it. What choice did they have but to use what grew in plain sight?

The cycad seeds I soak in a basin of water. I wait until their orange flesh softens before pulling them off. Underneath are smooth, toffee-coloured seeds, the shape of large acorns. I pass one from one palm to the other, trying to feel the electricity of their toxins – abdominal pain, muscle weakness, dementia. *You wanted me, Daniel, all of me. This is me. Poisoning you.*

I make myself a hot water bottle. Pressing the warmth against my stomach, I survey the beginnings of my own apothecary: the bunches of baby's breath, the neat row of jam jars; cycad seeds set out to dry, and beside them, on the desk, my angel's trumpets, the flowers sealed shut like silenced mouths. I feel very strong, very powerful, part of a long line of powerless women finding power. Hate us, fuck us, burn us, we can bring healing, give life or the opposite. We can main and harm and kill.

*

Dear Darling

From: Kit McDermott   14:25

I thought I'd cracked it when I had the idea of checking our joint account, I thought, I'm going to see you booking yourself into a hotel, buying a salad, I promised myself that if I found you, I'd be calm, I wouldn't scare you, wouldn't show up. I'd call you at the hotel, just ask, politely, if I could come and see you.

But there were no transactions, not since you left on Friday, and my heart plunged, I thought I was never going to find you.

Then, I saw it. A £200 cash withdrawal this month. I've looked back as far as the bank lets me – it's always the same, £200 goes out every month. I've ransacked our whole house but I can't find that money. I've never seen you with that much cash.

I thought you'd left us because of the baby. But this is something completely different, isn't it? Before Faye, before Millie, perhaps even before me. You've been planning this.

36

Botany

Then

He does not touch me again that evening. In the morning, he has an eight a.m. meeting an hour's drive away. I get up just to look at him, even that is new and fresh. I stand beside the pink sofa in the living room watching him rush about the cottage – he sprints up the steps because he has forgotten his laptop; he has no time to make himself a smoothie, so he turns on the tap, gulps water from the cup of his hand. Only when he's at the door do I speak. I say his name because I don't know how to say, *Don't go* or *Touch me*. He crosses the room, presses his thumb against my lip. 'Later,' he says. The promise, all the possibilities it holds, sends a thrill through me.

I watch him reverse out of the woods and then I sink into my usual chair at the desk. I don't open my schoolwork. I do what he did to myself. I toy with the sleeve he pushed back, I circle my wrist bone, press my thumb to my mouth. My arm, my lips are things transformed, why did he choose those parts, why that touch? I want to know what he's seen, what he's felt, every single thought he has about me. It's good he is away this morning. It gives me time to luxuriate in those touches over and over again.

But I am also aware that time is slipping away, I should prepare for what is to come. I am going to be kissed. I think of Olivia, one of the cool girls at St Matthews, she made a chart of first kisses, she asked everyone in the class. When she came to me, I didn't answer, unwilling to be entertainment. 'Why are you always so difficult?' she said, 'It's a simple "Yes" or "No."' I shook my head. She rolled her eyes, put a cross by my name. 'As if there could be more than one answer.' I take out a tube of lip balm, twist the pink stick all the way up and smooth it across my lips. I kiss the glass, cold and wonderful beneath me. *Ask me later, Olivia. Ask me later.*

I'm on the porch when he returns. I have taken a bath, my hair still smells of my apple shampoo, my skin is wrinkled and soft but I am wearing what I wore last night, the same long-sleeve T-shirt and shorts; if he kissed me in those, why would I ever change out? He slows when he sees me under the shadows of the eaves. He sets down the mesh cage, drops his bag, comes to a complete halt. He looks at me for what seems like an age. 'You're so beautiful,' he says, and suddenly, I am.

The cottage is cool – the stone floor underfoot, the kitchen counter I trail my fingers over, the polished wood of the banister winding upstairs. He holds open his bedroom door. Yesterday, after he kissed my arm, he dragged his duvet onto the study floor for me and I fell asleep to the sight of him working, the smell of ethyl acetate no longer repellent but a scent to be savoured, the smarting in my throat another form of his touch. But now, in his bedroom, there are no butterflies or jars or laptops and I think I've arrived. I am in the moment I've been waiting for.

He pulls the curtains shut, turns. 'This will be strange for you,' he says.

I shrug. I want it to be strange.

'You haven't done this before?'

I shake my head.

'Are you afraid?'

'A little.'

'Of what?'

I glance at the bed. I have only been here when the curtains are pulled back and I can see the leaves of the oaks, I have only come to mess it up and spy. Child's play. Now, everything is different. In the setting sun filtering through the weave of the curtains, the bed seems enormous, the plumped-up pillows, the folded throw are things from a hotel. So adult. 'I don't know. I'm not sure what to do.'

He steps towards me. 'That evening, in the museum, do you remember what you did?'

He is teaching me, he is returning me to the familiar, except this subject matter isn't butterflies or botany, it is the private science of him and me. The bed vanishes, overtaken by the memory of the carved pillars outside Lepidoptery, the vertebrae of the diplodocus in Hintze Hall below. I lift my fingers and lay them on his throat.

This time, there is no intolerable silence. This time, he makes a sound like nothing I've heard before, a purr, alive and trembling under my fingers. 'You see?' he whispers, 'You know what to do. Everything you do is right.'

A switch flips, all doubt, gone. I brush my fingers over his neck, let them rest at the base of his throat. He shudders. I loosen the line of pearlescent buttons I've stared at every Saturday for months. The openness of his shirt reveals the shock of his body, the definition of his abdomen, the curve of his biceps, the dark line of hair from chest to navel. I ease his shirt off. His shoulders are the most beautiful thing I have ever seen.

My hands drift to the clasp of his belt. It's unbelievably masculine. The thickness of the leather. The black stitching.

He catches my hand, then stiffens, steps back. 'Wait, wait, perhaps we should stop.'

I look up, confused.

'Before it's too late.'

Isn't it already too late?

'Nothing's happened.'

I don't understand. I've touched him, surely that's happened?

He shakes his head. 'This could be all.'

I stare at my hands, suspended where he has abandoned them, bewildered that the world of his skin can be so quickly withdrawn. I'm frightened. This will be so much worse than when he ignored me for weeks. How will I bear it now, after everything he's said, everything he's touched. Is this what men do? Kiss your arms, put their thumbs on your lips and then tell you it's nothing?

What I do next, I cannot pinpoint a source for. It rises from the shadowy swirl of movies and music videos, the whispers of cool girls, from biology itself, from science, it is as clear as a bell, solid as stone: a girl's body changes everything. I pull off my shorts and my top, I step out of my knickers. I stand in front of him in the falling light of the afternoon, trying to be brave. 'I don't want this to be all.'

He regards me for so long, I start to tremble, from his gaze, from the air on my skin, from the rising tide of my self-doubt – my nose is too large, my hair is too thin, my eyes are swamp water, how could he ever want *me* after *Mama*? But then, the tempo changes, he crosses the room. His hands are in my hair. He tilts my chin towards him, he says my name into my mouth before he kisses me. He is everywhere, his palms running down my ribcage, across the blades of my hips, his lips are on my neck, he is whispering, 'You're the one, do you know that, it was always you,' he is saying, 'I've loved you from the moment I saw you.' A shadow flits across my brain, that makes no sense, wasn't that in our living room, the day he first met Mama? But I push it aside, I can't think of her now. The backs of my thighs hit the bed. I lie down.

He pulls the sheets over us. I think of cocoons, layers upon layers of silk, the bed the first, the sheets another, his body the closest one. He supports himself on his forearms, his belt buckle stabs against my hip as he slides it off. With that practised efficiency I've always loved, he pushes off the rest of his clothes. 'This might hurt,' he says, reaching down.

It does at first. He is right about that and many other things – when he said it would be strange, when he implied there'd be no going back. Because while this is a return to the liquid world of his body – the taut muscle of his shoulders, his hair between my fingers, his addictive scent – it is also different. Pain tears through me, I cry out with it, I am dying, I am breaking apart but as he gathers pace, rhythm, I realise I am not dying, not breaking apart, I am being unlocked, surrendered. Towards the end, there is a shot of pleasure, my hips buck up to meet him and all the botany flashes in front of me that I thought I knew but didn't. Phototropism is every inch of my body arching towards him. Photosynthesis is his sunlight on my body harnessed into pure, sweet sugar.

PART III

Monday

37

Pollen

Now

My pulse is strong and rhythmic when I wake up, thrumming with purpose. Today is the day. Today, I'll show him. Today, I'll go home. I'll make Millie all her favourite foods, pancakes with chocolate spread, foamy milk with sprinkles, cheesy pasta, I'll do bedtime, I'll sing all the made-up verses of 'The Wheels on the Bus', let her fall asleep in my arms. Then, I'll go downstairs and watch an action movie with Kit, all I want is for us to have the same conversation we've had since we met. 'I could have a body like that,' he'll say, as we watch the Marine/warrior/gladiator leap off a building.

'If you didn't have a job.'

'If I didn't like pizza.'

'If you went to the gym for seven hours every day.'

He'll smile at me. 'Not worth it.'

I'll smile back. 'Not worth it.'

My strategy is simple. No more talking about the law, Daniel is immune to the logic of it. No talking about Kit either, he will twist everything. I'll simply show him why he doesn't know me at all. I'll tell him the secret I've kept from him in the place I kept it.

You don't trust him, he hurled at me yesterday. But it's Daniel I can't trust. With the biggest secret of all.

On the desk, the angel's trumpets bulge against the tape, straining to be loose. I pull on a pair of gloves, run a finger along the neck of one flower from sepal to petal. Carefully, carefully, I peel back the tape.

I've pollinated the flowers dozens of times. Kit bought my first pair of angel's trumpets for my birthday years ago, since then, I've been fertilising, cultivating, feeding until I have ten more shrubs. Still, my hands are shaking, the tweezers tremble between my fingers. I wait until I'm calm. Then, I ease back the petals to expose the insides of the flower. It's so quiet. All I can hear is the snap of the filaments as I transfer the sunshine-bright anthers into test tubes.

If I was fertilising, it would be easy, I would dab the pollen directly onto the stigma. But I am not pollinating, I am collecting. I turn out the tube of anthers onto a folded piece of hotel paper, use a paintbrush to coax off the grains and then tip the pure pollen back into the tube.

It's the scopolamine that makes the pollen so poisonous. In the eighteenth century, scopolamine was used as an anaesthetic, in higher doses, it causes dry mouth, blurred vision, tachycardia, arrhythmia. And that's just one of the tropane alkaloids in the pollen. The others – atropine, hyoscyamine – can lead to paralysis, delusions, visual and auditory hallucinations, death. I read once that a man who drank a tea made from two flowers stumbled out of his grandmother's garden house, blood streaming down his body. He'd amputated his tongue and his penis with a pair of pruning shears.

I like this story; my mind turns it over and over. Perhaps it's the garden house, I can imagine it so clearly, the pots of seedlings, the buckets, the loamed scent of soil, it blurs so seamlessly with my own greenhouse. Other times, I think I like it because of what he amputated. Why not a finger or a toe? Why his tongue, his penis? I think he hurt someone. The amputation, then, a self-inflicted punishment. A silencing. And an unmanning.

*

From: Kit McDermott   **05:35**

You know those few seconds between waking and sleeping where you don't quite know where you are? It was like that when I woke up just now, and then Mills rolled into me and I remembered why I'm in her bedroom and that you'd disappeared and that Faye is dead and I felt it right in my chest, the enormity of my grief.

You would freak out if you saw her bedroom. It's a lair. I've pulled Mills' mattress onto the floor beside me because she keeps coming to sleep on the floor with me, but that means the entire floor is now our bed, we share it with countless rabbits and unicorns, the names only you and her know. Their noses dig into my back, their tails sprouting from between the pillows.

We've reverted to our primal selves, no rooms between us, no walls, nothing as civilised as her pillow and mine. My body is hers – blanket, pillow, mattress – right now, she is sleeping in the crook of my arm, her heels flung over my ribs. I wake up at strange times in the night by her burrowing upwards, to lay her cheek against mine, I've started shaving twice a day because I'm worried about prickling her. I am exhausted but I wouldn't have it any other way. I don't know who needs who more.

I feel like I am in hibernation. That I will sleep and when I wake up this will all be over.

38

Pin

Then

He says I can come to the field with him but he warns that things are different now. We will not be alone. The field is swarming with researchers and assistants; the Blues will start to lay their eggs in the next few days and everyone is waiting, under Daniel's orders, to track the caterpillars' path from hatching to ant colony. We can't hold hands or touch on the coastal path either; it's the only way to get to the thyme. Every day, at least one person Daniel knows joins us on our walk to the field.

The older researchers – McPherson, David – with their balding heads and floppy hats, don't bother me, they clap Daniel on the back and talk about publications in *Insect Conservation and Diversity* and *Proceedings of the Royal Society B: Biological Sciences*. The assistants, on the other hand, make me feel awkward, out of place. Wildly overqualified with their degrees in zoology, their masters in conservation ecology, they net the Blues with carefree precision. Suzanna is Lithuanian, with pale skin that burns easily, she is constantly smoothing suntan lotion over her arms while cracking jokes with Daniel. Imogen has a wholesome, English prettiness and improbably large breasts, which she squeezes into tight, ribbed tank tops. But the worst is dark-haired Rachael, who is not pretty at all but is some kind of entomological prodigy, always making some opaque comment about the growth strategy of larva. She has a small, grave voice and whenever she speaks, Daniel quietens the others to listen to her. It is she who finds the first egg, a tiny pearl at the base of an unopened bud. Daniel calls everyone over to congratulate her. I want to tread on her sandwiches. Open her cage of Blues.

It is very bad in the field. He has no time to help me perfect my netting, he has real assistants to net, identify, log data. I dare myself to not go with him in the afternoons – I could stay at home, go swimming, see Alex – because the fact that he is within touching distance, the sheer proximity to him makes my skin ache. But I never do. I live for the moments when he catches my gaze across the thyme, when he asks me if I'm drinking enough, if I'm bored, what I'm sketching. When he calls for me, I always bring my illustrations. Shielded by my sketchbook, he draws a finger down the back of my hand or clutches my knee.

I am not alone in my desperation. Those long hours in the field, where we pretend to be what we are not, make him frantic. We are barely inside the cottage before he is dropping his nets, pushing the door shut, no time to go upstairs. His hands are in my hair, running over my body, he slides down my knickers, he says, 'I've been thinking about this all day,' before he sinks his mouth into my shoulder.

Later, we will do it again but slowly, the evenings are dedicated to it, the exploration of the other. While the sun is setting and the egrets come to roost, he says, 'Lie down, let me look at you.'

The first time he said it to me, I was shy. This was all I'd wanted, ever since those Saturdays at the museum. But under his microscopic gaze, I pulled the sheet tight around me, he'd seen Mama for God's sake, how could I possibly compare? I squeezed my eyes shut.

'What's wrong?' he asks.

It took a while for me to voice how much I despised the long paleness of my skin, my dull hair, my browny-green eyes. I could only do it into the cotton of the pillow, so I didn't witness his expression.

'Let me see,' he said, solemnly. I let him turn me round. He spread my hair over the pillow, circled my eyes with his thumb. '"Browny-green"? You can do better than that. After all, it was the botanists who named colour.' By then, I was already lost to the way he was looking at me. 'In the dark, they're Vandyke brown. In shadow, they're sap green. In the light . . .' he tipped my chin so my eyes caught the last shafts of dusk. 'Just what I thought. Burnt ochre with shards of sap green.'

I am discovered. Reborn.

It is not just my eyes he looks at; it is all of me. His looking is touch without touch. Insignificant parts of me, functional parts that I have never given much thought to – the back of my ear, the side of my ribs, my ankle – come alive, shivering up to meet him. Under his gaze, all my insecurities disappear; I don't feel ugly. I am exactly what he says, deserving of experimentation, investigation, obsession. 'You're a spectacular collision of mutation and genetics,' he says. 'Utterly beautiful.'

But what I like more than anything is when it is my turn, when I, tender from his ministrations, push him back against the pillows, tell him to lie down, let me look. His body laid out beneath me makes me think of untrammelled snow; I am the first person to break its surface. I run my tongue over the ridges of his chest, cup his feet in my palms, press my cheek against the dampness of his thighs. When I feel the want in his hips, the click of his body inside mine, I wonder if there is a point when all the laws of science are broken, if in fact we learn all the laws just to break them.

He is teaching me to pin butterflies. He sets out a selection of pins, no. 2s, no. 3s, long and silver with brown, nylon heads. He passes me a Blue fresh from the killing jar. The wings are soft and pliable but the body between the forceps is biscuit-crisp. I resist the urge to squeeze it. Crumble it to dust.

'Find the centre of the thorax, good. Now insert the pin. That's it.'

I flinch at how the body gives, those lessons in butterfly anatomy Daniel gave me in the museum are imprinted on my mind so that as I push in the head of the pin, I cannot forget that I am piercing gut, gland, heart.

He hands me a Styrofoam board with a groove cut down its centre. I push the pin in until the wings are level with the sides of the board.

'Okay, this is the tricky part,' he says. 'Do you want to do it or shall I?'

If I really wanted to be a lepidopterist, I would try it myself but I do not. There is something too animated, too visceral about butterflies, they seem too close to us to feel nothing when I am killing them, splaying apart their wings, pinning them to boards. Besides, my interest is less in the lesson than its teacher. I hand him the forceps. 'You do it.'

'We'll do it together.'

He stands behind me, the full warmth of his body against my back. He holds my fingers on the forceps as we gently separate the forewings and the hind and then, I've had enough, I am finished with learning. I put down the forceps, turn around.

'My little botanist,' he says, gently. 'You're not concentrating.'

I wind my arms round his neck.

'You'll never learn how to do it.'

I start unbuttoning his shirt. Recently, these butterfly lessons have started to lose their appeal, they bring back in technicolour the memory of him running from me through the thyme and my desperate weeks of solitude. Only his body can overpower how improbable this all feels. How knife edge.

*

From: Kit McDermott   09:18

I've just left the police station. I told the policewoman everything – the antidepressants, the sketchbooks, the lock on the greenhouse, the withdrawals. After I finished, she gave me this look – it was pity. Like poor mug, he never knew her at all, no wonder she left him, he's fucking clueless.

She's absolutely right. I have no idea what's going on.

She asked me how I didn't know you were withdrawing money. I told her I never dealt with our finances – our salaries went into the same account our bills came out of and there was never a problem, why would I check the bank statements, do people still do that? Until now, I never thought what we were doing was unusual. Now, I wonder if you took over the finances to hide your withdrawals.

The policewoman said people who withdraw over long periods are making plans. She said people who use cash don't want to be found.

You don't want to be found?

The low point of that conversation: her asking me why I think you've been planning to run away. If I've ever hurt you. If I've ever hit you

Hit you? I've loved you since the day I laid eyes on you.

39

Pastries

Now

I pull on my gloves as soon as I leave the hotel. Not the thin, disposable ones I used for botany but the heavy-duty ones I use to tackle the rose bush and brambles. I can't stop collecting. I pull out a handful of nettles sprouting beside the drain outside his house, bundle the leaves into a plastic bag, shove it into my rucksack.

He opens the door. He's unshaven. Violet shadows bloom under his eyes. He wears a crumpled T-shirt and checked pyjama bottoms. The only time I've ever seen him like this was at the end, when we'd fight and he'd get migraines. He wouldn't go to the field on those days, he'd stay in bed with the shutters closed, the butterfly nets empty at the doorway. *Lolly*, he'd say, *you're driving me mad*. I'd be good then, bring him fresh fruit smoothies, jugs of cold water. Now, I watch him shield his eyes against the sunlight, press his fingers to his temples, and think, *You deserve this*.

'You came back.' His voice is high and scratchy. For a second, I think he might cry. 'I was worried, I didn't think—' He presses the back of his hand against his mouth. 'I thought I might not see you again.'

It dawns on me how high the stakes are for him. Each admission and denial, every attack he launches is a risk – he could win me or push me away. If his gamble doesn't pay off, what else is there for him? His mews house, however lovely, is nothing more than a prison. I am the only thing he has left. His rarest, most precious thing.

He rubs his eyes. 'I used to pray, let me see her one last time, just once, I'll make everything right. But I've had days with you now, such a gift of time, and still, I'm messing it up.' He bangs his head lightly against the door. The gesture shocks me, I glimpse suddenly, what he might have been like in prison – quiet, destructive, haunted. Despite everything he said to me yesterday, all his lies and insinuations, I want to cup his stubbled face in my hands.

'I'm sorry for what I said about Kit.'

I hold my hand out to stop him.

'I want to say—'

'—It doesn't matter.'

'Why?'

'Because I need to take you somewhere. Then you'll realise once and for all.'

'What?'

'That you're wrong.' I slide my eyes away from his soft stare, the bed smell of his clothes. Adjust the rucksack that holds a hundred ways to hurt him. 'Get dressed. I'll wait for you here.'

*

He defeats me as soon as I see him. He is wearing a chocolate suede jacket. He left his door open while he went to get ready, that complete trust in my harmlessness; I stood in his doorway, leafing through Ziploc bags, choosing the next poison. I settled on the nettles I picked outside his house; I liked how fresh they were, each barb, a hypodermic needle. I dragged them across the collar of his navy blazer; I was sure he'd wear it again. But he isn't. I clench my fists. A rucksack of poison for nothing.

He pushes on aviators as he steps out. He looks like an off-duty race-car driver. Two girls in their twenties turn to stare at him as we walk down Holland Park and I think, *You know nothing about this man*, how different he looked ten days ago in his prison jumpsuit, ten minutes ago in his checked pyjama bottoms, the formidable strength he has to pull himself together, and I'm frightened that I am what has sustained him for almost two decades, that the memory of us has protected him in prison when so many other inmates haven't made it. How dangerous that is.

He stops outside a bakery that wasn't there eighteen years ago, his eyes bright. 'Do you remember?' he says, gesturing at the croissants. Before I reply, he's slipped in, he's ordering. When he emerges, he holds out a pastry to me. Apricot. I blink at the glaze, the yolk of fruit, the thick band of *sucre perlé*.

Early Saturday mornings, he'd nudge me sleepily into the car and drive to Falmouth. He'd park on the quay and head to the bakery for the only carbs of the week while I snoozed in the passenger seat, the sun warming my cheek. He bought four pastries the first time – butter, almond, apricot, a chocolate twist. 'I didn't know which one you'd like,' he said, opening the box. He chose the apricot, took a bite before lifting my hair up and kissing me on the shoulder. Awake and wanting him, I took the pastry out of his hand and dropped it back in the box. 'You haven't chosen one yet,' he whispered but, by then, there was no decision to be made, I'd already tasted the sweetness on his lips. 'Apricot,' I said, my fingers on the nape of his neck. 'My favourite is apricot.'

The pastries, the kissing in the car, the sleepy silence of the quay. In the fairy tale my fourteen-year-old mind was spinning, I thought that was the alchemy of us, our collision created it. But now, when I look back on those Saturday mornings, I am struck not by the magic of my seduction but its practicality. He wanted me outside; it was boring to always be in the cottage. Out was exciting. But it had to be early when no would see.

'You don't like them anymore?' he asks. He's already bitten into his. His lips are studded with sugar.

I squeeze it between my fingers. The fruit bulges.

I don't eat pastries now. I won't even go into a bakery. 'Too rich,' I'd say to Kit and Millie, as if it is the plump glossiness that is intolerable, the richness of the butter, when it is the memory that is intolerable. The glaze on Daniel's lips. Powdered sugar falling between my breasts.

I drop it in the nearest bin.

He looks from the bin to me. 'I haven't got this right, have I? I've thought about this for so long and I still can't get it right.' He lifts a smoothie from the bag, like the ones we used to make each other. 'I'm guessing you don't want this either?'

I shake my head. Take a hot swallow of my coffee. The liquid burns all the way down.

40

Names

Then

'What are you doing?' I ask, one evening, lying beneath him.

'Measuring.' His face is serious. His hand is his ruler. He has stretched his fingers out, thumb to little finger, he places it over my throat, my waist, my hips.

'Your findings, Mr Prior?'

'Your waist is the span of my hand.' He strokes my legs all the way down to my feet. 'I can fit your ankle in my hand.'

'Your conclusions?'

'You're entirely captivating. You're extraordinary. You're beautiful. Everything about you is beautiful.'

I flinch.

'What's the matter?' he says.

'Don't say that.' I pull the sheets over me.

'What?'

'That everything about me is beautiful.'

'I don't understand.'

'Mama used to say that to me.'

'I didn't know.'

'Do you think about her? Because I think of her all the time.'

His face changes, surprised at the sudden turn in conversation, and then he sighs. He pulls on his boxers, his T-shirt, sits at the foot of the bed. Discussion about my mother inappropriate while we are both naked. 'I think of her every day.'

'What do you think?'

His shoulders slump. 'I think about how long I waited for her by the pool. How I went to the room to check on her. The sound of the telephone.' He puts his hands to his temples, presses. 'It was hard to understand, the nurse only spoke Italian, but finally, I got it, *Incidente, incidente*, she kept saying. Later, I wondered if I hadn't been so dense, if there hadn't been traffic, if I got out and ran, would those seconds have made a difference? Would I have reached her before she—?' His hands are over his mouth and I am sobbing, I asked him for his thoughts but now, I can't bear to hear them.

'Sorry, sorry—'

'It's my fault,' I say, 'I shouldn't have asked.'

'If there are things you want to know, you should ask, I want you to ask.' He grasps my forearm. I put my hand over his. 'There are good memories too. I think of the first time I heard her play the violin.'

'The Tchaikovsky.'

'I'd never heard anyone play like that.'

'She plays that for auditions. She chose that to impress you.'

Then, I stop. Because she did impress him and he impressed her, they'd still be together if not for the accident, not him and me. And then, I ask the question, the question I think about in the darkest part of the night while he sleeps beside me. 'What would have happened if she'd lived? To us?'

'There's no point thinking like that.'

'But I do. I think about that all the time. If she hadn't died, we wouldn't have happened. What does that mean? Did we want her to die?' My nose is wet, I am crying, I keep trying to wipe my face clean but it is slick. 'Sometimes, I hate myself, hate what we're doing. Because it only happened because she died.'

He holds me then, tight, as if to still my heaving ribs, the shudders rippling through my shoulders. 'Stop, my darling, stop, it's not true,' but I don't know what he is denying: the bad part of myself; us; the undeniable sequence of events that have led us here. Perhaps he is just saying words to comfort a child, a rhyme, a lullaby.

'I wish I wasn't her daughter,' I say into his shoulder.

'I know.'

'I wish I was someone else.'

'That's okay.'

'Sometimes my own name hurts. Hearing you say it hurts.'

'I'm sorry.' He is rocking me slowly, back and forth. 'I don't want to hurt you. I never want to hurt you.' Around me, I feel him tense. The rocking slows. 'How about we try something? I don't know if it would help, but it might, it could.'

'What?'

'I could call you something else.'

'What do you mean?'

'A different name. One that's only between you and me.'

'I don't know.'

'Let's try,' he says. He holds my face in his hands. Our foreheads touch. 'It has to be something that's not too different from your name but different enough.'

'Okay.'

'How about "Laura"?'

I wince. 'That was the second name on Mama's list. She was going to call me "Laura" if "Lauren" hadn't suited.'

'Laurie?'

'That's what my friends used to call me.'

'Lana.'

'Too American.' I think, bizarrely, of my old favourite movie, *The Little Mermaid*, the scene when Prince Eric is trying to guess Ariel's real name. Except he isn't guessing my real name. He is creating it. Finding me another.

'Lola.'

'Too Spanish.'

'Lolly.'

It is silly, frivolous, a red, licked thing, so different to 'Lauren', the opposite of what my mother would have wanted. It sounds fun and carefree, like this summer, pastries and sun and the sea. 'Lolly,' I repeat.

'Lolly it is then,' he says with a finality which confuses me, because I'm not sure, I want to test it out. But then he says it into my mouth just before he kisses me and I think *He's right, that's it.* He decides it. He gives it life.

*

Dear Darling

From: Kit McDermott 10:31

I'm at work. My parents came yesterday, Cass called them, she doesn't think I'm coping. My dad told me to call in sick but I couldn't think of anything worse than being at home, with Millie asking me where you are and my mum always crying.

But now I'm at work, I want to be at home, among all your things – your clothes, your jewellery, your perfume – I haven't put any of your things away. I keep trying to read emails, speak normally to Peter and Tom but it's impossible, I drift off when they're speaking, can't finish sentences. I got called into a meeting and I literally could not get out of my chair. I was terrified. Nothing feels safe, there is no ground, no floor.

I need you, Laurie. Please.

41

Extraordinary

Now

'Are you going to tell me where we're going?'

'You haven't guessed?' After surfacing from the warren of the London underground at Marylebone Station, we're on a train to Buckinghamshire. The train carriage is empty. 'You've been here before,' I say.

'Oh? I don't recognise the destination.' He stares out the window. An hour from Marylebone and London fades into countryside – fields, sheep, church spires, empty platforms. His suede jacket is on the seat beside him; he hasn't worn it since we got on the underground. Instead, he's opened the top window, rolled up the sleeves of his shirt. I glance at his wrists. The hives have gone down but their outline is still visible. More noticeable are the scratches, spreading across his veins like the drag of a blade. I feel a shot of power then. He has twisted me up but I have twisted him too, I have broken through his skin, driven him to that addictive stage where he cannot tell the difference between relief and pain.

Dear Darling

'Wait a minute, are we going to Wyatt? Where you went on that holiday camp? Where you went to school?'

I nod.

'Wyatt School, Lady Margaret Road.'

I stare at him. 'How do you know that?'

'I wrote it enough times.'

His letters. He kept it up the entire time I was there, they each began, 'Dear darling'. The first one that arrived in my pigeonhole, I slid into my bag like the secret it was but later, when the letters arrived like clockwork, I began to savour the ritual of destruction – the gleam of my scissors, the tiny squares I cut his fountain pen words into. The sound of blades against that thick, cream paper was so sweet. Now, as we travel towards my fourteen-year-old self, I feel her strength pulse through me. So young and I knew. How to draw a line against him. How not to let him in.

'Are they expecting us?'

'I called ahead.'

'Why are we going to your old school?'

'Things are easier to tell *in situ*.' A breeze from the long window is cool against my shoulders. I pull out my clip, let my hair loose.

'Extraordinary,' he says.

'What?'

'These moments with you, they're both ordinary and extraordinary. Like your hair. I don't remember you letting it loose like that but now I see how it falls, it's so familiar. Do you ever get that? Things you've forgotten but then, when you encounter them, you think *Yes, yes, I knew it all along.*'

The shape of your mouth.

Your scent.

How you say 'Lolly' as if it's the only thing you've ever wanted.

I clutch the fabric of the seat, fix my eyes on the landscape slipping away. 'No. I don't get that at all.'

42

DRIFT SEEDS

Then

I am on the cliff face. I've drawn all the different varieties of thyme in the field and I am at a tipping point: I want to be with Daniel but I am also bored. I've started straying to the edges of the field to draw the wildflowers of the hedgerows or the white sea campion and pink thrift on the cliffs. So, when the assistants come to eat their lunch and enjoy the sea view, they don't see me in a cleft of rock nearby. I think of announcing myself when I hear Suzanna, she's always so friendly, but, as their conversation progresses, the possibility of declaring myself vanishes.

'David's fit.' Suzanna, with that distinctive European lilt.

'You think everyone is fit,' replies Imogen. 'You'd do Phersie.'

'There is a difference between *doing* Phersie and *thinking* Phersie is fit. Phersie isn't fit.'

'He's almost dead, Suz.'

'I'd do him, just to tick it off the list. Prior on the other hand . . .' Suzanna emits a low growl. I want to slap her. 'He is another level.'

'No one would say no to that,' says Imogen.

'What about you, Rach?' says Suzanna. The tone is friendly but there is the slightest edge to it and I understand that Rachael is being invited not just into the conversation but somehow to redress a power imbalance between them that has thus far been heavily skewed in her favour. 'Would you say no to Prior?'

Rachael says nothing for a few seconds. When she speaks, it is muffled, through a mouthful of sandwich: 'I don't like him.'

'You're insane!' Suzanna explodes.

'How can you say that?' Imogen continues. 'He adores you! If he'd talk about me the way he talks about you, I'd be all over him.'

'Don't you think there's something . . . off about him? He's *too* polished. Have you noticed he never talks about his dead wife?'

A stillness falls over me. The way she says 'dead' so casually is unforgivable.

'It's been, what, two months and not a sign that he's upset.'

'People grieve in different ways,' says Suzanna.

'But they do grieve. It's like she didn't exist.'

'Maybe he's holding it together for Lauren,' says Imogen.

'Something off about her too, don't you think?'

My skin prickles.

'What's she doing in the field? Isn't she supposed to be at school?' I hear Rachael screw open her Thermos, the hot pour of tea. 'The way she follows him round with that sketchpad, runs across the field when he calls her—'

'She's just a kid, Rach,' says Imogen.

'It's weird. So intense. So needy.'

Her words burn holes in me, lit cigarettes against my skin. I stare at the corner of my sketchbook long after they are gone.

Dear Darling

I hate them, hate them, I am the observer, observing them, not the other way round. I run back to the cottage before the afternoon is over, round on Daniel when he comes in. I repeat the conversation. He laughs it off. 'Just a bunch of bored girls, why does it bother you?' But I will not be examined by Rachael. Not by Daniel's protégée. The best up-and-coming scientist he has ever encountered.

Alex isn't there when I return to the beach. I don't swim. I spend the entire time looking for *Forager*, the familiar blue stripe of the hull, the orange life buoy strapped to its side. I want to feel normal again. A few days later, I spot the boat mid-river. I run into the water, waving manically. The boat turns towards me. I swim up to it.

'Where've you been?' he says without saying hello, without masking his annoyance.

'Away.'

'You didn't tell me you were going away.'

'I didn't know.' This is, at least, partially true.

'You didn't return my calls.'

'I lost my phone.' This is a lie.

He turns off the engine, crouches down. 'I came to the beach to look for you.'

'Sorry.'

He shakes his head, as if he didn't care anyway. 'You're back though, right?'

He makes it sound like it's a choice. Like everything that's happened is something I can come back from.

*

We're on *Forager*. Alex has just picked me up from the beach where I wait for him every afternoon. He navigates round the moored boats; the river is full. He turns off the motor. 'I have something for you.'

'What?'

He draws out something from under the seat, hesitates, then throws it at me from the other side of the boat. It misses my lap, which I assume is where he is aiming, catching my knee before sliding onto the deck.

'Sorry,' he says, his face growing red.

How many years will it take for Alex to be comfortable with girls, to become someone like Daniel, who can give a gift without throwing it? He is a caterpillar before he pupates, he doesn't realise that the awkwardness of his body, his self-consciousness, is precious in and of itself.

'It's okay,' I say, gently. I pick it up, dry it against the leg of my jeans. It is a pamphlet, no more than twenty pages, entitled, *Drift Seeds*. On the cover is a pair of seeds the exact colour of conkers, although their shape is unusual – flat and heart-shaped. 'What's a drift seed?'

'They're seeds from the tropics. They travel on the currents thousands of miles until they wash up here.'

I feel a shiver of curiosity, the fresh green of a new shoot. 'I don't understand. How do they survive?'

'It's all in there,' he says. Regaining his confidence, he takes the book from me, turning a few pages to a section on buoyancy. He's already read it. 'They float. Some of them have air spaces inside or their husks are fibrous or they have water-repellent coats.'

'You mean, they've evolved to travel thousands of miles?'

'I think so,' he says, slowly. 'Chris, my dad's friend, found one the other day.'

'In Cornwall?'

'Porthcothan, in the north. His wife collects them, she thinks they're lucky, they're really rare though, she's only found a handful in decades.'

'You saw it?'

He nods.

'What did it look like?'

'Exactly like those,' he says, pointing to the cover. I flick to the section on identifying drift seeds. *Coeur de la mer*, sea hearts. They come from Central America, the Caribbean, South America, Africa. Rapt, I turn back to the beginning, start to read.

'I was thinking . . .' he says shyly, and I realise he's been planning this, perhaps for days. His hands are clasped tightly together. 'We could look for them. On the beaches. If you want.'

I cover his hands with mine. 'Yes. A hundred times yes.'

Daniel doesn't like that I am not in the field. 'I miss you,' he says, holding my hand. 'Forget the assistants. The days are too long without seeing you in the afternoon. Come back.' But I don't want to hear Rachael's voice in my head, that hint of disgust.

When that doesn't work, he says it isn't good for me to be in the cottage for so long.

I tell him I am not in the cottage; I am in the sea. I show him my sketchbook, how it is bursting with kelp fronds, leafy furls of rose weed, drift seeds I've copied from Alex's book. He isn't interested. 'I don't like you swimming.'

'Why? I'm getting good at it.'

'What if something happens to you in the water?'
'I don't go very far.'
'I'm not there.'
'What could you do if you were? You can't swim.'

In bed, he tries other strategies, he whispers that swimming reminds him of those weeks we spent apart, he tells me he'd press his face against my cold swimsuit each evening while it dripped over the bath, trying to find me in the water, the seaweed, the shingle. 'It hurts me,' he says, 'I feel like you're slipping away.'

If that is meant to convince me, it does not. Because I, too, am haunted by those weeks. Sometimes, as I walk through the corridors of the cottage, I am suffocated by the memory of my own loneliness, the dark heart of my grief, even if I am heading to the bedroom where Daniel is waiting for me. I want him haunted too. Let the sea remind him of my absence. The possibility that I could be gone.

His dislike for swimming and my insistence on it solidifies between us. Now, when I get back from seeing Alex, he doesn't take me in that wild, desperate way he used to when we came back from the field. If I try to kiss him, he flinches. 'Wash up,' he says as if he can smell on my skin the seaweed rotting on the strandline. Once, while I was having a bath, he took my apple bodywash wordlessly from me, cut white circles over my skin, made the lather rise. He wants the sea erased.

But because I am petty and fourteen and I don't like how he is making me feel, I am fierce about my secrets. I never tell him about Alex or snorkelling or the mutations of the oaks on the foreshore, I don't tell him about my search for drift seeds, that they are so rare, people have always considered them charms. I rebel. I don't keep his rules. I buy chocolate and crisps with the change he leaves round the house; I hold the vitamins he gives me on my tongue, feel their edges dissolve, spit them out when his back is turned. Sometimes, I will not wash one of my hands so that later, in the dark, I can put my wrist over my mouth. Taste the salt on my skin.

*

From: Kit McDermott   11:25
Whenever my friend Peter talks to me, I think of his wife. You remember. One day, she simply decided not to speak to him anymore. They lived with each other for six months until their divorce was finalised, and not a single word passed between them. Peter said he never knew why.

You were peeling potatoes when I told you. It was summer, you were wearing shorts, standing perfectly poised, your left foot scratching the back of your right ankle, peel falling from your hands. I said she sounded awful, how insane, to stop speaking to him like that, no explanation. I'll never forget your response because I'd never thought about it like that: 'Either he's telling you half the story,' you said, 'or something is seriously wrong.'

I'm asking you for one single word. One word more than what Peter's wife gave him. What's the other half of our story? What is seriously wrong?

43

School

Now

Down an avenue of rhododendrons, the manor house of Wyatt rises between the oaks, the grey Victorian stone, the rose window of the chapel. The lake shimmers under the trees; the memory of the first time I felt that water on my skin shivers down my spine. Four years of schooling and all I can think of is when Wyatt was just a holiday camp. When I was angry with my mother but she was alive. When my feelings for my stepfather were just a crush. My transgressions were so innocent then.

Daniel removes his aviators to take in the school, 'I forgot how grand this is.' With his suede jacket and chocolate loafers, he belongs here more than I do. When I planned coming back, I looked up how much Wyatt's fees are for boarding – an obscene £50,000 a year. True, he paid for me eighteen years ago but he still did it while he was in prison, no questions asked, when I, as a lawyer with a mortgage, would struggle to pay this for Millie. I never thought about it at the time. How he could afford boarding fees as a lepidopterist in prison.

Dear Darling

It was easy getting into the school, Mrs Hannington arranged everything. I phoned her yesterday after I came back from Sky Garden, the office wouldn't put me through at first. 'It's a Sunday,' the receptionist said flatly. 'She's with her family.' But I insisted, she capitulated and, when she finally connected me, there was a brief pause before Mrs Hannington said, 'Of course you should come. I'm free at twelve. Just go to the porter. I'll have everything ready.' She's true to her word. The porter hands us two visitor lanyards and a prospectus, as if Daniel and I are new parents thinking about sending our daughter here. The reversals, half parallels, almost possibilities strike me in a series of low blows.

We walk into reception, high-ceilinged and wood-panelled. Glass cases display trophies, ribbons, photos of winning lacrosse and netball teams, all recent. So strange. Four years at Wyatt loom so large in my memory but there's nothing to show for them here. Then, I see it. Above the cabinets, in gold letters, are the names of every headmistress and every head girl since the 1980s. Including me. 'Lauren Tan – 2011'. My name injects me with a solidity I haven't possessed in a long time. I was here. It really happened here.

'You were head girl?' Daniel says behind me.

A girl walks past us in school uniform. It's still the same – the navy pleated skirt, the striped shirt, the crest with the school motto: *Ad astra per aspera*.

'You never told me.'

'How could I?'

'You could have written.'

'Is that what you expected? All my school news?'

'Expected?' Anger ripples through his voice. I remember when that started to creep in towards the end, and I see he is stuck in the vortex of us as much as I am, nothing ever past, everything always present. The aviators, the suede jacket, the silvered hair don't just conceal a man in a prison jumpsuit, they hide a man waiting for one letter, one message that never came. 'You could have let me know how you were. You could have asked if I was okay. Even if you decided you never wanted to hear from me again, you could have written to say that. What did I expect? A crumb. I expected you to throw me a crumb.'

'I didn't owe you anything,' I whisper, although there's barely anyone here. 'I didn't promise you anything.'

He takes a hurt inhale of breath.

I stare at the cover of the prospectus, tell myself, *I'm right, he's wrong.* But I'm not sure I believe it. Promises were made, weren't they? Perhaps not out loud but in under-cover light, in the softness of each other's skin. If you say, 'I love you' over and over, what else does that mean if not forever?

And then I'm astonished at how hard I have to battle this lovesick fourteen-year-old, how fearful I am of her. I've dismissed her for years, such an imperfect victim, too needy, too willing. But the more time I spend with Daniel, the stronger she grows. Have I come to confront him or vanquish her?

You've forgotten what he made you do, I say to her. *I will show you.*

I start walking, training my eyes on the map on the inside cover of the prospectus. I'm struggling to understand it, I can't layer over the school's recent renovations with my memory, but then I find the English department in the same place, Shakespeare sonnets and Chaucer essays on the wall. I lead us past one of my old form rooms; inside, the girls are sitting in a horseshoe arrangement around the teacher's desk, some with their hands up, others writing or fiddling with their hair. By their height, their confidence, they're about fifteen, sixteen, so young in their white socks and bare knees. My heart beats very fast. I was younger than them. Thirteen when I first met Daniel. Fourteen in Cornwall.

'Look, what are we doing here?' He squints under the strip lighting, massages his temples. Another migraine. When they got really bad, he'd put his head in my lap like a Great Dane; I'd run my fingers through his hair. It would be so easy to give him that relief, his body is begging me to do it – the inclination of his neck, the top knot of his spine edging out from his shirt. I won't. I want him to suffer.

'I've already told you,' I say, placidly. 'There are things I want to show you.'

'You haven't shown me anything.'

'I'm taking you now.'

'Where, though?' He rubs his hand over his neck; he's still feeling the poison from the ivy leaves. 'I don't want to walk through your school. I want you to tell me what's wrong with your stomach. I want to finish what we started yesterday.'

So, he's not sorry for what he said about Kit. Not sorry at all.

He puts his hands over his eyes, a makeshift dark room. I've bewildered him. I should have fallen in line when he undermined my marriage. Instead, he finds himself in my territory. I'm dropping grenades, sending bullets flying.

'It's ironic, don't you think?' I say, taking him further down the corridor.

'What?'

'You say you wanted to hear all my school news. But now I'm showing you, you're reluctant. So, which is it? Do you want to know what happened here or not?'

He peers out at me from behind his hands. 'You're playing games. Word games, lawyer games.'

I push through the double doors. This is what I'm looking for. The courtyard. The grounds beyond. 'I'm not playing games. I'm not playing at all.'

44

Door

Then

I know something's the matter as soon as Daniel steps out of the butchers. I am attuned to his body, there's a synchronicity as he steps into my orbit, any disruption sounding the alarm. Now, it blares. His features are rigid. He doesn't smile at me, doesn't even look at me, he is looking over my shoulder. I trace the laser beam of his stare, across the road to the jetty, where Alex is shouting my name as he climbs out of his boat.

I don't wave back. I am paralysed, dumbly aware that I should do something, I am scrambling to figure out what that might be and then those seconds where I could have walked away are lost. Alex has crossed the road. He steps onto the pavement in his waders and boots. 'I thought that was you! Shall I bring the snorkelling gear on Monday? Dad says it's going to be calm, if we go during slack tide, there'll be good visibility for the eelgrass meadows.' He pauses because I am not saying anything.

It is Daniel who steps in. Daniel who clears his throat, breaks the silence. 'Are you going to introduce me to your friend, Lauren?'

My name on his lips confuses me, aren't I 'Lolly' anymore? Then, I am unravelling, sycamore seed skittering to the ground, 'Lolly' is just for him and me, but I am also Lauren, his stepdaughter, his wife's daughter, Alex's friend and the crash of the two names, two worlds, splits me wide open.

'Lauren?' he repeats.

They both stare at me. I stumble over simple words. 'This is Alex.'

'Alex who?' asks Daniel.

Alex laughs. He realises what we both realise: I don't know his surname, he doesn't know mine, we've never needed to exchange surnames, or histories, or truth. He puts his hand out and shakes Daniel's. Alex's hand – large and calloused and fleshy – swallows Daniel's up. 'Alex Moore.'

'Alex,' Daniel repeats, without warmth. He takes in the breadth of Alex's shoulders, his sandy hair, his green eyes. 'Lauren, I think Alex asked you a question. Snorkelling on Monday?'

My cheeks flush.

'If you don't want to go snorkelling, we can go swimming in the creek,' says Alex, 'the weather's going to hold.'

Daniel flinches. And I understand, suddenly, why Daniel hates swimming. It is the swimsuit. For me, the plain, black costume, streaked at the waist from wear, holds no significance, no memory but the chlorine of the public pool where the school took us for lessons. But now, I see it is the singularity of the clothing that's the problem. How it is one piece away from the bareness of my skin.

'Snorkelling,' I say quickly. The wetsuit, the mask, the ridiculousness of the flippers surely add many layers of cover.

'Okay, I'll pick you up. It was nice meeting you.' Alex waves and then, is gone.

In the car, the silence between us vibrates. Half of me is in overdrive, spinning defences, long-winded rationalisations, but the other half is detached, curious about the precise texture of Daniel's anger. I've never seen him angry before and the scientist in me, or is it the teenager, is experimentally bold. What will I discover about him, about me.

At the cottage, he puts away chicken thighs, beef medallions, he starts washing fruit. I don't help. I lean against the island on one foot. He turns off the tap, shakes his hands of the water. He doesn't turn round. 'Why didn't you tell me about him?'

'I don't know.'

'You don't know?' He spins round. 'You don't know? Let's try an easier question, see if you can answer this one, Lolly—'

There it is, his name for me, except I've never heard him spit it like that, like it belongs on the ground.

'—How did you meet him?'

'Those weeks when we weren't talking.'

'When you started swimming?'

I nod.

He lets out a long, defeated sigh, as if he knew all along, his instinct has served him well, if only he'd trusted it and not me. 'You've been seeing him all this time.'

'I stopped for a while . . .' his eyes meet mine, he knows when I stopped, it was when I started with him, when I was with him all day, every day, 'and then, I started again when I stopped going to the field.' The field, Rachael, what she said, flashes through me – he has made me intense and needy and weird. 'What are you angry about? That I kept a secret? Or that the secret is a boy?'

His mouth falls open.

'I didn't tell you because I knew you'd act like this.'

'Like what?'

'Jealous!' I spit the word out, like he spat my name, tit for tat, though I've never thought about it like this. It feels unreal, distant, I'm not sure I believe what I'm saying or if I'm just parroting something I've watched, because none of it fits with any of those stories – he is my stepfather and my lover. Still, I can't stop. 'You want me all to yourself, cooped up in this cottage or on the field. It's too much. I'm allowed to do things that aren't with you. I'm allowed to have friends that aren't you.'

He rubs his jaw. 'You think I'm angry because I don't want you to have friends?'

'Yes.'

'I'm trying to protect you.'

'You don't know him!' I explode. 'You don't know anything about him! We talk about plants! We swim!'

'We swim!' he repeats, a cruel parody of my voice. 'You parade round in a swimsuit every day and you think all you do is swim?'

My eyes sting with tears. 'We're friends!'

'He isn't friends with you.' His voice is softer, scarier than I've ever heard it. He crosses the kitchen. I edge round the island. Days ago, we did exactly this, played chase, he caught me on the sofa, pushed back my hair, laid a trail of kisses from shoulder to ear. But that isn't what's happening now. His face is pale, his jaw is rigid. I catch my side on the corner of a cabinet and then he is right in front of me. 'All he wants is *this*.' He yanks down the strap of my summer dress.

I am not wearing a bra. In that split second, with my dress hanging off one shoulder, we remember the same thing, that time he said, *You don't have to wear underwear with me*, so I didn't, he liked putting his hand on my knee as we drove back from Falmouth, sliding it lazily up and down my thigh. But while the memory makes me weep, the shameful way it shatters against me clutching at my strap, it has a different effect on him. His body tenses. He lurches past me and punches the kitchen door. The wood explodes.

I scream.

He clutches his fist with his left hand. He backs into the kitchen cabinet, slides down. 'Oh my God, oh my God,' he is whispering. He covers his eyes with his elbow. 'What's wrong with me?'

His bewilderment unravels me, I can't remember why we're fighting. I drop down onto the floor beside him, put my hand over his bleeding knuckles. 'Nothing's wrong with you. Nothing.'

He shakes his head. I pull open his arms, get into his lap, wait for his body to register mine, his sigh when he feels me around him, *I love you against me*, he always says. It works. His arms clutch my back. 'I'm going insane,' he whispers.

'You're not.'

'My head is killing me. I'm losing my mind. I'm out of control.'

'It's okay.'

'It's not.' He inhales my hair deeply, desperately, like I am breath, I am air. 'You can see him. You can see whoever you want.'

I take his hand, bring his knuckles to my lips. His blood in my mouth is bright and metallic and I wonder why I've kept Alex a secret, it feels stupid now, a childish game when this man, raw and bleeding in front of me, is all I could ever need. I shake my head. 'I don't need anyone but you.'

He presses his lips to my forehead. It is a gesture he does many times a day, when he wakes, when he leaves, before he goes to sleep. But this time, it isn't brief or tender. It's hard. As if he wants to deliver the full force of himself into my skull, right through my body, all the way down.

When I was eleven, Mama dated a conductor, a man with stringy brown hair that he ran his fingers through to give it volume. It seemed to go well, until he showed up at two a.m., pounding against the door with the flat of his palm, 'Let me in, you let me in.' We found each other in the dark of the living room as we watched the door shake and then she pulled me into her arms and whispered solemnly, 'Promise you'll never be with a man like this. Promise.'

Is Daniel 'a man like this'? I push aside whether I can apply Mama's advice to her own husband, wonder constantly about what she would think. Was she afraid a man who hits a door would hit her? I don't think Daniel would ever hit me. The strap, wrenched down my shoulder, was rough but not intended to hurt.

Perhaps it was the reaction of violence that mattered to her, that it was an option.

I watch for this. A tractor driver pulls out in front of him without signalling – he doesn't shout or swear. His article on the Blues is rejected by an entomology journal – he slumps into the pink sofa, presses his fingers to his temples. Soon, nothing reminds me of how he punched the door, except the ugly hole in the door itself, its splintered edges. Even that disappears. One Saturday, we come back from Falmouth and the door has been replaced. It's as if the punch never happened. A bad dream long past.

But the fight has changed us. Daniel starts getting migraines; his mood swings. In one afternoon, he'll send me an extravagant delivery of hothouse flowers that I will draw and paint while he brings me iced lemonade. But hours later, he will read something in my face, an expression, a thought: 'You're too innocent. You don't know what men are like. What they want,' and in these moments, it feels like the same fight we had in the kitchen has not ended, that it is an elevator in a building that never stops.

The more he talks about Alex ('fisherboy', he calls him) the more I want to see him. If only for the few hours of relief when I do not feel documented, studied, when I can laugh about his catch or the tides or tell him about the boy growing vines of monkey-ladders from a drift seed he found off the north coast. Daniel's words circle in my head, *All he wants is this*, but the longer I am apart from Alex, the more convinced I am that Daniel was wrong. The fact of our friendship, that there was no more to it, is the substance of my relief.

It's not just words or thoughts that have changed. Sex has changed, it's charged now, dangerous, just another way he rages against me and I must prove my surrender. There are no more hours spent in bed, no more evenings where we explore each other's bodies. Now, when he comes back to the cottage, he doesn't take me against the wall. He pushes me down on all fours and takes me silently from behind before going straight up to the study, the wet trail of him trickling down my thighs. Sometimes, I don't care, my want for him is keener now he is the only person I see every day. Other times, I stare at the knots of the paisley rug and wonder how it is possible for him to enter me without seeing me.

Evenings are dedicated to his work. There's a problem with the Blues. 'The population is much smaller than we thought it would be,' he says, barely looking up when I ask him how it's going. 'I thought I was preventing the extinction of a species. But I'm not. All I'm doing is tracking their disappearance.' I try to seduce him, I wear my shortest shorts, my thinnest T-shirts before pushing open the door of the study. The sight of him sitting at that trestle table sends me back to that first night, it is enough for me to bridge the strangeness that has descended between us. But not for him. He doesn't turn round. I trail kisses up his neck, push my hand under his T-shirt. He holds my hand still. 'Not now, Lolly.' When I hear him say my name like that, flat, I want to die.

He comes closest to being mine again in the middle of the night. Prising open the sleepy curl of my body, he runs his hands over me like he used to, he whispers, *You're rare, astonishing, I'm so in love with you, my little botanist,* and in those seconds, half awake, half dreaming, I try and make myself believe everything is fine, everything is the same.

But it isn't. There is none of that mastery I loved, that control, that unshakeable belief in the alchemy of us. He says he can never lose me, he'd die if he lost me, that there's only ever been and will only ever be me. He begs me to tell him that he is enough, he makes me swear I don't think of anyone else, that I don't love anyone else. I do. I say all the right things, I repeat his words back to him, *You're rare, astonishing, I am so in love with you, there is only you, how could there be anyone else?* But no matter what I say, I cannot deliver him from the rising tide of his own doubts. He is drowning.

*

Dear Darling

From: Kit McDermott   12:03

Perhaps you haven't been hiding things. Perhaps I've shut my eyes to the flares you sent up, the signal fires you built, put my hands over my ears to block out the sound of sirens because all I've ever really wanted is you. But now you've gone, now I've lost you, now you're probably not reading anything I'm writing to you, I can finally bear to admit it: there were moments when I thought something was wrong.

45

OTHER ROOM

Now

Hawk House looks like an ivy-clad medieval hunting lodge; its arched doorway, decorated with metal studs and black iron bolts, looks like it's missing a moat. I hated it when I first saw it, how foreboding it looked, so different to the simplicity of the woodcutter's cottage, the pine forest, the field of Blues. But appearances are deceiving: the cottage was dangerous; Hawk House, safe. Now, I see the heavy wooden door and remember me and Jennie flying out of it after we finished our exams, the giant teddy bear Lisa won at the local fair, Mrs Hannington brimming with the news that I'd been elected head girl. Good things, so many good things after the unspeakable.

A pair of girls comes out, before the door shuts, I glimpse the entrance hall where Lisa convinced us to have a midnight roller-skating party and, behind it, the polished oak staircase leading up to the dorms. The first room I stayed in with the other girls was on the first floor. I step back, nearly tread on Daniel, because now I think of it, that first room had a view out to this gravel, this avenue of limes. There, on the sill, is a jewellery box, a bottle of perfume, deodorant. Mine was lined with pine cones, maple leaves, conkers. Behind, is a cherry oak wardrobe, I can't believe they still have those. I always hung my uniform up, no clothes slipping off the hangers, no sports bags or lacrosse sticks pooling at the bottom. Neat. Just like Mama. Just like Daniel.

Then, I want to find the other room, the room before that dorm. I follow the building round to the right, treading on the freshly planted begonias, the sweet peas, trying to avoid the open windows of the common room, I don't want to scare the girls. 'What are they doing?' I imagine them whispering to each other as they glance up from their breaktime apples and biscuits.

'Call security,' I want to say to them. When Millie is older, I will tell her instinct is the greatest sense she'll possess, if you trust nothing else, trust in that. Kit and I were once on the tube with a young woman in her twenties, blonde dreadlocks, a boho skirt, she talked to herself, loudly, 'I'm going the wrong way.' Everyone was staring at her. Then, she wrenched down the red bar of the emergency alarm. The driver stopped the tube. The carriage erupted with boos, hisses, even Kit shook his head. But I felt insanely jealous. She sounded the alarm for something so small when I had never sounded it. Now, all I am is scene, catastrophe, emergency.

The room I am searching for is at the far side of Hawk House, part of the housemistresses' quarters. Until I moved into the dorm with the other girls, I didn't realise it wasn't a bedroom at all. It was Mrs Hannington's study.

I search for something to stand on. Under the ledge is an overturned bucket. I brush off rainwater, rotting leaves and then,

I climb on, press my face to the window. The walls have been repainted, the curtains are cream instead of floral and there is no trundle bed, just a bookcase and a desk, a small armchair. Still, it is terrifyingly familiar. Eighteen years later and the light falls the same way, softly illuminating the wood panels, pooling on the desk.

Daniel comes behind me, the gravel stills. He watches me watch a room where only my memory is moving. 'Okay, you need to tell me what's going on.'

What did I expect coming back here? Not this. Not the feeling of growing backwards, getting smaller, younger, forgotten details flying back. I see the long crack on the left wall that my bed was pressed against – I used to chase it with my thumb, thinking what a huge mistake I'd made, thinking I should have stayed with Daniel. I hear Mrs Hannington read to me, she was my English Lit teacher, she wanted to catch me up because I was behind on my Brontë, my Shakespeare. 'My lips, two blushing pilgrims, ready stand,' she'd read, and I'd think of the lips of this elegantly dressed man standing behind me. Even after. Even after.

I shouldn't have come. I could have pretended for the rest of my life that I made it up. But that's gone now.

Daniel's voice is unbearably gentle. 'What happened?'

I let go of the ledge, brush flaked paint off my hands. My voice is a dulled version of itself. 'We have an appointment.'

46

BIRDS & BEES

Then

The first time it happens, it's late Sunday morning. I reach for him, the rich brown of his hair, the weight of his calf. He's not there. The bed beside me is empty.

I slide my legs out of the covers, walk to the bathroom, stare at my reflection. Every morning, I look more strange, more unfamiliar to myself. These nightly disturbances have taken a toll; yesterday, I woke up to him pushing my T-shirt up and pressing his forehead against my stomach. 'I can't lose you, Lolly,' he whispered into my navel, 'I couldn't bear it.' My eyes are enormous, my lips, pulpy. I bring the back of my hand to them, wince. They feel so tender.

I reach between my thighs. Pain dawns there, I lift my right leg up, balance it against the top of the bath. The insides are raw from his stubble, two bruises the exact shape of his fingers bloom, and then the imprint of him on my skin seems to collide with the sound of a bottle opening, the sharp scent of ethyl acetate floating in from the study, where he is killing butterflies.

I throw up in the toilet bowl.

He is behind me quickly, his hand is on my back, stroking big, comforting circles. 'Are you okay?'

I shake my head.

'What's wrong?'

'I feel awful.'

'There's something going round,' he says. 'McPherson was off for two days and now, Suzanna's down.'

He leads me back to bed, tells me I need rest. 'I'll check on you later, my darling,' he says. I almost cry. I'd be sick every day, just for him to look at me in daylight as he is now.

Later, something else wakes me, a smell – frying, cooking. My mind explodes with the veins of chicken breasts, the bloody ooze of steak, the textured muscle of meat. I don't make it to the toilet. I fling open the window, push my head outside.

Truth comes to me hanging half in, half out. My heartbeat slows as I breathe in the resinous scent of the pines, the wild garlic beyond, but my mind is busy, scrambling to fit in this wild card of my sickness, shuffling and reshuffling the deck until I realise it fits perfectly, just into a very bad hand.

The sex.

The sickness.

I can't remember when I last had my period.

I blink at the pines. There are two types of cones among the glossy sprays of needles: smaller, yellow ones growing in heavy clusters at the tips of the branch, and large, reddish-brown cones. Male. Female. I don't know whether to laugh or cry. How is it possible to know how pines are fertilised while ignoring that everything – trees, flowers, butterflies, my own body – is straining for two things? Survival. And reproduction.

I retch over the side of the cottage.

I crawl back to bed, pull over the checked quilt. A few weeks ago, all I wanted was to be the girl in this bed. Now, I'd give anything to go back to the evening when he touched me in his study, further, further still, to that golden afternoon in the field of thyme when I asked Daniel to help me net a Blue. I'd drop the net. Let the butterfly fly free.

My mind crawls over all the warnings I've ignored. 'Kissing is fine, beyond that, no more,' Mama used to say to me, as she dressed for rehearsal. I thought she was talking to herself rather than me, she was the person about to go out, I was staying at home. 'Men only think of their fun, not the consequences. They'll get you pregnant and then—' she clapped her hands together like that was it, a life ruined, over. 'Do you understand?' I nodded solemnly.

Now, I press a pillow to my mouth, whisper, 'No, I didn't understand. I didn't realise it could lead to this.'

Is that true? Should I have known? We were taught contraception at St Matthews, Aditi was my lab partner in biology, we took turns sliding condoms on a banana, egging Tanya on when she threatened to catapult it at Mrs Griggs. I remember the serrated edge of the foiled packaging, how easily it tore, the smell of the rubber as I unrolled the fop of it, and then I layer over each time I've had sex with Daniel – the cottage, the woods, the car. Not a single instance was interrupted by the sound of a packet opening or him rolling it on. Even now, as I run mad about the life fluttering inside me, I see so clearly why it was impossible. It would have changed the moment. It would have broken the spell.

Pots clang downstairs, he is doing the dishes, tidying up, cooking for me, something plain to quell my stomach. Looking after me, adult things, and then I realise that where things are fuzzy to me, for him, the inevitable march from the exploration of each other's bodies to pregnancy is crystal clear. He is thirty. Contraception is not bananas in biology but a mitigation of risk. He must have used it before. Then, why didn't he with me?

The thought, when it comes, is frightening. *He wants me pregnant.* It would bind me to him, isn't that really why he's angry about Alex, he wants me all to himself, to have no other choices, that's what he whispers to me in the dead of night, *I can't lose you*, his desperation seeping into his kisses, the urgent way he parts my legs. My promises aren't enough. The surrender of my body is not enough. Only this will bind me to him.

I take in the bedroom, the chest under the open window, the floorboards, the enormous bed. I used to love this cottage. Now, it is nothing more than a sealed tomb.

The next day, when Daniel goes to the field, I go straight down to the beach. I press my elbow to my nose so I don't smell the meat of a half-rotten crab or the bladderwrack drying on the rock. My body has turned traitor, things which once delighted me are now repulsive: the suck of the tide; clam holes; mussels puckering open to drain sea water. I need things still. I need things to stop.

Alex comes after hours. When I am at my worst, slumped against the rocks, my head in my hands, about to give up, go home.

'I almost didn't see you here.'

The sun is a halo around his brown hair. I start to cry.

'Hey, hey, what's wrong?'

I hold out my hand, try to get him to stop asking me questions.

'Are you all right?'

I shake my head.

'What's going on?'

'I need your help.' I stare at the wet shingle. A shard of quartz glints in the sand. 'I'm pregnant.'

*

From: Kit McDermott   **12:05**

There was that time you ran out of Pepe's. You were eating a slice of Hawaiian, I was eating pepperoni, when you suddenly stopped mid-sentence, dropped your slice and legged it. You were back before I could pay the bill, you were laughing, 'Sorry, I thought I saw someone I knew,' but I could see you were trembling. It was like you'd seen a ghost. I didn't ask you who it was.

    I should have asked.

47

Headmistress

Now

We're outside the headmistress' office now; I give my name to the secretary. She calls through. The bell rings, girls flood into the corridor. He puts his hands over his ears. They're too loud for him, too busy, rushing past him, perhaps they recall the clamour of a prison dining hall, the exercise yard. I turn pitilessly away. Maybe there is some justice. Everyday things should put him on edge, they should make him jumpy. Just like they do for me.

Mrs Hannington opens the door. She looks different to how I remember her and exactly the same. The mass of blonde hair that used to float around her like a nimbus is now smoothed back and lined with grey and she has traded her floaty blouses and long amber necklaces for a pressed white shirt and pearls. But her eyes are still the same – placid, observant. She holds out her hand, but last minute, pulls me into a hug. In her arms, I'm fourteen again.

'It's so good to see you.' There are tears in both our eyes when we pull apart. 'And who is this?'

Dear Darling

I wipe my palms on my jeans. Suddenly, this feels wrong, bringing him here, not telling him who she is. When do these secrets just become straightforward lies? But it's too late to retreat, I'm too far in. 'This is Daniel.'

'Welcome,' she says. It occurs to me that Mrs Hannington and Daniel are similar ages, both in their fifties. In another life, they might have been colleagues, friends, lovers. 'Come in, come in.'

The headmistress' office was always intimidating when I was at Wyatt. Even as head girl, I never got used to it, I'd have to gear myself up before I entered. Now, as an adult, I can break down why it is so impressive. It's three times the length of the managing partner's office at Dulwich & Sullivan, and everything in it is luxurious, from the polished escritoire framed by an expansive view of the lake to the casual seating area – a wool sofa, two deep armchairs, a glass table over a Turkish rug. Three of the four walls are filled with books: Angela Carter's *Bloody Chamber*; Jean Rhys's *Wild Sargasso Sea*; Rebecca Solnit's *Men Explain Things to Me*. I steal a glance at Daniel, does he know these stories, these essays, how they hum with rage, can he anticipate what he's walking into? But he doesn't register them. He is looking at the portrait of Mrs Hannington hanging over the fireplace. In it, she wears a suit jacket and a smile that seems to capture both the force of her personality and her warmth.

She gestures for us to sit on the sofa. I perch at the edge, my abdomen is already twinging. Daniel sits beside me. Our knees almost touch. Eighteen years ago, not a day went by when they didn't touch.

'Coffee, Lauren, Daniel?' she asks, standing in front of the silver service on her escritoire. Daniel asks for a water; I ask for a coffee. When she hands it to me, I press it close to my stomach, my body seeking its small heat. Since I lost Faye, Kit made three hot water bottles a day, in the morning before he left for work, when he came back and before bed, and I remember Mrs Hannington making me a hot water bottle after I came back from the clinic, she presented it on the tray with a cup of sweet tea. The ordinary ways they both tried to pull me out of extraordinary grief.

She pours herself a coffee, sits opposite us on the armchair. 'I wish we'd kept in touch.'

'I do too.'

'I've thought of you many times over the last, how many years? Fifteen?'

'Fourteen.' There is some arithmetic I am always working out even as it moves away from me: it's been fourteen years since I last saw Mrs Hannington; eighteen years since I last saw Daniel; almost four weeks since I lost Faye; two days and nineteen hours since I last saw Millie and Kit.

'How have you been? What do you do now?'

'I'm a lawyer.'

'What kind?'

'Corporate.'

'M&A?' she asks.

The specificity of her question surprises me, in my mind, she is sitting at the front of my English class, reciting Milton, her blonde hair shaking with the rhythm of iambic pentameter. I've forgotten she was one of the most intelligent people I used to know, her interests wide-reaching, from philosophy to economics. 'It's not actually corporate,' I explain. 'I just say that so people understand.' My mistake. She's not 'people'. 'It's banking regulation.'

'That would explain why you were involved in the deal to save Silicon Republic.'

'You read about that?'

'It was all over the news.' She smiles, takes a sip of her coffee. 'All right, I'll admit it, I do keep tabs on my favourites. That sounds terrible, doesn't it, I'm not supposed to have favourites. But I do.'

I bite the inside of my cheek. There are points in my life where knowing I was someone's favourite might have saved me. We need so little to survive.

'I'm so proud of you,' she says and I think, suddenly, of when Mama stuck the poster I drew of *The Tempest* on the fridge, it was there for months. After she died, I found it in the pocket of her trench coat I pulled from the boxes in Daniel's office, the folds soft from how long she'd kept it. I scramble to push down grief.

'I always knew you'd do something valuable. Something important.'

Daniel stiffens beside me.

'Do you enjoy it?'

'Parts of it. Sometimes, it's a bit much.'

'What about it is too much?'

I press my coffee cup to my lips, think of the all-nighters I've pulled, the number of mornings I met Kit in the lobby, traded a kiss for fresh clothes. I didn't realise how hard I was working until I had Millie. After that, I saw every billable increment in missed dinners, bedtimes, lullabies. 'It's just hard to juggle.'

She is quiet, then, I remember the quality of her listening, the way she made me feel like I could say anything to her, she is doing it again, inviting confidences. But this isn't the time. I'm here for another reason. 'I wondered if . . .' I am stumbling over my words because she and Daniel are both staring at me, but I can't help it, my heart is beating so loudly, I can barely hear myself think. 'I wondered if we could talk about what happened when I came to Wyatt.'

She puts her cup and saucer down delicately.

'It's come up a lot recently. For years, I couldn't talk about it, I just . . .' my hand makes a sweeping motion. 'But now, it's become something I need to work through. I know it's strange coming here, so out-of-the-blue, but I wonder if you wouldn't mind telling me your version of events. Because sometimes—' My tears anger me, why have they sprung up now? This is nothing compared to what I've forced myself to say these last few days. I press my fingers to my eyes, 'I remember in broad strokes what happened but the details are hazy.'

'Of course,' she says gently. 'Let me think where to start.' She fiddles with the back of her pearl earring. 'I think it was the summer holidays when I first met you. Wyatt had all but emptied apart from a few girls who weren't going home. I got a call from the headmistresses at the time, Mrs Parkinson, saying you'd arrived, asking me to come and meet you. It made sense that it was me, you were a Hawk House girl so one of mine, and I knew you a little, I'd been sending you English work. But I could tell by her voice that something was wrong, though she didn't tell me what, probably because you were right there.' She squints at me, as if to superimpose the girl she can see against the fourteen-year-old she met.

'You told me you'd asked for directions at the station and walked because you didn't have any money for a taxi. You wondered if you still had a place. We asked what had happened, where your stepfather was, but you said you didn't know. You just repeated the same question, very quietly, very clearly, was there a place for you or not?'

My mouth is suddenly dry, I run my tongue against its roof, I want a drink but I don't put my coffee to my lips. I can't let them see me tremoring.

'So, I took you to a dorm, rang the kitchen for dinner, while Mrs Parkinson tried to get through to your stepfather. I sat next to you, making horrible attempts to engage you about what you liked, the work you'd sent in. You were so polite. I thought you very self-possessed. But so vulnerable.'

I don't remember this, of course, he doesn't either. Yet we both see it. A girl, drawing herself up to answer questions. Trying to be brave. Daniel tugs the collar of his shirt like he is loosening a noose.

'A few days later, we got a call from the police, informing us that your stepfather had been arrested.'

Daniel puts down his glass of water.

'It might surprise you but we're quite used to dealing with these issues. Mrs Parkinson was at least. And since I've been headmistress, let's just say we're prepared for everything at Wyatt. Even for what came after . . .' she spreads her hands on her knees, 'when you asked me to take you to a clinic.'

Beside me, Daniel is absolutely still.

Mrs Hannington looks at him and then at me, she is checking if she should carry on. My pulse is racing, part of me doesn't want her to, but I force myself to nod.

'They gave you tablets because you were less than ten weeks along.'

'Along from what?' I whisper. We all know the answer. But I need her to say it.

Her eyes on me are wide and intent. 'You were pregnant.'

Daniel stands up abruptly. His knee catches the edge of the coffee table, his glass topples, for a moment, he cups water in his hands to stop the spill and then the enormity of what she's said dawns on him, the ridiculousness of saving the rug when he and I are both ruined. He wipes his hands across his blazer, 'I'm sorry, I just need to, I have to—' He rights the glass and then stumbles round the sofa, he has to put one hand over the other to steady himself. Then, he's gone.

I stare at the water trickling off the edge. The smudge-print of his lips on the glass.

Mrs Hannington reaches over. Wipes the water with a napkin. After a few minutes, she gets up and closes the door. 'It's him, isn't it?'

'Who?'

'The man who did that to you.' Rage blazes in her voice, her eyes are hard as she watches him through the window, making his way out of the grounds. She looks at him as if he is a creature in a box, something with too many legs or too few and I wish he was still in the room, I'd cup his chin in my hand, turn his brilliant navy eyes towards her, say, 'Tell me, my love, is this really just maths?'

'When did you realise?'

'When you introduced him.'

She's an exceptional actress. She's sat here, opposite him, pretending she didn't know.

'You used to say his name when you dreamt.'

Dear Darling

I still do, sometimes. On the pillow beside Kit, I dream of Daniel. His name breaking out from memory to life.

'He's your stepfather, isn't he?'

My mouth falls open.

'I suspected when you were in Wyatt. Something about the timing of it – your arrival, the arrest; the pregnancy – it seemed more than coincidental. Too many things in quick succession.' She pushes away his glass with the backs of her fingers, like she can't bear to touch it. 'And when I told you he'd been arrested, you didn't cry. You were silent. Like you were numb already.'

'Why didn't you say anything?'

'To you? Never. You were far too fragile, you wanted it behind you, over, it took so long to get you well, I couldn't risk it. We did have a meeting about it though, with Mrs Parkinson, the school board, and we decided to say nothing about it. With the length of his sentence, he wouldn't be able to pull you out. We never told the police, we didn't want you taken into care, in the school holidays, we just looked after you here.' She presses her palms against the back of the door. 'It's different now; we have a duty to call the police. But for you, I don't regret it. Wyatt was the best place for you, in the circumstances.'

They knew. They all knew. I press my fingers over my mouth. Why have I kept all these secrets, for what, for whom?

She sits beside me on the sofa. Puts her hand over mine. Her skin is velvet and cool. 'What are you doing with him, Lauren?'

'There are things I need to speak to him about.'

'He's dangerous. Remember what he did. Not just your age, the abortion, but what happened afterwards. You weren't well for months.'

'Months? You mean days. I only stayed in your study a few days.'

She looks at me, her grey eyes clear and unblinking. 'You stayed in my study for almost a year.'

I press the heels of my hands against my eyes. I remember certain things – the curiosity of Jennie and Lisa when I rejoined the dorms, how quickly that faded when I told them I'd been ill, how I failed art year after year because I refused to lift a paintbrush, a chalk, a pencil. But all that must have been after my stay with Mrs Hannington. And then I think memory must have a will of its own, speeding up time, making it run slow, blotting out sections of reel. 'A year,' I repeat, dumbly.

'You don't recall?'

'No.'

'You were hollowed out. A shell. I worried about you for years afterwards.' Her fingers tighten round my wrist. 'That's why I'm saying he's dangerous. The way he looks at you—'

'—I know. Like he loves me.'

She shakes me, like she's waking me from a dream. 'No. Not like he loves you. Like he's obsessed. Love and obsession are different things. You know this. Iago and Othello, Mr Rochester and Jane Eyre. He doesn't see you clearly, only what he wants to see. And once that illusion is shattered—' She seems to realise she is squeezing my wrist, she lets go with a start. 'You get what you need from him and then you leave.'

I feel suddenly very frightened. Like I've been ignoring warnings, signs. Now, I'm about to go into the woods. It's pitch black and quiet.

'Don't stay a minute more.' She pulls me into her then, I feel the familiar generosity of her body. I want to stay in her arms forever. 'You remember our school motto?'

'*Ad astra per aspera*,' I reply instinctively.

'Through hardship to the stars,' she whispers. 'Be finished with your hardships. It's time for the stars.'

*

From: Kit McDermott   **12:08**

That time Emma messaged me to say she'd taken you home. I was there within the hour but, when I knocked on the door, you looked so normal, so calm, you were surprised I'd come over. Said it was nothing. But later, when I spoke to Emma, she told me it was serious. She said she'd never seen you that way, it was a full-blown panic attack, you could barely breathe. I believed you instead of her. But now, I wonder if I made that choice because I didn't want to believe there's a side of you I have no idea about. A side I didn't want to see.

48

Soft

Then

'You're what?' says Alex.

'I'm pregnant,' I repeat, but he heard me the first time because the shock of it destabilises him. He stumbles on the sand.

'I don't understand,' he says, as he sits down. His eyes on me are wide, he is trying to process all the things I've shared against the enormity of what I haven't. 'You never said anything about—'

A man, a relationship, sex.

'Who is he?'

I bite my lip. I can never tell him. My secrets are so much darker than his.

'Lauren?'

I shake my head.

He puts his hand on my elbow. His voice is so gentle. 'Who is he?'

I wrench my elbow away, my whisper, savage. 'Don't ask me.'

He freezes. He's never heard me like that before, so hurt and hunted, and then I can't look at him anymore, can't see how much I'm frightening him. I bury my face in my hands. Behind my palms, I'm praying, *Stay, please, don't leave*, and then, I feel his hand on my shoulder. The relief is so overwhelming, I almost cry out with it.

'What do you need?' he says.

He is everything I need him to be – practical, resourceful. He asks if I've taken a test and I think Mama's death, these weeks in Cornwall, Daniel, have made me soft in the head, like the smashed flesh of a bruised peach – it *could* actually be noro, I could be worrying about nothing. I tell Alex I can't get to the pharmacy and it wouldn't matter if I could because I don't have any money. He drives me to Falmouth in his father's truck. He buys the test.

Pitched over the café toilet, trying to plunge the test into my urine, I look at my reflection, see the cliché I truly am. I believed what Daniel and I had was rare, astonishing, that I was rare and astonishing. But I am not. I am ordinary. So very ordinary. The sink is smeared with liquid soap. I fold a length of tissue, place it on the edge and then lay the test on top of it, as if cleanliness will save me now.

Pink cross.

Pregnant.

Alex doesn't have to ask me what the result is. I fly into his arms, bury my head against his neck. I want to sink down through his skin, into his body, I want to be him not me. Lock the door on myself, the basin, the test. Leave myself behind.

In the truck, he asks me again whose baby it is, if I'm going to tell my stepfather. I tell him I can't, my stepfather won't understand. Alex doesn't piece it together. It is incomprehensible because it is disgusting. I am disgusting. *Your mother's husband. Your stepfather.*

The hedgerows come into view, the post office, the fish cellar, the beach and then he drives up to the cottage, through the woods. I want to say stop, stop, we're going back too fast, I'm not ready, I can't do this, but I don't. He parks outside the cottage. He rubs his palms on his legs, he's sweating. 'I think we should tell my dad. He's really cool. He'll help.'

'No!' I grip his arm. 'I just need to get away from here. Tomorrow, I'll be gone.'

'Where? Your stepfather is here. You don't have any other family.'

All this thought of escape and nowhere to go. I think of Mama, what she used to say. 'You're the only family I need.' I believed her, but where has her fierce isolation left me? I shut my eyes, wish that childish wish of wanting my father, that would give me an option when I have run out. I want to crawl into my box room with the maple leaves tacked on the window, listen to Mama's violin through the walls but the flat's rented out now and Mama's dead. The only place I can think of is Wyatt, where I was before Daniel told me about Mama, where, for nine days, I was happy. That decides it. 'I'll go to boarding school.'

'You go to boarding school?' His features harden at another thing I've left out, another secret I've kept.

I take a deep breath, make my voice steel, strong. 'I need you to bring as much money as you can, pick me up tomorrow morning and drive me to the train station.'

'What about your stepfather? Are you sure he's going to the field?'

I look beyond him, out of the truck window, to the pine wood beyond, the flowers and ferns and plants I have dissected and sketched and labelled. I know what will delay Daniel. 'I'll deal with him.'

'I'm not sure. I have school and I just don't think—'

I do what will silence all his thinking. Because it is the thing that has silenced my own, made me soft and stupid. I lean over the gearstick and kiss him. His lips stir beneath mine; his hands move to my waist; in my mouth, I feel the smallest flutter of his tongue. Then, over his shoulder, I see Daniel.

*

From: Kit McDermott   **12:20**

I remember the week you lied about going to work – you'd been off for two days before I found out. I walked over to surprise you for lunch but I could see from the street that the light in your office was off. I was just about to call you when Mirel came out of reception. She looked confused when I said I was looking for you, she said you'd called in sick since Monday. I checked my phone. You'd messaged me minutes before about how your memo was driving you mad.

I didn't pull you up on it. I don't remember why I didn't or what I thought was going on but now, it seems really obvious you were having an affair. Nothing else makes sense. You're beautiful, smart, sexy as fuck, I've spent most of our relationship wondering why you're with me, when I'm clearly not smart enough, witty enough, good enough. Perhaps I didn't ask because I didn't want to know.

49

Secret

Now

I don't take anything in as I leave Mrs Hannington, the reception, the girls are a blur of light, colour, movement. I push through the double doors. The sun is blinding. I glare back at it, like I've told Millie never to do. Burn my retinas. Erase the study, the clinic, the dull ache in my stomach.

Someone touches me, I flinch, but it's not him, just a girl already walking away from me. I look round for him and then double back to reception. He's not there.

Coward.

Does he think he can get away from this that easily?

I haven't finished.

Not by a long shot.

My backpack swings as I sling it back on.

The lights are off at his mews house but the curtains are drawn. He might not be here; I don't have to hurt him, I could go back to the hotel now, climb between fresh, clean sheets. But I am only pretending, stretching out the last few seconds before time snaps back into place. He's in. His lights are off because of the migraine I've given him. His head is about to feel a lot worse. I take a deep breath, press the doorbell.

He isn't wearing the dove-grey shirt, he's exchanged it for a linen one, creased at the waist and rolled at the sleeves. He covers his eyes as he opens the door. Light from the streetlamp cuts shadows on his skin. 'I can't really do this now,' he says.

'Do you want me to go?'

We both know what his answer is. Always. He stands aside to let me in.

I am frightened following behind him, I feel like I'm going back in time. In the corridors of the cottage, I'd pull his shirt free from his belt, slip my hands round his waist; he'd tense under the cloth, the draw of his spine under my lips. My skin prickles. He rubs the back of his neck. He is thinking of this too.

In his living room, it's difficult to process what's changed, what's memory; apart from the lamp on the far side, the living room is sunk in darkness. The bones of the house look the same, the corridor that leads to the kitchen, the stairs downstairs. But as my eyes adjust to the shadows, it's clear that where once the interior of the house was light and neutral, now, it's rich and dark. A pair of chocolate leather Chesterfields claim the centre of the room, a captain's chair is angled towards the fireplace and above the seating area is a large pendant lamp in a milky glass, which looks like it once belonged in the cabin of a ship.

'Sorry,' he says. 'I can turn on another light.'

'It's okay.' On the walls are his published articles, hanging in gold frames. The coffee table is set with lepidoptery journals. I want to push a stack over. Watch them slide onto the rug.

The only thing missing is his butterfly collection, he used to keep them in an enormous antique collectors' cabinet, the drawers shallow and wide to display as many butterflies as possible. There's nothing like that in here now but I know they must be here. I cast round for them. The wall across from me has nothing on it, just plain walnut. I cross the room, run my palms over it, it's not a single piece but wooden panels. I press my palms against them, they spring open. Underneath, is butterfly upon butterfly, rare or extinct, their names coming to me like the lyrics of a forgotten song: Emperor of India; Island Marble; Xerces Blue; Zebra Longwing; Saint Francis' Satyr.

'You know all my secrets.'

I am your secret.

He's beside me, the butterflies have energised him, but it lasts only a second, he slumps onto his couch, shuts his eyes, and I think Daniel behind closed doors is Daniel in the dark. However much he loathed prison, the truth is, he's recreated his prison cell, here. It's the only place he feels safe.

'Sorry,' he says quietly. 'I'm having some kind of reaction.' He rubs the back of his neck, he's still itchy. 'And the school . . .' He shakes his head. 'It tires me, being round that many people.'

'Is it a migraine?'

He nods slowly, covers his hands with his eyes. Cowering from ordinary things, he looks older than I've ever seen him before.

'You need to drink; have you had anything to drink?'

He shakes his head.

'I'll get you some water.'

He doesn't protest. I go to his kitchen.

In contrast to his living room, the kitchen is bright and sleek – white marble counters, black cabinets. I open his fridge, his cupboards, his drawers. Everything is where I think it should be, the utensils in the top drawer of the island, cups and glasses above the kettle, it is the exact way I organise my kitchen, perhaps I do it that way because of him.

I smash my palms on the cool marble of the counter.

No more.

The surfaces are clear apart from a wooden bowl of fruit, the blender. He still likes smoothies. My heart pounds. Will I get away with this? How much do I want to stop my hurt? How much do I want to hurt him?

I push those thoughts aside, I can't think of them now. I fill a jug, take a glass.

He is in the same position when I return.

I hand him the water. 'Drink.'

He takes a small, pained sip.

'Come on,' I say tenderly, like I'm talking to Millie. 'All of it.'

He stares at the water's skin. 'I don't feel good.'

'I know.' I sit on the captain's chair opposite him. 'You won't until you drink.'

He looks at me, that molten navy. 'One of my favourite memories of you was how you'd look after me when I got my migraines. Sometimes, I think you're the only person who knows me.'

He's right.

Amber light floods in through the window, a horn sounds from the avenue, but in the dark heart of his house, no one else exists. We are the only people in the world.

He drinks obediently; I hear each swallow. He puts down the glass. 'I'm sorry.'

'For what?'

'Hurting you. I never wanted you to go through anything like that.'

I shut my eyes. It's happening now, isn't it? A reverse alchemy. The transformation of the gold of our past into lead, the dismantling of our fairy tale, and although this is what I've come for, my heart is cracking.

'When I think of you taking a pregnancy test, going to the clinic, staying in that tiny room at Wyatt with a teacher—' He breaks off. 'I would have done anything to take that from you.'

I turn my face to the wing of the captain's chair.

'Lauren,' he whispers. It's coming, we can both feel it, we're edging closer to the precipice now, hand over hand on the rockface until even that disappears, the drop below us sheer. 'Did you know you were pregnant at the cottage?'

I nod.

He lets out a small, terrible laugh. 'I spent all my time in prison turning over every single day we spent together, trying to figure out how I lost you, how he could have lured you away.'

Lost. Lured. Eighteen years on and he's still making the same mistake, to him, I'm no more than a butterfly, baited away by smashed bananas and sugar water, precious but stupid.

'I know I behaved badly towards the end.'

Is that what he's calling what he did to me the day before I left him?

'But I didn't foresee this.' He runs his hands over his face. 'Why didn't you tell me? We could have dealt with it together. You didn't have to be alone.'

I think about how he looked after me after Mama died, the meals he made for me here in this house, the walks in Holland Park, the extravagant set of drawing pencils. Is he right? Would it have been better staying with him, going to the clinic, getting better on his couch? I'd have never felt the hot shame of strangers knowing. Then, I remember why I didn't tell him. Why I left. 'That's a lie.' My voice – raw, hoarse – cuts the velvet dark between us. 'You knew what you were doing. You wanted me pregnant.'

'What?'

I stare at his clean, almondine nails, his powerful fingers and then, I stand up, flick on the wall switch. The room floods with light. He gives a low moan, covers his eyes with his arms but I prise his arms from his face, I want him to hurt, I'm so tired of the civility of this. Slap him, slam his skull against brick, wrap my fingers round his throat, that's the way it should be, no tenderness. Because what he did to me is violence. Everything else is pretend.

'All those times we had sex, you never wore a condom, never once talked to me about contraception! You knew what was going to happen! You were a scientist, Daniel, a fucking biologist! So don't tell me it wasn't something you wanted. Planned even. You made it happen. And I wasn't going to be like my mother, pregnant and trapped. I wasn't.'

He is blinking rapidly. 'That's what you think?' he whispers.

'Yes.'

'Why on earth would I *want* you to be pregnant?'

'So I'd be more dependent on you. So I'd be bound to you. You'd have made me have it, ruined my life more than you've already ruined it.'

'No wonder you're angry at me.'

'Angry?' I am swaying a little, dizzy with my rage and the open cabinets of butterflies, their jungle colours, their bright, dead wings. 'Anger doesn't touch how I feel about you.' I am panting now, the exertion sending spasms of pain through me, I wrap my arms round my stomach, try to stop the vibrations.

He reaches for me in the broad light of his living room. If I'd let him, he'd press me against the soft linen of his shirt, it flickers through me for an instant, what it would be like. But it's just a trick of time, a memory of my fourteen-year-old self, already slipping away. I step back. 'Don't.' Then, it's time. Time to put everything together. 'You still haven't figured it out, have you? Why I'm hurting?'

He looks at me for a long time in a way I can't read. But when he finally speaks, I understand it is a terrible pity. 'It's your husband, isn't it?'

'What?'

'He's hurting you.' His right leg is shaking, he looks at it like it doesn't belong to him, like he might not be able to control what he's about to do. 'He hits you, doesn't he? That's why you've run away. That's why you came when you got my letter.'

Then I wonder if Daniel has heard a word of what I've been saying or if I am nothing more than an embellishment to a story he's telling himself. Because no matter where I take him or how many times I try to explain, nothing has dissuaded him from believing that *another* man's hurt me, *another* man is dangerous, when he's the most dangerous person I've ever met.

'Daniel,' I say slowly. 'Kit has never laid a finger on me.'

He squints at me, disbelieving.

'It's my baby,' I say, and it feels like I am in a building seconds after it's been bombed, watching the blast ripple through the bricks, the roof cave, I'm about to be buried alive. 'I lost my baby.'

'What?'

'I had a stillbirth,' I say and then I hate myself, hate that I know the precise term, the precise definition, I shouldn't know this, no one should know this. How many babies has this happened to, how many mothers for language to press together these two words? Why should vocabulary be such a testament of loss?

'When?'

'Four weeks ago.' The row of beds flash across my retina. The blue paper curtains. The sound of the monitors.

'I really believed in the beginning that everything would be all right, I was sure I was being silly, I was over-worrying, not counting the kicks properly, I was ashamed I was in the Maternity Assessment Unit, I thought I was wasting their time when there were other mothers, other babies who needed their help more than me. But Lucy, the midwife, she was so kind, she said, "You were right to come in," and for once, I felt like I had a real maternal instinct, I might actually be a good mum. She hooked me up to the monitor. I knew instantly something was wrong, I could hear the sound of the monitor of the woman in the bed beside me, that regular, echoey swish, a sound mine wasn't making. Lucy was unplugging me, ushering me into a private room, telling me I needed an ultrasound, a doctor. That's when the panic set in. I called Kit, telling him he needed to come, he was on speakerphone when the doctor said the umbilical cord was constricted, the baby wasn't getting enough oxygen. "We need to go," the doctor said.'

My nails are in my palms, raising crescents of blood, and I don't care because it should hurt, there should be blood, when you're telling something as appalling as this.

'Later, I realised, "We need to go" was code, because the entire back wall was suddenly filled with nurses, doctors, midwives, they were getting me up, undressing me, pulling a hospital gown over my head, and I was crying, I kept saying over and over again, "Why is this happening, I don't understand why this is happening?" But, after they injected anaesthetic into my spine, after they pulled the blue curtain over my ribs so I couldn't see them cutting into me, or their expressions when they saw she was dead, I knew why it was happening. It was my fault. My body had turned on the baby, it had cut her off, killed her. It knew I was a bad mum; I couldn't deal with her sister, I'd killed her sibling and, even though I kept it a secret, it was like every vessel in my body knew, every artery and vein, my fault, my fault, my fault. But also, yours.'

He is crying openly now but I am not. There are no tears left. I've cried them all for that tiny, clean baby they gave me, those small limbs, that new skin, still rose-coloured and warm. She looked like she was sleeping.

He says over and over again, 'I'm sorry, I'm so sorry,' and as I watch him weep into his hands, it occurs to me that I've accomplished what I set out to achieve. Because he can see it now – how the grenade he planted inside me eighteen years ago has finally gone off, all the people it's obliterated – it's enough. Call this off. Go home. But the loosening of my hate frightens me. Who would I be without it? It was my companion when I went home without my baby, my dearest friend as I lay crying in the greenhouse. I cannot let it go now. Will not.

'Does your head still hurt?' I say.

Dear Darling

'It doesn't matter.'
'You haven't eaten anything, have you?'
'Lauren—'
'I'll make you something.'
'I really don't—'
'—Don't worry. I know what you like.'
I go to the kitchen.

*

From: Kit McDermott   12:31
An affair makes sense. Months before we got married, you were listless, distant, you didn't seem to care about the details of the wedding, the honeymoon, you just went along with whatever I decided. The only thing that energised you was clearing out the front and back gardens, the only thing you asked from me was to help you build a greenhouse, and I confess, I was ecstatic carrying panes of glass, putting it together, watching you smile as you carried in seedlings because you never asked me for anything, because finally, finally, there was something I could do for you. I thought all that digging, raking, planting was you working something out of your system. I didn't think it might have been someone.

And if I'm brutally honest, horribly honest, I wonder if you're thinking of someone else when we have sex because you never look at me, you close your eyes, you shut me out, and even though I've never said anything to you, I don't know how I'd bring it up, I think about it all the time, how at our most intimate, you're not there, you're gone.

50

SHIRT

Then

How long he's been standing there, I don't know. He has stopped in the middle of the cow parsley, the umbrella blooms waving in the wind, the sun, a lucent orange through the pines, it would almost be beautiful, were it not for the tunnels of his eyes. 'My stepdad,' I whimper.

'Shit.' Alex sees him, jerks back. 'Let me talk to him.'

I love him for that. But he can't intercede for me, he doesn't know the truth, I've never told it to him. 'No. But come tomorrow at eight.'

'I'll try.'

'Promise.'

'I promise.'

I slide out of the truck. He reverses out of the clearing.

Then, it's just Daniel and me, facing each other in the clearing.

He moves first. He cuts a path through the woods to the cottage, mowing down cow parsley, grass, dandelions. He rattles the door handle as he fumbles with his key. I wonder if this is another door that will surrender to his force but it springs open. He flings his gear down, rounds on me. 'You said you'd never see him again.'

'This is the first time!'

'You said you never needed to!'

'I don't.'

'I. Saw. You.'

'That was just—'

'Friends?'

My mind is splintering, equal parts panic and fury; I wouldn't have to kiss Alex if I wasn't pregnant with Daniel's child and then I see that what I have with Daniel is a steel trap, sharp-toothed, jawed, always clamping round me. I turn away. 'I don't feel well.'

'Now, you're not well? When I'm here?' He advances on me quickly now. His eyes are wild. 'After you've spent the whole afternoon letting him do God knows what?'

'I told you, I haven't done anything with him—'

'You let him kiss you! His hands were on your waist!' He squeezes my wrist. I pull myself free. 'Did you let him unbutton your jeans? Put his hands under your shirt?'

'No!'

He grabs my collar, jerks me towards him, I'm bewildered by the power of his hands balling up the cotton at my shoulders. There's an appalling series of sounds. Ripping. The pop scatter of buttons. A strangled noise from my throat. Thoughts spark, fly. I think of the gentle way he undresses me every day, how it is a courtesy, he could just as easily be doing this. I think that this is Mama's shirt, she bought it from a vintage shop in Paris, she loved the blue and white ticking stripes, the thickness of the cotton. I think of what she would say if she saw me now.

He is holding my face between his hands, he is kissing me and crying and saying sorry, but then he stops because I am not responding, no part of me is moving except my hands, which flutter helplessly round the openness of my shirt.

'Lolly?'

He pulls my shirt shut. Pats down a button that's no longer there.

I turn away from him. Walk up the stairs.

He spends hours pleading with me, battering his palm against the bathroom door. I drown him out at first, I run full baths and then drain them. Eventually, I do nothing at all, just slump down the wall, let the apologies, excuses, justifications wash over me, wondering if the craziness he's saying is because he's been talking for so many hours, or if this is really what he thinks.

'It was an accident, I just got worked up, you have so much power over me but it was wrong, I see that now, I should have trusted you, because you're you, you're innocent, *he* kissed *you*, *he* kissed *you*, that's what happened isn't it, that's what I saw, he forced himself on you, darling, open the door, let me in—'

Hours after, he tires. He stops suddenly. The handle rattles as he pulls himself up.

'I need to lie down; I've got a migraine. But I love you. Come to bed. I can't sleep without you.'

I hear his footsteps in the corridor, the click of his door opening, shutting. I wait, ten, fifteen minutes. Then, I walk past his room, head downstairs, out of the cottage.

It's sunset now, the light is disappearing fast, but I don't need much time, I don't even have to go far, they're right here on the doorstop, growing beside the cow parsley – the edible and the poisonous. The flowers are astonishingly similar, white umbels the size of my hand, the leaves are almost identical – it's only the stems that give them away. Cow parsley is green, covered in fine hairs with a deep groove, but hemlock's stem is smooth with a spattering of purple blotches. I pull on a pair of Daniel's gloves. Pick a bunch of leaves. Grass brushes the backs of my hands.

At the cottage, I look back at my sketchbook, the notes I've taken on hemlock water dropwort. A single root can kill a cow. A child died after her parents rubbed leaves onto her skin – they thought they were dock leaves. But I don't want to kill him. I just need to buy myself time, slow him down. I choose the smallest leaf, slice it, blend up only a quarter with one banana, two kiwis, a handful of blueberries. It glugs as I pour it into the glass, like the chug of vomit.

He is lying fully clothed on the covers of our bed, one arm flung over his eyes, as if to shield himself from the sun, although it's long since set. I set his smoothie down, climb onto the bed beside him. He lays his head in my lap. I stroke his head like he loves, pushing my fingers through the thickness of his hair, running my nails down his back. He whispers, 'I'm sorry.'

'It's fine,' I tell him, though, it's not. Something dead has settled in me, silt covering my insides. I just want this to be over. I take the glass. 'Sit up,' I say. 'I've made you something.'

Ella King

He reaches for it in the dark. 'I love you.'

'I love you, too.' As he puts it to his lips, I make clear pictures in my mind. The sky above the creek. The water pushing away from the rudder of the boat. A train thundering me away.

51

Smoothie

Now

In the kitchen, I am petrified. What if he walks in, asks me what the hell I'm doing? Will I deny it? Or will I look full in his beautiful face and make my confession? *Yes, I'm poisoning you. I've been doing it for days. I did it eighteen years ago.*

My hands are shaking. I don't drink smoothies, I never make them at home, just one more thing, like pastries and men with dark hair, that I'm expert at navigating. A few years ago, my friend, Elias, who sat in the office across from mine, started making smoothies for breakfast at the office. He'd take hours to drink it, I'd look up to see his glass still full of swampy gunge, a trail of raspberry seeds clinging to the side. I couldn't bear it. One evening after he'd gone home, I pushed his blender in his bin. He talked about it for days – who it might have been, why they'd taken it. He never did land on the right motive. The right culprit.

Banana first, that's the base, my mind squirms remembering that from Cornwall. The memories are very close now, very intense – the stricken look on Kit's face, the tiny baby I wanted to hold forever – I can't wait any longer. I get out the test tube. The pollen is still bright and fluffy; it tinkles against the sides. I flick open the top, pour it over the bananas. There is no information on the internet about the potency of pollen, no guidance on dosage, I'm not sure how much Daniel will have to drink before he slips into a coma, how many sips before the hallucinations start. The Andean tribes of Peru hallucinate animals – hunting dogs, pumas, bears, bulls. I wonder if he'll see the first butterfly he ever showed me – the Queen Alexandra's Birdwing. Or if it will be the last – the extinct Cornish Blue.

He hasn't moved since I've left, his face is still in his hands, but he looks up as he hears me. The light from the street splits his face, one half obscenely bright, the other in shadow. 'I thought that was what you were making.'

'I saw the blender.' My heart is pounding. 'It's the only thing I've ever made for you.'

'It's perfect.' He takes it from me.

I switch off the main light, keep the table lamps on. A small kindness in these last few moments.

'I know what you're about to do,' he says.

My pulse races.

'You're about to leave.'

Close. But not close enough.

'When I was in prison, I'd dream about waking up that morning, the emptiness of the cottage, the dizziness, the smell of my own sick. How I called your name over and over but you never came.' He plays with the smoothie, winding it in slow circles, the movement mesmeric. '"Dream" is the wrong word. It was my worst nightmare, waking up without you. It still is.' He drags a finger slowly round the top of the glass and then looks at me intently. 'So, if this is the last time we're going to see each other, there are things I need to say.'

I've been so caught up with hurting him, I've failed to comprehend what he has – this is the end of us. It hits me like a high-speed train – I won't be able to speak to him or hear his voice, I'll never see his dark eyes again or the breadth of his shoulders – and then, though I am the one who's done this, I am drawing the curtain on us, the preciousness of these last moments together disarms me, all defences down. I lean towards him, a plant craving the last rays of sun.

'Do you remember those vitamins I used to give you?'

I'm not sure if I've misheard him.

'I gave you a round Vitamin C tablet, two cod liver oil tablets and a multivitamin. But when our relationship started, I started giving you another one.'

It was pale pink, small.

'That was the pill.'

For a second, I just blink at him before horror slivers through me. *He changed my body, my chemistry.* The entitlement. The audacity. The insidious control.

'I'm sorry I didn't tell you. I didn't want to worry you.'

I don't believe him. He didn't care about worrying me. He didn't want me to see the consequences of what we were doing. He couldn't risk me saying no.

'They didn't work obviously, perhaps I missed a day when I gave them to you, I don't remember now—'

But I remember. I didn't take the pills he gave me, not always. It felt like seeing Alex or going swimming, important to do the opposite of what he wanted, perhaps I sensed what he was doing and rebelled. But it backfired. I search for the sofa behind me, cannot find it. I sink to the floor.

'I should have told you, I know that now.'

I bury my face in my hands.

'But darling, don't you see what this means? There was never a plan to trap you.'

Behind my palms, things slowly click together. He is owning up to this transgression to absolve himself of a greater one. And then the scientist in me takes over from the frightened hurting child, recognises the sense in what he did, his scalpel-sharp efficiency. Because, he's right, isn't he? If I'd taken the pills, I would have never got pregnant, I would never have had an abortion. If I'd just done what he asked, none of this would have happened.

'I think that's the tragedy of all of this. If I hadn't become so possessive towards the end, you'd have come to me when you found out, not him. I wouldn't have lost my mind trying to find you, I wouldn't have gone to prison. It wouldn't have been the end of us.'

Misunderstandings. Possibilities. Counterfactuals. There have been so many mistakes.

He presses the side of the glass against his lips. 'One last thing before you go, I need you to listen to this, it's important. The thoughts you had about your baby, that you lost her because you're a bad mother, because of the abortion, none of that is true.'

I stare at him in the dark. No one has ever said that to me before. No one has stood before the whirlwind of guilt and shame that has always swirled inside me and simply told it, 'No,' and I don't understand how it is *him* who's saying it, the man who's ruined my life, the man I hate more than anyone in the world.

'The reason you've found everything so hard – being a wife, a mother, losing the baby – is you've kept so many secrets. And, when you were most vulnerable, on that delivery table, they overtook you.'

Tears stream down my face.

'Your secrets are my fault, I admit it, I did something very wrong, I committed a crime, it's my fault you could never tell anyone. If you came to show me that, you've done it, I see it now, the harm, I'm sorry, truly. But . . .' His voice quivers. 'I am also hoping, praying that during these last few days, you'll have realised something else. Because of all the things you've told me and I've told you, there are no secrets between us anymore. Which means now, more than at any other time, we have a chance. To make something out of this.'

I cannot breathe.

'I love you. You must know that.'

'You can't say that,' I whisper.

'I'm the *only* person who can say that. Because I'm the *only* person who knows you.'

I put my hand out to silence him but it's too late, his words roar inside me.

'I know why you find childbirth hard, motherhood hard, being a wife—'

I press my knuckles to my mouth.

'—I'd be there for you helping you through, unknotting, untangling you, I've done it before, I'll do it again.'

A case of colour pencils. Primroses. A thyme field, golden with dusk.

'Don't you see? We can still have it. Our rare, astonishing life.'

I try desperately to hold on, I think of Millie and Kit but they flitter away, there is too much pain there – Millie thrashing on the floor, the look on Kit's face when they took Faye away. Daniel says, 'Darling,' and the word rings in my head, I could be *that*, his darling, not who I am now, everything that's happened is no more than a bad dream, and then he whispers, 'Lolly,' and at my old name – forbidden, transgressive – the fourteen-year-old girl I've shackled for eighteen years, sick and wrong and wanting him from the start, breaks free.

He slides onto the floor beside me. 'Be with me.'

I search for my hate but it isn't there. Perhaps it never was. Or maybe it was just a road I had to travel along, a country I needed to pass through to find the place where I belong.

I take the smoothie from him.

Put my hand in his.

There is shock, recognition, astonishment. Because in the cave of his hand, it feels like home.

*

From: Kit McDermott　　　　　　　　　　　　　　**12:39**
But even an affair doesn't make sense of it. It doesn't explain the nightmares you wake up screaming from, or how you've never learnt to drive, or how you make excuses to get out of taking Millie to the playground. I told you once, that playgrounds are important, she needs to know where the boundaries of her body are, where she starts and where she ends and you looked at me like I'd slapped you. What makes sense of that?

Dear Darling

My mind is exploding trying to figure this out. Cass said I need to stop writing to you, according to her, I'm not doing anything except message you all day and I sort of growled at her, told her it's the only thing that makes me feel better.

But now, I think she's right. I can't keep this up.

So, this is my last one.

If you're reading these messages, I want you to know, I'm sorry for what's happened to us. I'm sorry we lost Faye.

I'm sorry if I haven't loved you as much as I should, if I didn't love you enough to ask you hard questions. But I'm not afraid anymore. Nothing you can say will frighten me. Because nothing is worse than not being with you. Come home.

52

HIT AND RUN

Then

This is how you die from a hit and run. The bumper of the car strikes your legs. You're astounded that the words you learnt at school – *speed*, *mass*, *velocity* – are really talking about this. That your body, which always felt invincible when you ran into the sea or did a kick flip on your skateboard, simply surrenders. You didn't realise metal was so absolute.

Your legs, already broken, are swept from under you as your torso contours to the car's bonnet. Your ribcage cracks. You wish you'd kissed that girl at the school dance. You're moving at the speed of the car now, everything inside you is moving at the speed of the car, all your soft organs, until, one by one, they're halted by bruising, tears, ruptures.

Your head hits the windshield. Your skull fractures, you have a concussion, which you could come back from if your brain wasn't already swelling. You want your mum.

The last thing you see through the glass of the windshield are the navy eyes of a stranger. You don't know that, after a night

Dear Darling

of what he thinks is food poisoning, he is looking for a girl. A girl who, at the very moment you die, is hundreds of miles away on a train. A girl who, after the man is arrested, will never stop researching hit and runs.

Later, when she is a lawyer, when she is pretending to be an adult and not the fourteen-year-old she feels like she is, she will use all her resources to find your name: James Saunders, seventeen. Just an innocent boy in the wrong place, at the wrong time. Collateral. You will be with her at the zeniths of her life and the nadirs – her abortion, her graduation, her wedding day, the birth of her first daughter, the loss of her second. No matter where she is or what she's doing, she will see, in retinal flashes, the hundreds of collisions that pulled you apart. In all those moments, she desperately wants to say one thing to you: 'I'm so sorry. You could never have seen him coming. No one could.'

PART IV

53

DRIVE

Now

It's easy to slip into a younger version of myself, like sinking below the surface of warm water. In the passenger seat of his car, I roll down the window and hold my hand to the wind, watch its steadiness against the zip of motorbikes, cars, lorries. Tarmac clears my mind, no past behind, no future ahead.

That evening, he drove me to The Spitalfields. I gave him everything – address, room number, key card. He packed up all my things, slung my bag over his shoulder. It looked so small against his hip.

In the lobby, he took out his soft tan wallet, slid his credit card into the machine. I didn't want him to pay, I had money, all that cash, but my mind had disconnected from my body, signals firing without being relayed. I couldn't have put my hand in my rucksack and taken anything out. Couldn't.

The only time I hesitated was outside, between the glass doors of The Spitalfields and the open door of his car, it felt so final, I am going away from Millie and Kit, this can't be right, this is the opposite of what I want. I rocked on my heels, whispering, 'I don't know, I don't know.'

Daniel turned off the engine. He came round the car and crushed me to the dove-grey cotton of his shirt. Against him, I was speechless at the relief his body brought me, I can have this always now, even in broad daylight. He held me for so long that the breadth of his chest, the ram of his heart stopped feeling like the cracking open of a secret. It started feeling like a promise.

He talks to me as he drives, he says, 'You're a butterfly hurtling into my windscreen, I am swerving off-road,' 'I'm going to make you better like I did before, do you remember, do you remember?' He calls me 'Lolly' now without asking, without discussion. Lauren is gone. Soon, his voice fuses with the other sounds of the motorway – the swoop of traffic, a low horn, a siren. I don't know where we're going but the further we travel, the less it matters.

At service stations, he asks if I want to stretch my legs, eat something. I don't reply. He returns with treats, things he'd never eat, as if I'm a small animal he is tempting out of a hole – a bag of jelly babies, a bar of chocolate, fries. Untouched, they grow stale and hard against the car's leather interiors. At the next stop, he drops them in the bin.

In his car, I dream of Millie. She is having a tantrum at the bus stop, thrashing her head from side to side, smashing her heels against the pavement, the air ringing with the pitch of her screams. I try to wrap my arms round her, a desperate attempt at comfort, but she sinks her teeth into my skin, 'No! Not you! Daddy, I want Daddy!' I grasp the bite mark on my arm, blinking back tears, I take my eyes off her for no more than a second but it is a second too long; when I look up, she's gone. A bus is pulling

Dear Darling

away, window after window goes past and then I see her at the back, hands plastered against the glass. Her mouth is moving, she is saying something to me but I can't make out what, I am running, my mind white with panic and then the doctor whispers, 'We need to go,' because I am losing the baby. I jolt awake, a shout in my throat. Daniel says, 'It's going to be all right, you're going to be all right,' and I try to stop trembling, try not to fall asleep but I am so tired.

54

Loft

Now

The first thing I see is the sea, an iridescent turquoise so luminous I have to shield my eyes while they adjust to the light. Across the water is a shingle beach, backed by a forest of pines. It is the view from a set of French doors and then other things come into focus – a plush grey carpet, a carved wood dresser. Over my waist is a striped yellow throw. I touch the fabric beneath me – crisp, white cotton. I'm in a hotel.

'You're awake.' He sets down the journal he's reading, crouches beside me. He strokes my hair, a gesture that is both familiar and transgressive – his powerful fingers, the dark hair below his knuckles. Kit's hands are different, the hair so gold, it's imperceptible except by texture, by touch. A tear trickles down my cheek. Daniel wipes it away. 'You're okay. You're safe.'

'How did I get here?' My throat is so dry.

'You were asleep when we arrived. I carried you in.'

The image makes me wince. 'I don't remember.'

'You were exhausted.' He pours me a glass of water.

I gulp it down.

'Now, for some food, you need to keep up your strength, darling. There's not much around, pretty limited take-out options here. Or I can whip something up for you? A healthy breakfast, maybe? A salad?'

I cast around for a kitchenette, but don't see one.

'You can have whatever you want. I picked up a few things when you were asleep and the owners left us a welcome hamper with granola and fruit. You should see the kitchen now, it's absolutely huge, there's a utility room, a wine cellar, the whole place looks nothing like it looked before, it's been completely remodelled.'

I stare at him blankly.

'You don't recognise it?'

The way he says it sounds a faint alarm; there's a pulse of excitement I don't understand and then, the pieces click together. Pines. Shingle. Sea. 'It isn't the sea,' Alex once told me. 'It's an estuary.'

No.

It can't be.

'The cottage went through a couple of owners until someone finally pulled it down and built this, they still call it a "cottage" but it has six bedrooms, it sleeps twelve . . .' He tells me about the underfloor heating, the wood burner, he doesn't seem to notice the dawning terror, because I can see it now, the same view, the light on the water, I am exactly where the master bedroom used to be, and then I remember how I flung open the window here when I had morning sickness, the pink cross, the clinic, 'We need to go.' A sound comes from me, keening and low.

'Lolly? Lolly?'

I am shaking my head, it doesn't feel like mine at all, it is a rag doll shaken in the jaws of a dog.

'What's wrong?'

'I can't be here!' I stand up, but my will is too ferocious for my body, which buckles under me.

He holds my arm. 'You're okay, you're okay. Look at me.'

I tear my eyes away from the French windows. Focus on the perfect circle of his pupil.

'It's me, it's me, you're with me now, I'll look after you.'

'I don't want to be here,' I repeat, only now, in his grasp, I am just whispering.

'I should have realised, you have bad memories of this place, I'm sorry. It's different for me.'

'I can't, I can't.'

'That's fine, darling.' He strokes my hair. A long, mesmeric stroke. 'Your happiness is everything to me. Everything. Why don't you choose one of the other rooms? I'm sure we can find you somewhere else.'

I hold his hand, follow him out. Each step through the hallway makes me feel stronger, better, this isn't the cottage, not the narrow corridor of memory, it is wide and broad, well-lit and thickly carpeted. There is no study to my left with the trestle tables and killing jars, no single box room at the back. In their place are four huge bedrooms with high, sumptuous beds. I don't want any of them. A breeze blows through the house, I follow it, up a flight of stairs to a level that wasn't there before. A loft space opens before me, it is the entire length of the house, the walls, a cream clapboard. There is a bathroom to the left, a seating area and then, all the way at the end, a pair of neat twin beds fitted snugly under the sloped alcoves. The breeze is coming from an open window. I look through. The view is entirely different from the French windows downstairs, I can still see the water but there are no pines. I could be anywhere.

'Here?' he says, incredulously, just like he was when I chose the box room eighteen years ago. He doesn't like it. The loft is too low, he has to crouch beneath it.

I pull back the quilt. Slide into bed.

55

Estuary

Now

'Where's my phone?' I say to Daniel the next day after breakfast. Staring at the estuary, I am seized by the urge to identify its colour, I know how names can capture an object, hold them fast. But water is not an object, the limits of ordinary language insufficient to describe that chimeric blue, so I think again of the botanists, they came up with the first colour charts, they understood the importance of identification, categorisation.

He is arranging my plates on a tray, I'm not sure he has heard me. 'Daniel, where's my phone.'

He stops, clears his throat. 'I'm not sure that's a good idea.'

'What?' A single strand of anger vibrates in me. I am not asking for permission. 'Why not?'

'Darling.' He lays down the plates, comes back to my bedside. 'I don't want anything to upset you. Your husband, your daughter, the baby . . . you had a breakdown and no one noticed—' A sob rises in my throat. '—I've got you a little better, but you're still so fragile.' He kisses me on my forehead. 'What do you want it for? Is there something I can help you with?'

I raise my chin to the water. 'The blue.' My voice is strange and soft. 'I want to look up colour charts. Saccardo's *Chromotaxia*, Burchell's for Brazilian plants.'

He smiles, relieved that I am speaking about botanists again, not the law or banks or regulation. 'I will get these for you. You just tell me what you want and I'll get it for you. That is all you ever need to do.' He covers his hand over mine.

A day later, he brings me a package, slides out the books from the cardboard, parts the pages to show me the charts. I learn all the names for blue. But, as I watch the sea, I go beyond blue. The water is verditer when the estuary is full. Verdigris when the tide is low. Streaked with dragon's blood, vermillion and yellow ochre at sunset. Almost indigo before the light falls.

Daniel is right. I get better. I still dream but I don't shout anymore. The dreams have changed. Now, there is a man standing behind Millie on the bus. When I first saw him, I thought he was a stranger and I'd scream, but soon, the identity settles – it's Kit. Sometimes, he wears his light grey suit he's always looked so handsome in, other times, he's in jeans and the baseball cap I bought him. But although I wave at him, he doesn't recognise me, he reacts like I'm a crazy person, wrapping his arms round Millie, shielding her from me, from the desperate way I call after the bus.

Kit said, 'Dreams don't mean anything, they're just mental admin, the brain processing the day.' How true that is. Because eventually, I stop running after Millie. I blow her a kiss and, with my bursting heart, I wish her all the love in the world. I am processing that she is better off without me. I am processing that I am gone.

56

SHAMPOO

Now

The first time Daniel orders take-out, I think he'll ask me what I want – Kit and I always order from different places, he'll want burgers when I'll want Korean. But Daniel doesn't. He just hums 'The Girl from Ipanema' while he looks at his phone. He is choosing. This is what I've wanted all along. To have no responsibilities, to make no choices. I am not a wife, not a mother, not even an adult. Just a child.

He tidies up after me, cooks for me, feeds me, in these simple, domestic tasks, there are no glimpses of the vulnerability he showed me in London. He doesn't seem anxious, he doesn't sit in the dark, there are no migraines. He devotes himself to caring for me, he draws up a meal plan, cooks, cuts my food up into bite-sized portions. At lunch, he makes protein salads – heirloom tomatoes with prosciutto, cress overlaid with slices of beef, so rare, I taste the sharp iron of blood. Dinner is usually fish – lemon sole, sea bass, haddock – with a single glass of wine from the cellar. No carbs. I crave hunks of soft white bread, slathered with butter. Oven chips. Kit's Sunday morning waffles thick with chocolate spread.

At breakfast, he never brings coffee, only freshly squeezed juices or smoothies and, without fail, he'll make eggs, which I cannot stand. Kit knows why, once, Mama chased me around the kitchen with a sliced-open *pídàn* preserved egg, an Asian delicacy, the white a brown jelly, the yolk an ashen grey and, since then, I haven't been able to eat egg on its own, cannot separate the preserved egg from a normal one.

Today, he brings sourdough soldiers and half-boiled eggs. I dip the bread into the eggs, open my mouth. The yolk oozes from the bread, slides over my tongue. I think, *Look at what's happened. Your old hates, old desires, gone.* I meet Daniel's eyes and swallow.

'You should probably get a shower.'

He says that to me after he dabs egg whites from my mouth. He is staring at my empty plate, trying hard not to look at me, and I think I have broken down too much, I have let myself go too far. There was indulgence for me when we arrived but now, two days later, the novelty's worn off. Breakdowns are exhausting. Not just for the people having them.

I push back the covers. Daniel has sat down with a lepidoptery journal but I know he is watching me and I try to be any version of the person I was before I lost Faye, I can do it, the walk to the shower is no more than a few seconds, I lift my head up, try not to stumble. But, in the bathroom, any sense that I might have fooled Daniel is dispelled. Days-old eyeliner is smudged across my temples, mascara crusts at the corners of my eyes. My hair is lank and oily.

I peel off my T-shirt, the same one I wore at his mews house. My breasts are full and heavy, my nipples dark; even though I never breastfed, my whole body remains on high alert for Faye. I run my fingers over my stomach. The spasms have stopped now, it doesn't hurt as much but it's still numb. The midwife said this was nerve damage from the C-section, completely normal, it will get better if I sensitise it, rub it. *Rub it?* There is only one person who would have done that for me and he is in London with my daughter. I can't even look at it, the sad flop of skin, the angry scar. And I remember being here in this cottage, watching myself pull up my swimsuit, the flatness of my abdomen, my small breasts.

I stand under the shower. Try to recall what to do. There are expensive toiletries in the shower caddy in black glass bottles boasting essential oils of lemon, mandarin, rosemary. But beside those, there is a bottle of supermarket shampoo. I flip open the cap. Apple. Like I used eighteen years ago.

I know what Daniel's doing: he wants Lolly. The question is for me. Do I want her back? Do I want him and me?

I turn over the shampoo, let it spill out, mix with the water, fill the bathroom with its sweet, cheap condensation. I will do what he wants. I will let him bring her back.

I wear the clothes he buys for me – T-shirts, sweatpants, sweatshirts, plain knickers, no bras – they're expensive editions of the clothes I used to wear when I was fourteen – but strangely, he's bought them all in white. 'A new start,' he says, when he leads me to the full chest of drawers, 'a new you.'

I shower every evening; I change into these fresh clothes but I hate the white. It shows everything, my whole body is on display, perhaps that's what he wants, until it isn't. I catch him staring at my nipples through the fabric, I wait to see that familiar jolt of desire. But I don't. I'm struggling to identify exactly what I am seeing flit across his face, because it is so foreign to me, so unfamiliar, neither Daniel nor Kit have ever looked at me like that, until I realise what it is – disgust. I hug my arms over my chest. Try not to cry.

He handles it. One day, I come to the chest of drawers and find that every single item has been replaced in black, all the white gone. It reminds me of the door he punched through. How, one day, it just wasn't there anymore.

Everything is better in black, I am more comfortable, he is more comfortable, his eyes linger on me a little more, don't slide instantly away. But he doesn't sleep with me in the loft though there's an empty bed across from mine, he's in the master downstairs. Sometimes, if I think too hard about that, it feels suffocating, dangerous, it echoes too closely how things were when we first came to the cottage – parent's room, child's room, parent, child. I press my hand over my racing heart. Tell myself things are different now. We're adults. We have chosen each other.

Except, he never touches me. I tell myself he will soon, it's only been a few days, it will be like how it once was, but perhaps because I am fixated on it, I think he's touching me even less than before. He doesn't stroke my hair like he did when we first arrived or try to hold my hand, he doesn't repeat those things I've now let myself want, *You're rare, beautiful, astonishing, I'm still in love with you, it was always you.*

I try harder. I brush my teeth, I shower, I feed myself. I eat downstairs now. I let him show me the wine cellar excavated into the floor of the kitchen, feigning enthusiasm at the motorised door, the spiral steps. I listen to him talk for hours about new papers he's thinking of writing. Then, if the moment allows it, I reach for him, the stubble on his jaw, the softness of his lips, all that desire rushing back, he must feel it too, I was sure he felt it too.

But each time, he takes my palm, kisses it, hands it back to me. 'When you're better.'

Doesn't he realise? He is my healing, only he can close over the black hole of Faye, Millie, Kit. But he won't heal me.

57

MAP

Now

Daniel tells me that he's going to the field. 'The field?' He's spent the last few days in the loft with me; he is on his laptop while I read the books he bought. He's planning a comeback to lepidoptery, he's thinking of ideas for a research paper, arranging meetings with old colleagues. But I didn't realise there would be fieldwork. 'Not for Cornish Blues. Didn't they go extinct?'

'You've been paying attention.' He looks at me intently, just like he used to. My body shivers. 'They went extinct eighteen years ago, sometime after us.' He pauses, as if the end of our time together was as seismic as the extinction of a species. 'Now, it's just Holly Blues. Still, I think there's something there,' he says. For a split second, I feel like the last eighteen years haven't happened, no prison, no Kit, no children - he's snipped all that from the reel. A chill runs up my arm.

He isn't there when the couple arrive at the next-door cottage, he doesn't know that they have a baby, a baby who can't stop crying. Just hearing her makes my breasts swell – I can't read, I can't sketch. I press my forehead against the wall. When Millie was a few months old, she had colic. None of that reflux medicine worked, all that gave her an ounce of comfort was being strapped to my body, my back ached from it. I crave that pain now. I want to go down there, say, 'Give her to me. I'll hold her.' Instead, I pull a pillow round my ears and stare at the walls.

That's when I see the poster.

I'd dismissed it initially. The loft is intended for children, there are alphabet prints on the wall, a cupboard full of games; I assumed it was just another children's poster. But it's more than that. It's a map of the Helford – the land, the estuary, the open sea, the locations labelled in cursive looping font. I stare at it for so long, I stop hearing the baby, the places settling in my mind like sediment. I know these places because of Alex. He showed me ancient oaks at Frenchman's Creek, he told me the names of seaweed at Bosahan Cove. Trebah is the beach he said not to bother paying to enter, Port Navas is where he lived. I hadn't realised how close it was to Durgan, no more than the tip of my index finger. And I think no matter how much money Daniel has spent renting the cottage, or how long we stay here on the estuary, we are in Alex's country.

I've looked him up many times over the years. He became a skipper, took over *Forager*, he posts about his fishing business – repairs he had to make, dwindling mackerel stock, how he's started to export green velvet crab to Spain because there is no market here. But buried among these are morsels of his life – a date with his wife, a photo of his son, the coastal walk he does each year to mark the deaths of his father and his friend. He still dives for oysters. There was a photo of him in his diving gear, the wetsuit on his body, a pelt.

But thinking of him in Cornwall is very different from scrolling through his social media in London; I have thoughts I've never had before. Has he thought about me in the last eighteen years? Would he recognise me? What would he make of me back here?

Once I start thinking about Alex, I can't stop. He is in the estuary outside my window, in the nautical décor of the cottage – the fishing net wall hanging, the shelf of sea glass, a lobster pot on top of the kitchen counter – I'd think it all kitsch if I had a different history. Instead, I remember how he knew exactly where to drop lobster pots off the side of *Forager*, how he used to throw crab shells overboard for oysters to lay their spats in. He always thought of helping something on.

'Lolly?' says Daniel.

I turn to look at him. He is watching me from the kitchen island.

'You seem distracted.' He pads towards me with a bowl of salad, walks straight across the round door of the wine cellar. He's assured me that it's perfectly safe, the glass is reinforced, but I always skirt round it, convinced I'm going to crash through.

'Have you looked at the books I bought you?' he says, spooning tomatoes onto my plate.

'Not yet.' He put *The Origin of Species*, *Botanising in Britain* and *Saving Orchids* on the end of my bed a few days ago. I haven't told him I've read the first two before. That I'm not interested in orchids.

'You've barely touched the sketchpad and pencils.'

I don't reply.

Dear Darling

He puts down the salad. His eyes on me are flint. 'You will not get better, Lolly, unless you try.'

Grief yawns wide within me. Can this man, who knows everything about me, really believe I can get over losing one daughter and leaving the other by reading and drawing? I will never forgive myself for what I've done. Never.

I push my plate away. 'I want to go out.'

'What?'

'Out.'

'I'm not sure you're well enough, darling.'

This is the tenderest he's been in days. I stand up.

'Lolly, I want you to get better but—'

'Do you?' I push his hand away. 'I wonder.'

58

STRANDLINE

Now

When I start going to the beach, Daniel comes out with me in the mornings, although after two days, we're both glad that he is busying himself at the post office in Falmouth or the field. He doesn't like it that I grip his arm as we walk down from the cottage, he likes it even less when I tell him it's because the twisty Cornish roads, guarded by hedgerows, make me think of the boy he killed. He doesn't like the feel of the sand or the sun on his laptop or the fact that whenever I hear a child shouting, my head swivels.

'You need to stop,' Daniel says, putting his hand on my shoulder after I jumped at the sound of a boy calling his mother over to see a crab he's found.

'I can't help it.'

'She's not here.'

'She might be.'

He stares at me through his aviators, although I cannot see his eyes. 'You need to be with me, in this moment. Not somewhere else.'

Wasn't that my struggle in London? That I was a half person, my attention always divided? I thought if I came with Daniel, I would resolve that once and for all. Why am I still in pieces?

Once Daniel leaves, I don't startle anymore. I give myself over to people-watching. I see Millie in every child, Kit in every man. He is the twenty-year-old student who buys iced frappés for him and his girlfriend. He is the grandfather who takes an order of six ice creams, remembers all the different flake and sauce combinations. He is the dad digging an enormous hole for his two sons. Kit once carved a car for Millie in the sand, sculpted a bonnet, seats, lifted her wriggling into the centre, then buried her, and suddenly, this life with Daniel – books and drawing and bans on carbs – seems unbearably empty.

I start walking the strandline, like I'd do if Millie and I were at the beach, I start collecting. I taught her what Alex taught me, that the strandline – the jagged bands of seaweed – are the best place to find anything because sea glass, shells, drift seeds get tangled. When Daniel sees the buckets I am bringing back to the cottage, he's pleased. 'I knew it would work, bringing you here. Can you see? You're coming back to yourself.'

I am. But not to the fourteen-year-old he wants me to be; I don't collect pine cones or seaweed. Instead, I pocket pink striped shells for Millie. Bits of Lego for Kit – a red flipper, a scuba tank, a life raft. Pure white scallop shells for Faye. And for myself, tiny shards of blue sea glass, incredibly rare, from centuries-old poison bottles.

'Why are you just collecting those four types of things?' asks Daniel, coming up behind me, as I wash them in the sink. 'It's not botany.'

'I just like them,' I say lightly.

'Sometimes I have no idea what goes on in that head of yours.'

I keep washing the sand off.

'You know what it reminds me of?' he says, his eyes trailing up and down my collection. 'Voodoo.'

He's so close. This wreckage calls me home.

59

SEA HEART

Now

I'm floating at the secret beach now, my old favourite, when I see him. I push myself upright, my feet catching on the slimed rocks beneath me. Water ripples through my hair, I could be dreaming or drowning.

He is standing above me. His face in shadow, it might not be him, and then the sun moves over his features and I know it is.

'Lauren?' he says.

Alex.

He's grinning. I'd forgotten his grin but, now I see it, I'm not sure how I could have forgotten it. 'I can't believe it! It's you!' He is growing a beard and he's smaller than the image in my head. But then, I was only a child when I knew him. 'How many years has it been?'

'Eighteen,' I say automatically and then my brain crashes into that number. Until I said it, I hadn't realised that when I lost Daniel, I lost Alex too. My oldest friend. Possibly my only friend. A wave crests at my chest, splashing water over my cheek. I wipe it away.

'I was on *Forager* when I saw you. I had to paddle out and check.'

'Do you often check on floating women?' I say lightly.

'Only ones that could be you.' He's smiling but the look he gives me is serious and I have the sense that just being here with him is dangerous; I am on the precipice of something, about to fall in. But I can't help it.

He holds out his hand. I take it. Standing in front of him, everything passes between us – the pregnancy test, how he came to the cottage that morning, drift seeds, seaweed, *Forager* – and then, I let go of age and time and throw my arms around him. He hugs me back, so tightly I nearly forget everything that's happened.

'I've drenched you,' I say, when we come apart.

He plucks at the wet patches on his faded Adidas T-shirt. 'I'm a fisherman, I don't care. You, on the other hand, are soaked.' He lifts his chin. 'Do you feel like coming on *Forager*?'

'Always.'

I swim behind him, through the water, I can feel the force of his strokes. He lifts himself effortlessly onto the boat and then he steadies me as I clamber in. I am so clumsy, I want to apologise for being so much heavier, so much older than I once was, but I stop myself. Absurd. We're both older, heavier.

'Sit down,' he says, after he's helped me over the side. 'Let me get you a towel.'

I don't sit. I greet *Forager* in the only way I know how, trailing my fingers over the knots in the bench, the iron chains, the spill of nets.

Dear Darling

He hands me a towel, an old T-shirt, board shorts, a hoodie. I change in the cabin. The hoodie is a faded violet, once blue perhaps, tears splitting the rim of the hood. I slip it on. It smells so clean.

We smile stupidly at each other when I step out.

'Well, how are you?' he starts.

I want to tell the truth. I want to say, *I lost my baby. I left my husband and my daughter. I'm here with the man you helped me escape from*, and I wish there is something else I could say that's true, that means, *I'm treading water, I'm surviving, please don't ask me anymore, I can't bear it.* Instead, I say, 'Fine.'

He smooths the aluminium of the gunwale. I have not been convincing.

'You've done well,' I say quickly, gesturing to the newly painted deck, the hatch. 'You did exactly what you said you were going to.'

He scratches his chin. 'I said that, did I? That I wanted to be a skipper?'

'All the time.'

He laughs softly.

'Do you love it?'

'Nothing beats pulling a catch from the sea.'

I believe him.

'How about you?'

'I'm a lawyer.' Another half-truth; I'm nothing now. Maternity leave has slid into bereavement leave, which, surely, after my disappearance, has come to an end.

He lets out a low whistle, runs his hand through his hair. 'Didn't see that coming. What happened to being a scientist?'

'I moved past it.' As if botany was a teenage fad, no more than a hobby.

'Are you here on holiday?'

I nod.

'With family?'

My heart is in my throat. 'They couldn't make it this time.'

'Well,' he says, stretching out, his body still so lean. 'Lucky I saw you.' He appraises me from the other side of the boat. 'You look exactly the same.'

'Impossible.' I cross my arms over my scar-ridden stomach, conscious of my thickened arms, the fat under my chin, all the things Daniel sees and now, I see too.

'Yeah, you do.'

My cheeks flush.

'You know I called you hundreds of times after I left you at the station.'

'I thought you might have.'

'You never answered.'

'I threw my phone away.' I remember opening my palm, letting it slip in the gap between the platform and the train, hearing it thud against the tracks.

'Will you tell me what happened after?' he asks gently. 'You don't have to if you don't want to. It's just that I've always worried, wondered.'

I slip my hand into the hole of the life ring, feel its solid rubber under my fingers, I wish it could save me in the way I need to be saved but wishing is for children and I am all grown up now. 'I had an abortion.'

He flinches and I hate myself, my words, my tone of voice, why did I say it so coldly? I don't know him anymore, I have no idea what his beliefs are, his politics, but then he says, 'Lauren, I'm so sorry,' and I realise I've got this completely wrong. He isn't flinching because of *what I did*. He is flinching *for me*. And I think this is so much worse than his judgement, seeing the desperation of my choices reflected on his features.

'I wish I could have been there for you.'

His words leave me breathless. *Been there for me?* During that time in Mrs Hannington's study, I never let myself think about him, never let myself miss him, and I understand then, the tyranny of my shame, all the things it's shut out.

'You know, I tried to find you. But all I knew was your first name and that you were from London and you liked plants. Wasn't much to go on. There are a lot of Laurens.'

In my chest, a firework bursts. 'I found you on Facebook,' I confess. 'I read all your posts, watched all your videos.'

'Why did you never message me?'

'I didn't know what to say.' I still don't.

His fingers toy with the rope. He is itching for the nets, for the winch, not this. Normal people don't have space for the broken ones, like Daniel and me. That's how it should be.

But Alex surprises me. He is as brave as an adult as he was as a child. 'Were you okay?'

I meet his eyes, that transparent green. This is another chance, isn't it? To let someone in. I could never do it, not completely, not with Alex or Mrs Hannington or Kit, I only ever gave them a sliver of me, never the whole. Even now, I still haven't learnt that lesson, I can't do it.

'It was rough,' I say. He waits to see if I will say any more but I can't. 'It's not like you've had it easy either. I read you lost your father. What happened?'

He rubs the side of his face. 'There'd been weeks of heavy snow, poor visibility so finally, when the forecast was calm, Dad and I were raring to get out. It was flat at the start and sunny, but then the swell grew suddenly, I'd never seen the sea change that quickly and then there was an entire horizon of water coming towards us, it sounded like a train.' He cups one hand over his ear, as if he can still hear it. 'I got tangled in the net, I was towed under but when I surfaced, I couldn't find Dad. Nothing around me but fish boxes.'

My hand is over my mouth.

'After that, I made a rule – no fishing with family or friends – it was too much, I'd already lost a friend to a car accident, he died right before my eyes, and then to lose Dad—' He breaks off, twisting his thumb and forefinger round his wrist and that single gesture takes me back to when we were children, sharing hard, hurtful things.

I cross the boat, put my hand on his shoulder. Instantly, he stops twisting and then he and I are thinking the same thing, that we are in each other's bones, under each other's skin, that on this boat, on these estuary waters, we forged a friendship that meant something then. Maybe it still does.

'I wish I'd reached out,' I say.

'Yeah.'

'I'm sorry.'

He shrugs. 'You're here now. We're both here. Still standing.'

Barely.

'I read you got a new boat,' I say, changing the subject.

'You saw that, did you? *Sea Heart*'s nearly ready to go, I just need to get the engine replaced, the old one was spilling its guts all over the bilge.'

'Why the name?'

'I thought you of all people would know.'

I must look confused because he says, 'You don't remember?'

'Remember what?'

He reaches into the pocket of his shorts, holds out his fist, drops something flat and circular into my palm. It's a drift seed, the colour of melted chocolate, a black seam round it. The width of my lost baby's palm.

'*Drift Seed* wasn't the best name for a boat. But *Sea Heart*, that's a solid name.'

I feel its shine in my palm. 'You kept looking.'

'I never stopped. Haven't found many over the years, no more than eight. This one's the best, it's the first one I found after we started. Won't go fishing without it.' He sniffs. 'When we got hit by that wave and I was towed under, all I could think about was that drift seed, it was there, in my pocket, I prayed to it, that I would come through, see my wife, Martha, again—' I wipe tears from my eyes. '—And I did. Then, when Martha lost the baby—'

'She lost her baby?' It is foreign to me. That it could happen to another person. I've been so consumed by my private grief.

He nods. 'I gave it to her. I met an Icelandic fisherman who told me it was a birth charm. Then, we had Seb.'

'I lost my baby,' I say suddenly, and it is awful and freeing. I hadn't realised how much I'd wanted to say it.

'When?'

'A few weeks ago.' I look back to Durgan, the curve of beach, the cottage. How small it looks.

He says nothing for a long time, just watches me, our bodies swaying with the rhythm of the boat. Then, he closes my hand over the drift seed. 'Take it.'

'I couldn't.'

'It's yours.'

'But it's your lucky charm.'

'I have seven others. Besides, I started looking for them for you.'

'Thank you.' I slip it into my pocket.

He walks back to the cabin; he is writing something down. When he comes out, he says, 'Do you remember when we were kids and I used to ask you how you were? You always said fine and I believed you. But you weren't.' He presses the paper into my hand. 'This is my number, my email, my address. You don't have any excuses anymore. Don't do that thing you do.'

'That thing I do?'

He looks at me with so much emotion in his eyes. 'Vanish.'

I don't tell Daniel about Alex. I tell him I found a sea heart. Daniel smiles. 'Your focus is coming back; do you feel it?' To reward me, he buys me the book I ask for on drift seeds. When the package arrives, I tear it open.

Alex was right about sea hearts being birth charms. In Iceland, they call them *lausnarsteein*, in Norwegian, *losningsstein*, and the meaning of both is the same: a loosening stone. To loosen a baby safely from its mother, just as this seed has been loosened from its tree and carried safely to a shore thousands of miles away.

Dear Darling

I worry it constantly, brush its shiny casing with my thumb so often, I am afraid I will break it when thousands of kilometres of sea have not. At night, I lay it against my cheek, I press it to my lips, the scar across my stomach, during the day, I hold it secretly in my pocket. Maybe it will stop me from drowning too.

60

STUDY

Now

I'm not sure if it's real or memory when I see it.

It's afternoon. I've just come back to the cottage from swimming, I'm still in my wet clothes, leaving puddles all over the floor that I'll need to dry before Daniel returns from the field, any reminder that I have been in the water irritates him. I'm heading upstairs, when something catches my eye. The master bedroom door is shut, Daniel knows I don't like to see it. But the door of the room beside it is open. Inside, there's a flicker of blue.

I cross the landing. Push open the door.

It's the same simple set-up: trestle table; lamp; laptop. To the left are lepidoptery tools: glassine envelopes; bottles of entomological pins; spreading boards; a dish of wax paper. To the right is a bottle of ethyl acetate and a row of killing jars. Four are washed and dried, no streaks on the glass, but in the fifth, there is a layer of plaster of Paris soaked in ethyl acetate. And, on the plaster, is a Cornish Blue.

It can't be. It must be a Holly Blue, like Daniel said. Under the table is a pile of lepidoptery journals, a stack of field guides.

I find an old edition of *Butterflies of Britain*, turn to the section on Cornish Blues and Holly Blues, compare what I'm reading to the creature in the jar.

It *is* a Cornish Blue. Male. The vibrant blue of its wings. Velvety margins. Black spots on the upper side. The Holly Blue has black spots only on the underside.

My mind is whirring. This is important but I don't know why, it's like having an answer to a question I haven't asked and then, two parts of myself collide, my adult self – methodical, analytical – and Lolly. Not the Lolly Daniel wants but the real Lolly, who kept secrets, who went brazenly through his things. I run my hands over every inch of the trestle table, remove each of the journals and field guides beneath. When I don't find anything, I start on the rest of the room.

I find them almost instantly under the bed, I don't think he's even trying to hide them, it's just a convenient place to put them away. Two simple plastic boxes with snap-locks. I tremble a little pulling them onto my lap, I feel like I've been trawling through the dark, my net is full of monstrous things – tentacles and suckers and teeth – I don't want to look in but I have to. I unclick the latches of one of the boxes. There are a handful of glassine envelopes, the same envelopes on the trestle table. Inside each one, folded neatly in half, are dead Cornish Blues.

I don't understand. How is Daniel netting Cornish Blues when they're extinct?

My mind is lurching, I need answers now. I unlatch the second box. Pull out a stack of neatly stapled journal articles. Force myself to read every single word.

I wrap my arms round myself after I finish. Two things are clear. First, the Cornish Blues did go extinct eighteen years ago. But second, shortly afterwards, a programme was started to reintroduce the Blues to secret sites in the UK.

The thyme field.

My fingers are trembling as I reach for the last item in the box. It's very Daniel, a small, calf leather notebook, his initials monogrammed in gold, although I've never seen it before. It opens easily; the spine soft from use. My heart is racing so fast, it takes some time before I understand that what I'm looking at is a ledger, hundreds of pages long, setting out details of butterflies – species, sub-species, male, female, wingspan, the date it was caught. The first dates back over thirty years ago. The last dates to yesterday. This makes sense, he's a scientist, he was always going to record what he caught, surely, that's what we were doing eighteen years ago, recording the number of Blues, releasing them.

But it is the last two columns that explain why I've never seen this book. They set out the addresses where the butterflies were sent. And their price.

There is a sound behind me. I turn round.

He is standing at the doorway. The last of the light shines on his face – the planes of his cheekbones, his dark eyes. The rest is shadow. 'What are you doing?'

I shut the notebook. Let it sit on my palm. 'I think the question is, what are you doing?'

His eyes flitter over the trestle table, the Blue in the killing jar, the open plastic boxes, trying to decipher the conclusions I've drawn, the secrets I know.

'You're hunting them, aren't you? Driving them to extinction. For money.'

For a while, he doesn't respond. When he finally does, he speaks quietly, as if he isn't speaking to me at all but to himself. 'What am I supposed to do? I can't go back to being a lepidopterist. No one wants to hire a criminal. And you know as well as I do that the Cornish Blues are so valuable, they're as protected as snow leopards.'

'Snow leopards are endangered,' I say slowly. 'Cornish Blues are extinct.'

'Exactly, exactly!' He gestures excitedly, like I've suddenly grasped a concept he's been trying for hours to teach me. 'Eighteen years ago, when they were endangered, their prices were already through the roof, they sold for more than Queen Alexandra's Birdwings. But now, when no one knows if the reintroduction programme is working, when they're *technically* extinct, their price has skyrocketed.' He sounds like an investment banker, analysing fluctuations in investments, triple shorting extinction. No wonder he was so harsh about me going into law. I am nothing but a mirror. Hold me up and he sees himself. 'And with the connections I've made—'

Is that what he's been doing in prison?

'—It's much easier now to move the Blues across borders. Don't you see? At this point, when the Blues are at the tipping point between extinction and comeback, we're in the best possible place.'

We?

'It's an absolute gold mine. Hundred per cent profit. No poachers, no middleman, they're caught by us, verified by us, straight from the field to the collectors.'

'From farm to table.'

He stares at me. I stare back, until the truth is bare and trembling before us: I don't condone this, I want nothing to do with this. His eyes soften, I think I see triumph there and pride, my refusal to be corrupted a tribute to the man he's pretended to be, because he starts to backtrack. 'It's just until I get back on my feet.'

'Stop.' I'm suddenly so tired. I hold up his notebook. 'I read this. I saw the dates. You've been doing it for years. What were you selling back then? Museum specimens? Scientific samples? All those fancy dates you used to take Mama on, your house, the money for Wyatt, it's so obvious now. You would never have got that kind of money from being a lepidopterist. No way.'

He blinks back tears, I think he will plead with me, promise to be different, but the tension in the air seems to peak, then fade. He doesn't move. He stays at the doorway, looking down at me in the fallen light. 'I guess it was time.'

'What does that mean?'

'It means you're not fourteen anymore.' His voice is harsh now, harsher than I've ever heard it. 'Now you know what all this takes.' He gestures at the cottage around us. 'You said it yourself. There's no money in biology.'

I shut my eyes. Remember how, in a makeshift study very much like this, I dropped Blues into killing jars, watched the slow drain of their power, the final beat of their wings. I spread them on boards. I pinned them. For him.

'You were a god to me,' I whisper. 'A scientist. A conservationist. You were my hero.'

His eyes pass slowly over me. My bare legs. The towel round my swollen middle. The tangle of my hair, dark with sea water. 'I guess we're both not who we once were.'

61

Field

Now

At dinner, he pretends nothing's wrong. Or maybe he's relieved. My discovery of his secret is a burst dam, everything rushing out, he doesn't stop talking about how much he's sold the last pair for, the swarms in the field, how out of practice he feels. 'I used to net seventy butterflies in one day, do you remember?' I watch his lips move and remember all the times he spoke about the moral corruption of John Sloane, the habitats cleared for palm oil, how he always encouraged me to be a naturalist, a botanist, a conservationist. I think, *Who are you?*

He kisses me on the forehead the next morning before he heads out with his nets. I watch him disappear into the woods and then, when he is out of sight, I sink to the floor. I take in the room – the square window, the cotton weave of the corner sofa, the log burner – I let my gaze fall over each object very slowly because I know, as soon as I stand up, I will have to confront the wreckage of a single question: if Daniel's lied to me about this, what else is he lying about?

My fourteen-year-old thoughts rush in – I could ransack his bedroom, hack his laptop – but I know I won't find anything. Or, I could smash those killing jars, I could make a bonfire, there's wood outside, I want a conflagration with glassine envelopes, dead blue wings, neatly stapled lepidoptery articles, watch that disgusting notebook turn to ember. But what use would that be? What I need to do is cut through his bone, read in the gory mess of his brain, his torn-out heart, all the things he's done. But that's impossible.

I stand up. Pull on my trainers. Blood pounds in my head, so loud, I can't hear my soles crunching up pine cones or the crash of the waves. I will do the adult thing, the hard thing, I will confront him. I will tell him face to face that I can't bear any more lies, I will ask him, as the person who's been in love with him most of her life, what the fuck is going on.

I see the Blues as soon as the wood opens out to the thyme, secret location, what secret location, there should be a land marshal, security, they're so obvious to anyone who might be searching for them. Flashes of blue and brown flit in and out of the herbs, swooping low, before shooting out with stuttered, sudden flight. I lean against the turnstile, watching them. Breathtaking. If it weren't for Daniel, I'd never be able to appreciate this. But he is also wiping them out. Selling extinction. How can there be so much good among the bad?

He doesn't net with as much vigour as I remember but there's still an agility in his movements, an absolute stillness where he calculates when to twist his wrist, when to swoop down. He always knew where to put his body.

I watch him for hours.

Then, he turns. Not towards me. But behind him. Over the thyme.

It's a girl. She is walking towards him, dark, shiny hair skimming her waist, ripped jeans, trainers, wrists stacked with rainbow friendship bracelets, a slogan T-shirt, '1970' emblazoned in black. Serious. Beautiful. No more than fourteen.

He stops as she approaches. Puts down his net. Turns his absolute stillness onto her. A sound comes from me like a freshly slit throat, because that look, those eyes – starred navy, freckled cobalt – are what I left my daughter, my husband for – in that look is everything he promised me, *You're utterly rare, astonishing.* But he doesn't hear me. Because he isn't looking at me. He is looking at her.

He doesn't hug her. He knows to take it slow. She gives him a small, self-conscious wave. He smiles like he used to smile at me in the museum. Like this is normal, this is nothing.

He is chatting with her, I can't hear what they're saying, though I can imagine it, he is asking her more questions about her interests, no hard topics, everything easy. Her phone buzzes, she slips her hand in the pocket of her jeans to retrieve it and her hair falls over her face. She cannot see him but I can.

His lips part.

He almost had me. He almost convinced me that I was the one for him, I was all he thought about, all that held him together in prison when it had broken so many others, nothing else mattered, not age or consent, how could any of that matter in the face of our seismic, earth-shattering collision? He made me think it was my fault. If I'd just trusted him, waited for him, nothing bad would have happened, not the abortion or being a bad wife, a bad mother, because we would have been together.

We would not have been together.

Because I could never have stayed fourteen.

He points to a Blue darting in and out of the thyme. He picks up his net. He models how to wait, how to swipe. She bites her bottom lip when he offers it to her. Gives him a shy smile when he encourages her. She wipes her hands on her jeans before taking the handle. She's nervous. I was nervous my first time, too.

She catches one, first time, better than me, she has it against the ground. She calls to him. He extracts it deftly, elegantly from the gauze, cups it in his expert palms. He lifts his chin. She opens her hands.

I shut my eyes, turn round, rush back through the woods, sending squirrels scurrying, pine cones flying, I wish I was brave but I am not, I cannot bear to see the flutter of wings light up her face. How could I not have realised he's caught me, when I've watched him catch so many things? Needles fill my trainers but I don't care, I want to hurt. Stab through my soft stupidity, puncture my vanity, peel my foolishness back to the bone. The no-carb diet. The teenage clothes. The shampoo. I thought it might have been enough. It would never have been enough.

Something sends me stumbling to the ground, a tree root perhaps or a fallen branch, my hands scrabble for a trunk or some bark to stop my fall but find nothing. My chin rakes across the ground. I am sprawled out on the forest floor. I let myself weep then. For the clump of soil melting on my tongue, the beetle that runs over my hand. This is what loving him has got me.

Dear Darling

Bracken canopies over me, huge and ancient, filtering the light green. I reach out, touch the underside of the fronded leaves, brush my fingertips across scored rows of beaded spore cases. Distantly, I remember a fact from my botany days – when insects, like butterflies, damage the fronds, the bracken releases a poison that breaks open their exoskeletons, turns them inside out.

Nothing is defenceless. Nothing.

I spit soil from my mouth. Sit up.

62

CANDLELIGHT

Now

I'm waiting for him when he comes in from the field, I open the door. He stares at me, surprised, rests his nets carefully on the floor of the porch. 'Lolly?'

I am wearing a black dress. It is the only formal thing Daniel bought me, it has ridiculously thin straps, a soft, billowing skirt. If Kit saw me in this, he'd give a low whistle. But Daniel isn't Kit. He stops abruptly in front of me, takes excruciating seconds running his eyes over the scrubbed planes of my cheeks, my clavicles, my thinner arms. He swallows. I go up on my tiptoes, kiss his cheek so he can feel how small I am next to him, like he loves.

'You look—' He cannot finish.

'Do you like?' When I got back, I prepared myself very carefully, conditioning my hair, brushing it out, blow-drying it, applying the slightest hint of make-up. The pine needles, the mud are all gone.

'I do.' He shuts his eyes, inhales. The apple shampoo. I used it all over.

Dear Darling

'Come, sit.'

'You've made dinner?' He glances at the small, round dining table. In the shadow of twilight, he takes in the cutlery carefully placed on folded, checked napkins, the bowls of olives and artichokes, the enormous salad with quartered heirloom tomatoes. A smile plays on his lips. He's taught me well. I've done it exactly as he would.

I strike a match to light the candles, then snuff out the burning end. A vein of smoke drifts over the table. 'I thought we could celebrate.'

'What are we celebrating?' He shrugs off his jacket, sits while I pour water.

'Us.'

'I thought perhaps, after yesterday—'

'—Oh, don't worry about that. You were right. I just needed to think things through.'

'I knew you'd come around! You just needed to see the potential, how much we can make, when you see it in those terms, it would be insanity not to. Tomorrow, I'll show you how I contact the buyers, the kind of quality they want, it's easy really—'

'—Tomorrow,' I cut him off. 'Tonight, I want to celebrate.'

'Of course.' He's smiling at me, he takes his water glass, waits for me to lift mine.

'Oh. We can't toast like this.'

'Can't we?'

'It's bad luck. Everyone knows that.' My heart is racing very fast. 'Can you get something from the wine cellar?'

'There's not much good stuff down there anymore.'

'It doesn't matter what it is.'

'I can go out, buy something—'

'—Daniel?' I reach out. Spread my fingers over the base of his throat, evoke my museum seduction, the press of my index finger against his pulse, my thumb on the jut of his clavicle. Any opposition loosens in him. He is quiet. Pliant. 'I want us to celebrate now. You and me. The next chapter of our rare, astonishing lives.'

He blinks. This is the illusion of candlelight. In soft glow, in flickering flames, the fine lines around my eyes are almost invisible, the bulge of my post-partum stomach is in shadow. When he speaks, he's hoarse with emotion. 'You're right. Let me get a bottle.'

He stands up.

I follow. Stop at the edge of the wine cellar built into the floor.

Beneath the round glass door, the spiral stairs are dark with shadow but then, he flicks on two switches. LED lights illuminate the shelves. The door lifts up. It takes three seconds for it to open, three seconds for it to shut, I checked earlier this afternoon. He steps in, shuddering at the sudden drop in temperature, goes down the swirl of steps, past empty shelves, all the way to the bottom, where I have relocated all the bottles. He slides out a red, examines the label. 'I wish I'd known you were making a special dinner, I would have bought something, that would have been better than any of this.'

I press the switch.

One. Two. Three.

63

Cellar

Now

He stares at me from below, not quite understanding what's just happened. 'Stop playing, Lolly, it's cold down here.'

I drag a dining chair to the edge of the glass, sit down. He blinks at me. There is a beautiful handful of seconds when he searches for a catch that will release him, his fingers flutter over every surface because surely, there's a safety switch in the unlikely event you get stuck in the cellar.

There's no safety switch. I've checked.

Realisation settles over him, wings coming to rest. I wonder if he sees the irony of this, he who's imprisoned so many things. He holds out his hands in surrender, as if I'm playing a prank, all right, all right, you got me. 'What's going on?' he asks.

'We need to talk.'

'I'm happy to talk to you, always, I just don't see why it has to be in here.'

'You will.'

'Darling.' He circles the cellar while he stares up at me. He reminds me of a panther I saw in London Zoo that paced back and forth, measuring the dimensions of its captivity. It couldn't quite believe it had been caged. 'Open this door. You're not well. You're not yourself.'

'I'm the best I've been in a long time.' I stretch my arms over my head, feel the barest of twinges. All that pain almost gone.

'Look, is this about the Blues?' He rubs his forehead. 'Because I was up all night thinking about what you said and I wanted to tell you . . .' he makes an expansive gesture, 'you're right, Lolly, you're right, I'm not the man I should be. But I want to be better, you make me want to be better.' It's a clumsy lie – five minutes ago, he was ecstatic that he'd persuaded me to hunt the Blues, and I wonder if all his lies have been this transparent, if I've just been too blind to see them. 'That conversation we had yesterday, only *you* could have had that with me. Who else would have worked it out? I need you, you're only person who can hold me accountable, I need that, I need—'

'—I followed you today.'

That silences him. His lips part but nothing comes out.

'Who is she?'

'I don't, I don't think—' His hands cover his face, he is processing the bomb I've just detonated, the rubble in us both. 'I'm not sure that would be helpful to go into.'

'I think it would be very helpful.'

He pinches the bridge of his nose. A migraine. He hasn't had one since we've been in Cornwall because I've never challenged him and then I realise his migraines are just symptoms of his lies, mental screams before his mind twists every depraved thing into something acceptable. 'It's not what you think.'

'Let me guess. She's interested in butterflies. She doesn't know anyone else who is. You're helping her. Teaching her. Nothing to do with the fact that she's a *child*.'

'I – I –' His hands open, shut, grasp an empty shelf, and I see suddenly, the old man he'll become – stuttering, frightened, confused. He shuts his eyes. 'Nothing happened.'

'But you want it to.'

He shakes his head.

I say it then. The word that's fluttered inside me for years. I thought I was brave when I said 'consent' and 'rape' but now, as it darts to the tip of my tongue, I understand they're a kindness compared to this. I was saving him from it. Or myself. 'You're a paedophile.'

'What?' The old man vanishes. In his place is something wild – flashing eyes, bared teeth.

'A paedophile.'

For a second, he is still, just his right hand convulses. Then, his control goes. He flies at me, covering the distance of the stairs. The force of him, the speed, brings a sudden blank fear – I jump out of my chair, it topples over. 'Don't you call me that. Ever!' His eyes bore into me as he pulls his arm back and swings the bottle against the cellar door. The glass shatters.

I stumble, reaching clumsily for anything to steady me – the edge of the countertop, the cool brick of the wall – and in that moment, I realise how terrified I am, a primal fear of his hands across my throat, his fist on my face, and I am astounded that I was ever confused about his intentions towards me when now, they are so appallingly clear. This man wants to hurt me.

But he can't.

Because he was right about the cellar door. The safety glass, though shattered, is reinforced. Not a single piece falls.

I peel my fingers off the island. Blood is still rushing round my head, my heart is hammering but I force myself to look at him. His eyes on me blaze; once, I wouldn't have been able to bear that. But once, I wanted to be a thing in his jar. I walk slowly over to the shattered cellar door. Tap it with my toe. Nothing happens.

'Let me out,' he whispers. 'You let me out.'

I pick up the chair. Sit back down.

He drops the neck of the bottle; it smashes at his feet and then he smacks his palms against the door, over and over.

I fix my eyes on a single crack until the blur of movement stops.

He is slumped on the steps, his face in his hands. 'What do you want from me?'

'Everything.' I get off the dining chair, sit cross-legged above him. We are two people whispering in the dark, all that love and damage between us. 'Tell me,' I say very gently, 'how did it start?'

He puts his hand over his mouth.

'Please.'

He pauses fractionally; this secret could be another card to play. But then he wipes his eyes, gives me an odd, resigned smile and I know he's going to tell me. There's no one else. It must be such a relief. To tell the truth for once. 'It started with Lolly.'

The name cuts me in two.

'My father was a soldier, he was posted to a base in the Philippines. It was immense, thousands of hectares reaching over the Sierra Madre mountains, all the way to the Pacific. It was so vast, it had its own forest.' He laughs at the memory. 'Every few months, these illegal loggers would come with bulldozers and chainsaws and cart off truckfuls of timber. It caused a scandal. A military base, invaded by logging companies.'

His voice takes me back to the stories he'd tell me in his lab. I want to close my eyes.

'My dad wasn't that interested in me, I wasn't his kind of boy, didn't want to play football or wrestle, all I wanted to do was fill up jars from the forest with huge, prickly stick insects, giant crab spiders, yellow crazy ants, vicious little biters, once, they escaped through a crack in the glass and my dad went ballistic.' He chuckles. 'The forest was also where I first started catching butterflies – Peacock Swallowtails, Green Dragontails, Glassy Tigers, I didn't know what they were at the time, or how to preserve them. She taught me.'

A forest unzips in my mind, I am choking on wings and petals.

'She was a tiny slip of a thing, twelve, thirteen, I felt enormous next to her, though I was the same age. She was an incredible catcher. I dream about her sometimes, climbing trees, waiting for the perfect moment to squeeze their thorax, kill them instantly...'

Ruthless. Practical. All those things I'd admired about him.

'Her family were tenant farmers, she'd string the butterflies up, sell them for nothing to help out.' He laughs. 'They weren't even what she was looking for. She was searching for tiny orange flowers. Later, when I looked into it, I was almost certain she was looking for these miniature orange orchids, endemic to that area, extraordinarily rare.'

He gave me a book on orchids. He was always trying to make me into her.

'She said, "Lola" all the time, a name I hadn't heard before, so I called her an English word I knew, something that was close enough, "Lolly." Years later, I found out "Lola" means "grandmother" in Tagalog. She'd been talking about her grandmother, not herself. I never knew.'

The name he gave her, the name he gave me, nothing more than a mistranslation.

'Then, one day, she was gone. After the logging scandal, the military took a stronger line on protecting the base; her family were living on the reservation. They tore down her house without notice, without warning. I never saw her again.' He presses his fists to his eyes. 'After that, I struggled. Perhaps it was grief or sadness or being alone again but I never got over her. I had girlfriends in the Philippines and in London but they never worked out, they weren't like her, never interested in the natural world like she was, they were too old—'

Something in me snags. *They were too old*. I stare at him. My own morbid curiosity lured me down the jungle tracks of his mind but I refuse to follow him any longer. I will not go further and further into black. He was lonely. He lost his childhood girlfriend. That doesn't mean he wasn't responsible for what he did. It doesn't absolve him.

'Then, one day, I knocked on the door of a dingy flat in Queensway to value some rare Singaporean butterflies, and there you were. A botanist with butterflies.'

The words break me. They were the first words he ever said to me, I've held onto them as cold, hard proof that we were meant to be together right from the beginning, we were so similar, my passion for botany, his passion for butterflies, we were naturalists, scientists, our love forged in wings, in leaves. But we're nothing but ghosts. Ghosts in love with ghosts, in love with ghosts.

Dear Darling

I wrap my arms round myself.

'When I saw you in your living room, what you said, the way you clutched those butterflies, my heart almost left my chest. I thought, I've found her.'

I want the glass to swallow me up. I want all these jagged edges to rip through me. I want to be the nothing that I am. The nothing who left my child, my husband. All for nothing.

'You're so precious to me. More than the Blues. More than the rarest butterfly.'

You *sell* butterflies. You *kill* butterflies.

'Now do you understand why everything imploded in those last few weeks, why I lost my mind? I just couldn't bear it, all that time you spent with fisherboy—'

'—What?' I stiffen. I haven't heard his nasty name for Alex in so long.

'I couldn't lose you to him, not when I'd just found you.'

A shiver ripples down my spine, my body is afraid before my mind knows why.

'And then when you disappeared, I had to go after him, you see that, don't you, I had no choice.'

'What do you mean, you "had to go after him"?'

'In Falmouth.' His voice is very quiet.

'Daniel,' I say slowly. 'You didn't kill Alex.' He flinches but I carry on because the fear is white-hot and slipstream now, because it is suddenly urgent to break down what he's done into one simple sentence, to name subject, verb, object. 'You killed a boy called James Saunders.'

'Him?' He laughs the laugh of a broken person. 'He was a mistake, I didn't find out I'd hit the wrong person until they arrested me. But how was I supposed to know? I only saw fisherboy twice. They all looked the same, stepping out of their boat in their cheap T-shirts.'

There is a sudden quiet in the room before it blurs, I see only glittering stars of glass, and then things snap together. Alex said his best friend died in a car accident, he died right before his eyes.

Which means they were together when the car hit his friend. A *car*.

My hands make a shocked, incoherent movement. It wasn't a hit and run. Daniel *meant* to kill *Alex*.

'Don't look at me like that.' He reaches for me but I am pushing myself off the floor, I am getting off cracked glass. 'I did it for you. Everything I do is for you. You've never been able to see these things for what they are.'

'Which is what?' I whisper.

'Offerings, darling. Sacrifices at your altar.'

He's insane. Fascinatingly, appallingly insane.

'Tell me, who's loved you like I've loved you?' His voice is so tender. 'Who's *killed* for you?' Behind the glass, he traces the outline of my lips with his finger. Part of me leaps for him, still wild for his touch, but another is observant, watching, and then finally, finally, it speaks in the terrible quiet of my mind, it says, *In all the time you've been here, weeks, days, minutes, he's never touched you. Not once.*

'Except, Daniel,' I put my hand over his. 'I'm not fourteen anymore.'

He looks me full in the face, the plumpness under my chin, the fine lines under my eyes, he must feel fooled, the thrill of winning me over in London so close to the thrill of winning me over at fourteen. But it couldn't last, he saw who I really am: thirty-two; post-partum; depressed. He withdraws his hand. 'No. You're not.' He swallows. 'But we can do this, we can make this work . . .'

So strange. That the man who once made me feel so beautiful can make me feel so ugly.

'And there are pills I can take; I've been looking into it . . .'

I shut my eyes. Think of the easy humour of Kit's mango emojis.

'Then, there's Bella.'

The girl in the field.

'Now, I don't want you worrying about her, she's not a patch on you, she's quite slow really, she doesn't have the mind for science, but she could be useful in other ways . . .'

I picture her then, the stack of bracelets on her arm, hands outstretched for the flutter of a butterfly and my insides run cold. Because I do not see what Daniel does – Lolly 3.0, another version of myself. I see my children – Millie and Faye are closer to Bella in age than I am. Motherhood, once my enemy, saves me now. My voice is suddenly high and clear. 'I have a gift for you. It's at the bottom of the cellar.'

His confusion lasts for no more than a second; of course he's convinced me; everything is forgiven, forgotten. His socked feet swipe wet glass off each step as he goes down. He finds the silver Thermos at the bottom. Twists it open. 'What is it?'

'A smoothie,' I say. Except this time, I haven't bothered to mask it with mashed banana and berries, it's pure smashed flower, stem, root. 'You don't remember, do you?'

'What?'

'The night before I disappeared, you had stomach cramps, you were vomiting.'

'I had a bug. You had it too.'

'But I didn't have a bug, remember? I had morning sickness.'

He stares at me, uncomprehendingly.

'There was a train to Wyatt. I knew you'd never let me go so I got you out of the way.'

'You got me out of the way?' he repeats.

'I had to. I asked Alex to come and pick me up.'

He backs into the shelves, the bottles shifting behind him. 'Stop talking like this, stop it, it wasn't *you*, it was *him*, he took you from me.'

'That's what you still think? After all these years? You're so blinded by the fantasy of Lolly, you never figured out it was me who arranged everything.'

'No, no, you wouldn't. I know you.'

'Not all of me. Not the bits that don't fit. Like the fact that I've been poisoning you ever since I met you in London. You've been itchier since you met me, haven't you? The rashes on your wrist, on the back of your neck? That was me.'

His hand moves protectively over his skin.

'At your house a few weeks ago, I almost killed you with that smoothie I made you. And the night before I disappeared, I made you another.'

He blinks at the hideous gloop of it.

'The poison in there is the same I used eighteen years ago. Ironic because it was you who got me into poisonous plants. All those books you bought me. I saw the plant instantly, it was blooming just outside the cottage. Lots of poisons taste quite bitter but hemlock water dropwort tastes like parsley. You didn't suspect a thing.'

Dear Darling

He puts his hand to his throat. Like he can feel a noose.

'It's the oenanthotoxin, it affects your central nervous system. The first time I gave it to you, I just put in a few leaves, I didn't want to kill you, just delay you and it worked, you had abdominal pain, nausea, vomiting. But this one, I haven't diluted and I've included the roots, so you'll feel the more serious symptoms quickly – slurred speech, seizures, cardiovascular issues. It shouldn't take too long.'

His eyes on me are tunnels. 'Who are you?'

'I'm Lauren.'

He laughs, a laughter that slides into crying, hoarse and ugly and wet. His powerful chest is heaving, his astonishing eyes are shut, and it is magnificent and terrible, like seeing a mountain suddenly cave in. 'You said you loved me.'

'Yes.'

'You were never who I thought.'

'Neither were you.'

'Was any of it real?'

'I think we were both pretending.'

He clutches at the buttons of his dove-grey shirt. His whole body is shaking, is he having a heart attack, should I open the door? But then, he takes a sudden, wet gulp of air and slumps down on the lowest step. I watch the unmoving heap of him for what seems like hours. Finally, he pulls himself up. Makes his slow journey to the top of the stairs. So close to me, he sits down. Unscrews the Thermos. Pours himself a full cup of juice.

'What about you?' he asks, cupping the lid in his palm. 'What will you do?'

I shake my head.

'You can't go back,' he says gently. 'You know that, don't you?' Tears sting my eyes.

'You're not cut out to be his wife, her mother. You want to be, I know how much you do, but however much you try, you'll only hurt them.'

I stare at the sunburst of his irises, unable to hide the crushing fear, the flooding doubt. He's right. I was never a good wife, a good mother, I tried to get better, I left them to become better but all I've got to is here, to a man in a hole and the juice I've made to kill him. How can I go back? He lifts his hand towards me and, for a second, I think he will release me, this man – who's loved me and wounded me more deeply than anyone else – he will take back what he's said, he will convince me that I'm worthy of returning.

He doesn't.

He touches his fingers to the glass and says, 'Let's do it together.'

Something in me gives up then. All fight gone. I've been struggling against it for so long – whenever I stared at the electrified train tracks or imagined falling off a building or water closing over me. But I can't anymore.

I look out to the estuary, to the mudflats at low tide, the crimson sky, and I think of Millie growing up, the books she might read, the subjects she might study, who she might become. Of the hair on Kit's temples growing grey, the wrinkles deepening under his eyes. Of Alex and all the waters he will dive in, the scallops opening like treasure boxes, the drift seeds he'll find and I feel for the one he gave me in my pocket, I want to see it one last time before I get up and pour myself that drink.

It has everything of autumn in it – shined and conker brown – yet it is large and flat, unbelievably heart-shaped. Waves have roared at it, it has travelled thousands of miles under sunny and stormed skies, all to wash up on a beach, where a man who's been searching for them for a girl he once knew, finds it, keeps it and then presses it into her palm eighteen years later. Isn't this the lesson of the drift seed, of botany and science and love? Everything is impossible – seed to flower, cone to pine, caterpillar to butterfly – there are a billion ways to fail. But there are also a billion chances to grow. To tell the truth to Kit. To try again with Millie.

He looks at me with lake eyes. It seems so foolish now, to want a drowning man to pull me to shore. But my salvation isn't up to him.

'Pour it out,' I say.

He watches me closely, searching for clues, and then he moves quickly because it doesn't matter what I'm thinking, it never has, all that matters is that I'm not poisoning him. He overturns the lid first and then the Thermos. Liquid pools thickly at his feet.

'You were right,' I say.

'About what?'

'I can't go back to my family. But not because I'm going to hurt *them*. I can't go back if I hurt *you*. I can't be a murderer and mother. So, I'm making a choice. I choose them. Not you.'

'What?'

'You won't be here long. I'm sure they'll come quickly after I give my statement.'

'Who?'

'The police.'

The flicker in his eyes dies.

'You'll be free. Though, probably not for long, after what I tell them.'

'You can't do this.' His voice is breaking, he is where I was seconds ago, more fearful of living than dying. 'I can't go back there, I can't do that again, I barely got out in one piece, stop, darling, please, we belong together, we always have, I love you—'

I crouch down on the fractured glass. Put my hand against the enormous animal of his. Love for one last time the man I've squandered my life for. Then I walk away. Step out into the impossible dark.

64

THE WEDGE

Now

The Wedge is not the same as when I left it. The ivy is overgrown, stretching around the ironwork of the gate, the small patch of lawn yellow from underwatering. Under the window, my hydrangeas are dry and crisp, one touch and the petals will fall. But none of that matters. The lights are on. They're home.

I ring the doorbell, though I have a key. I've seen all of Kit's messages but I haven't dared to read them. I'm too frightened. One wrong word could banish me back to the cottage, to the man I locked in the glass cellar.

When Kit opens the door, he blinks. Then, he falls to his knees and weeps, buries his head against the wound of my stomach. He says my name over and over, my name, not the name of my reinvention, it fuses with his shock into a single word, *Lauren-LaurenLauren*. I drop to the floor, wrap my arms round his neck, our cheeks slick with each other's tears, because I am uttering one word too, *SorryI'msosorry*.

Then, there's a familiar patter of feet, yesterday, I'd have given anything to hear that sound but now I'm here, it's more than I could have imagined because it is also the silk of her hair, her temples, her cheeks. I let her obliterate me. 'Mummy!' she says.

I am home.

It's not plain sailing. After the jubilation of the reunion, Millie refuses to let me change her, bathe her, read her stories, all she wants is Kit. The only time she lets me near her is when she's asleep. Kit buys a mattress to put on the floor for me when he never bought one for himself but I don't sleep on it, I'm in her narrow cot bed, slipping my hand under her neck, curling my body round her, inhaling her scent. Guilt circles the lowest parts of me like dirty water round a drain, *You abandoned her, you left her, what kind of mother are you?* But now, another voice rises.

What kind of mother am I?

I am a mother who's come back from the edge.

It's been rough with Kit. At first, he says he doesn't need to know where I've been, he's just glad I'm home but, when I'm least expecting it, he hurls grenades at me. A few days ago, I was looking for one of Millie's pink knitted cardigans, the one with rainbows on the pockets. He watched me from the door of her room for a few minutes before he said, 'She's grown out of that. You'd know, if you hadn't left.' Quiet blowings apart.

So, I decide. To evolve. To change.

I start with his messages. I've avoided them until now, I toyed, briefly, with getting a new number, I wanted a blank slate. But blank slates are metaphors, not reality or possibility. We are composites of our history. I know that more than anyone else.

So, one evening, I shut myself in Faye's nursery. Sit in front of her empty cot. Under her mobile, I read.

The messages detonate inside me, the panic and anger, the fury and the breakdowns, there are parts I can never read ever again. But even as they explode, I am flooded by his love for our daughters and for me. And I pray that will be enough. Because when I tell him where I've been, everything I've done, everything that's happened, he will finally see the monstrous truth: I am not the woman he married. He'll have to decide then. If I'm really who he wants.

After I read the messages, I ask if Cassie can take Millie for the morning so Kit and I talk. He wants coffees and croissants – he's forgotten I don't like bakeries or maybe he's testing me. I don't say anything. I press against him as we walk in, butter, flaked pastry, apricot, I'm afraid, so afraid. But away from the display, there's a free table by the window and, through the window, there's a maple tree growing over the train tracks, at that height, that age, it's fought and won against impossible odds. I track the length of the trunk, take in its whorls, its wounds, follow the branches to the tips of the leaves, until the fear has passed. I'm still here.

Kit sits down, pushes a cappuccino towards me. The sight of foam, the hit of caffeine has made me smile every day I've been back.

'We can't go on like this,' he says.

'I know.' In my pocket, I push my thumb into the heart of the drift seed.

'I said I didn't want to know where you were. But—'

'—You need to.'

He nods. He trembles as he picks up his coffee, abruptly puts it down. 'So, if it's all right with you, I'm just going to ask you some direct questions, I've tried to come up with a better way of putting this but there just isn't.'

'Okay.' My heart is racing.

'Did you cheat on me?'

'No.'

'Have you ever cheated on me?'

'No.'

'Not any time we were together?'

'Never.'

He jerks back suddenly, his anger bewilders me, until I realise it would have been a relief if I'd cheated – he's prepared for that. Now, he's in the dark once more. 'You're going to have to help me out, babe.' He rakes his fingers through his hair. 'There's just too many ends that don't tie up. I feel like I don't know you at all.'

I reach for his hand. Lace my fingers through his. He stares at his skin against mine, he doesn't know whether to trust it or not. But, for once in my life, I do. 'You *do* know me. You do. But I have kept a lot of secrets. I've been ashamed, so ashamed.'

He brushes a tear from my face.

That simple gesture, between a husband and wife, makes me brave. 'I need to tell you about Lolly.'

Epilogue

One year later

Seb, Alex's six-year-old son, is stomping with Millie over the mudflats. We are in Port Navas for the summer, staying with Alex and his wife, Martha. It is a village of no more than ten houses, a convenience store, a post box and a creek.

Alex and Kit have become fast friends, entirely different but bonding over rugby and Kit's newfound love of fishing. Most mornings, when I get up, Kit isn't there. He's with Alex, out on the estuary and then the open sea.

After I told Kit everything, I wanted to never speak about Daniel again, I'd said all I wanted to say, close the book, it's done. But our therapist, a strident sixty-year-old called Diana (who reminds me, comfortingly, of Mrs Hannington), warns me of my instinct to bury my secrets, to let them grow unchecked inside me until I believe everything hard and difficult – losing Faye, Millie's tantrums – is about them. They are not. I must unlearn this. Because now, I am not just trying to survive. I am trying to live.

So, I talk about Daniel to Kit, even though it's awkward and hard and terrible. I will not drift into these places alone. There is no need. Kit is here.

Even so, there are things Kit doesn't know. A few days ago, Martha took the kids while Alex, Kit and I went out on *Forager*. When we glimpsed the promontory of pines, the secret beach, the village, Alex whispered to Kit and my husband came and stood by me as we passed the cottage. 'It's over now, babe,' he says, slipping his arm round my waist. 'It's over.'

And it is.

The police told me that after I gave them my statement, they drove to the cottage and let Daniel out of the cellar. They asked him to come in for questioning. He said he was thirsty. They thought he was drinking water. It was pure ethyl acetate.

I felt nothing when they told me, unable to process the magnitude of what they said while standing in my own kitchen, watching Kit chase Millie. But in the months that followed, his death would catch me unawares, the air trapping suddenly in my ribs. A train would arrive on the platform, depart, and I'd just be standing there, confused that the world had carried on when he was gone. Some part of me thought he'd always be in the cellar, forever behind glass.

And then I'd crawl over the details of his death, all the tiny choices he made at the end. Why did he give up then? Why did he drink ethyl acetate rather than running a kitchen knife through his jugular or walking into the sea? Perhaps it was comforting taking something he was so familiar with. Or perhaps he wanted to send me one last message: *Look at me, Lolly. I've killed for you. I died for you. I loved you. It was all true.*

It's not true.

Because his love never gave me life. This is life.

Millie is calling me. 'Mama, I see one, I see one!' and I feel again the trembling joy of discovery, of pulling out into the light something that has been hidden. She finds the edge of something, wrenches it out, she nearly falls back with the force but she is laughing. In her hands, is the enormous muddy prize.

'Wash it in the water, honey,' I say to her. She does, rinsing it with jagged movements. At the sight of it, she squeals, gallops over to show me. It is half a scallop shell, the outer ridges amber, the inside, pure opaline.

'Do you want to keep it?' I ask. 'For your collection?'

She nods. 'It's beautiful.'

Acknowledgements

This book wouldn't have been possible without so many people but I'm going to try to name a few. To Charlotte, you're the alchemy that transforms thoughts in my head into a book in a reader's hand, I can't comprehend writing without your particular brand of magic. To Hellie, your faith in me when I was just starting out and throughout this book is the fire that keeps me going. To Susanna, Alice, Sarah and the whole Harper Fiction team and to Ma'suma and the entire WME team, thank you for your unfailing passion and support, nothing happens without you. To Blanca, for taking me behind the scenes at the Natural History Museum, and to Thomas who sent me to her, heartfelt thanks. To Ela, Callie, Liv and everyone from my Faber Academy group, your Zooms, voice notes, messages and calls haven't just challenged me to be a better writer but have made this journey so much brighter. To Anna, I couldn't have done this without your encouragement, kindness and the pre-pick-up productivity hour, forgive me for tainting your cellar. To Patrick, for helping me with the school sections and quite literally everything else. To Annie, Rees, Alice, Tinashe, Inyoung, Will, Gemma and Pete, for listening to me rant, interrogating my choices and talking me back from many edges, I am so blessed to have you. To Lara and Cordy, you are everything to me, each word I type is in the hope of a better world for you. To Tim, there is no book I could ever write without the roar of your encouragement or the ferocity of your love. To my father – lions, chasms, unshakable promises – I still believe.